The Truth About My Daughter

Jo Skinner

HAWKEYE
PUBLISHING

First published in Australia in 2024 by Hawkeye Publishing.

Copyright © Jo Skinner

Cover Design by Natalie Chen

A catalogue record of this book is available from the National Library of Australia.

ISBN 9781923105249

Proudly printed in Australia.

www.hawkeyebooks.com.au

Praise for THE TRUTH ABOUT MY DAUGHTER

'Written with aching restraint and melancholic beauty, *The Truth About My Daughter* clutched my heart from the first page and refused to let go. A story about the fragility of happiness and innermost dreams, this intriguing migrant family drama depicts the slow erosion caused by buried secrets, old resentments, and fresh criticisms. Crafted by adroit storyteller Jo Skinner, every vivid line shimmers on the page, leading the reader to a bittersweet conclusion that feels like vindication.'
Anne Freeman, award-winning author of Returning to Adelaide

'A thoughtful portrait of the shifting kaleidoscope of sisters and family dynamics. How far would we go for those we love? An evocative Brisbane-based story brimming with authentic detail… about children: yearning for them, coveting them, losing them, giving them away… and the consequences.'
Cass Moriarty, award-winning author of The Promise Seed

'A bittersweet tale of family, sisters, lovers, all the ways life confounds us, but surprises us too. An out-and-out page-turner. Save it up for a cosy weekend. Jo Skinner is a talent, a kind and tender writer.'
Al Campbell, multi-award-winning, bestselling author of The Keepers

'The author shows a deep understanding of her characters' flawed humanity, infusing the novel with generosity and affection.'
Dr Fiona Robertson, author of the award-winning, If You're Happy

'A wonderfully compelling and consuming read with a message that lingers in your gut.'
Olivia Griffith, reviewer

'An inspiring read about family, found or otherwise. The book is unafraid to dig into the impacts of less-than-stellar family and how that toxicity can affect everyone in its sphere of influence. The romance is excellently crafted, and the story touches on many topics that readers can empathise with.' *Nita Delgado, reviewer*

Praise for THE TRUTH ABOUT MY DAUGHTER

'A gripping tale of family, secrets, and betrayal. Set across both rural and urban Queensland, and New York, it explores family life and the competitive nature of sibling rivalry. With two compelling timelines running, the plot has many twists and turns that keep the emotional tension high with the final reveal clever and satisfying. You can't help but love Fin, the novel's protagonist. Jo Skinner's novel is reminiscent of Sally Hepworth and Holly Ringland. Don't miss this read.'
Peter Long, award-winning author of Steve Hart: The Last Kelly Standing

'A rich and complex tale of life's ups and downs with the full scale of emotions and gripping characters. It will stay with you long after you've read it.'
Edita Mujkic, award-winning author of Between Before and After

'Be captivated by the raw emotion and Fin's poignant journey as she confronts her past and an uncertain future, while striving to safeguard all that she loves.'
Kylie Fennell, author The Kyprian Prophecy series

'Deeply poignant… about love, loss, and the ties that bind us, from an exciting new voice in Australian fiction.'
Dr Joanna Nell, Australian GP and author

'A breathtaking story… the evocative prose and bittersweet portrayal of Fin and her tangled family will capture your heart and stay with you beyond the last page.'
Kelly Rigby, editor

'When 'family is everything', challenges and compromises await at every turn. In *The Truth about My Daughter*, Skinner negotiates, fearlessly, the harsh terrain of family dynamics – the secrets, the cruelty, the power – finding both heartache and beauty.'
Amanda O'Callaghan, award-winning author of This Taste for Silence

To Michael, Lara, Eva, and Jonathan for their unwavering
love and support.

And to the late Jim Skinner who lives on in
our hearts and in this story.

PROLOGUE

Now

FIN agreed to meet him at Stones Throw. She dressed the baby in a pretty pinafore, added a headband, and strapped her into the second-hand pram. She arrived at the café twenty minutes early, keen to be first so she could watch him arrive and assess him from a distance. She wondered if she would even recognise him. It would be even more difficult with their faces covered.

She reached into her handbag and pulled out the photograph folded inside the letter. She lingered over the details of the creased black and white print. Her mother's lips formed laughter that Fin could almost hear, and joy radiated from her eyes.

Outside, Fin scanned the socially distanced queue waiting at the window for takeaway coffees. They were all suited, masked, and glued to their phones. None of them were in the right age group. Anthony had offered to come too, and she regretted saying no – she was tempted to send him a text. She wondered if she should head home and forget the whole thing.

Hands tight on the handle of the pram, Fin took advantage of a gap in the coffee queue and manoeuvred through the front door into the courtyard where she sat at one of the tables, grateful the baby was asleep.

When the tall man with broad shoulders approached her, she knew it was him, remembered seeing him before. He slipped his mask off and let it dangle from one hand, his smile cautious. He motioned for her to stay seated and his hand fell to his side. 'I am so delighted you agreed to meet me here.' He hesitated and peered into the pram, his smile filled with longing. He lowered his voice to a loud whisper. 'I was worried you might change your mind.'

He lifted a chair, careful not to let it scrape on the ground. When he sat, he shifted his legs sideways as his knees didn't fit under the table.

Somehow, Fin had imagined a frailer man. He sat very upright, his silvered hair distinguished, his eyes warm.

She held her breath and his gaze. Her lungs filled with air when his large, warm hand closed around hers.

1

Four years earlier

FIN gripped the steering wheel as she turned off the highway onto a stretch of dirt road. She was about to suggest they forget the visit to her parents' property when Anthony leant over and touched her arm.

'It's just lunch.'

She sighed, her heartbeat all over the place. The spot under his hand tingled. It was impossible to explain her family to anyone. It was never *just* lunch.

'You'll fall in love with my sister. Everyone does. She'll probably bring her latest boyfriend along.' Fin was speaking faster than usual. 'My father, though, is unpredictable. It all depends on his mood. He might drop hints about grandchildren.' It sounded like she was sucking on helium. 'My mother tiptoes around, smiling non-stop. She used to be a dancer.'

Anthony started to speak, but Fin pulled on the wheel and swung wildly to miss a blue-tongue lizard sunning itself on the road. She'd nearly landed them in a ditch.

'Would you like me to drive?' Anthony asked, eyes wide.

Her father, Victor, would approve of the man driving. She wanted to wave the offer away but could not resist the appeal of being a passenger and getting herself together in the final stretch toward The Estate. She pulled over where the verge flattened, the gravel noisy under the tyres.

She wriggled across to the passenger side while he opened the door and stepped out, letting in thick waves of heat before sliding into the driver's seat.

Anthony was a compact, lightly-muscled man, surprising for

someone who spent so much of his time buried in a book. His quiet presence filled the car and loosened the tight knot in Fin's neck. A comfortable familiarity hung about him, and she watched the fluid way he pushed the seat back, adjusted the rear vision mirror, and clicked on the indicator, ready to pull out onto asphalt.

He paused with his eyes on the road, and his brow furrowed. 'My family isn't perfect either, you know.'

The sound of the air conditioning hummed in the cabin. Ahead of them were still twenty kilometres of rutted dirt road, leading to her parents' godforsaken property.

He turned off the indicator and let the car idle in the dense heat. The sun glinted hard on the faded metal of the bonnet, burning Fin's eyes. Her thighs stuck to the seat. She bit her tongue, wanting to reassure him, but worried she would say the wrong thing.

The pause that followed was excruciating. Fin had an urge to jump out of the car and keep walking until she melted into the shimmering haze on the horizon. Maybe Anthony had already changed his mind about her. After today, things would fizzle between them. Nobody had a family quite like hers.

'Damon just turned twenty-five,' Anthony said finally, staring at some point in the distance. 'You know, I wasn't the best father. I wasn't always there for my son. I let him down after the divorce and didn't contact him for a couple of years. I think he hates me now.'

Heat triumphed over the struggling air conditioner and pressed down on them.

He turned and looked at her, his grey eyes smoky with regret. Beads of sweat gathered like translucent pearls in the creases on his brow. His fingers brushed her arm and left another delicious tingle. For a moment, she imagined arriving with Anthony and announcing she was pregnant at lunch today. How thrilled Victor would be. She bit her lip at the thought of George's wide-eyed surprise.

Fin swallowed the urgent desire to say, *you would be a wonderful father,* and focused on the soft pulse in his neck instead.

His gaze shifted back to the window, his hands positioned at three and nine on the wheel. 'Let's keep going and get through this lunch.'

2

Childhood

JOSEFINE thought the best thing about Mum having a baby was getting to spend a few nights at her best friend's house. Miranda unpacked her doll's tea set and laid everything out on the Petersons' polished kitchen floor next to a box of Christmas lights. The Petersons were always the first to decorate their house.

Although Josefine had known for ages about the baby, the reality was something she had never really considered. For as long as she could remember, Mum's belly was an enormous balloon pushing out under her breasts. Miranda's mum, Mrs Peterson, who was slim as a pleat, turned from the wall-mounted phone with one manicured hand over the speaker. She smiled. 'You have a baby sister.'

Josefine turned away from Miranda's Cabbage Patch doll, Adele Rose, and stared at Mrs Peterson. 'Do you think Mum will let me bring the baby to show and tell at school?'

Mrs Peterson laughed. 'She just might.'

Josefine returned to Miranda's doll and sighed. 'I wish I had one of these.'

Miranda poured the pretend tea. 'Why don't you write to Santa?'

Josefine stared at Adele Rose's adoption certificate and remembered when she asked her parents. 'Can I please, *please* have a Cabbage Patch doll for Christmas? I don't care if I don't get anything else.'

Before Mum – leaning heavily against the kitchen bench – could respond, Dad frowned over his newspaper. 'Bloody ridiculous. Never seen anything so ugly. You don't need a doll. You'll have your own baby brother to play with soon.'

5

Josefine's heart dropped like a plumb bob and understood the topic was closed. She also knew she would never be happy again.

Sitting on the floor in the Petersons' kitchen, Josefine held the tiny teacup so that Adele Rose could have a sip, and wished she could stay there for another week. When she realised that Dad had been wrong about the baby, it made her warm inside. She did not have a baby brother, but a baby sister. Picking Adele Rose up, Josefine gazed into her funny, compressed face and sighed to Miranda. 'You're so lucky to have one of these.'

Mrs Peterson stood in her shiny kitchen holding a tray with two glasses of pink Quick and iced cupcakes. 'Well, you have a real baby to look after now. Why don't you come and have some morning tea?'

She led the girls across the gleaming timber floor to a patterned tablecloth smoothed over the dining table. Mrs Peterson smelled like sunshine in her pretty floral dress, her lips painted rosebud-pink.

~

Dad drove Josefine to the hospital. He seemed creased like the pink card Josefine clutched in her hands. He hardly spoke. Josefine had made a card using pink cardboard and golden stars. She clutched it in her hands.

'What is she called?'

A grunt.

'I want to write her name in the card.'

There was a long pause while the tyres screeched and Dad hunted for a vacant spot.

'Bloody thieves. Expecting us to pay this much to park the car. We must remember not to stay too long.'

Josefine decided to wait and ask Mum instead, but then Dad answered.

'George.'

'But that's a boy's name.'

'She was meant to be a boy.'

Dad bought a bunch of flowers at the entrance and Mum was sitting up when they reached her room. There was a flush of pink on her cheeks, but her face was pale. The baby was a blonde, fuzzy head pushed against the soft mound of Mum's breast.

'Mum!'

Josefine rushed in and crawled in next to Mum and the tiny baby. 'Can I see her? I made her a card but didn't know her name, so I left a space. I used my neatest writing. Mrs Peterson helped.'

'Careful.'

Mum shifted across the mattress. 'Just let her finish. She's having a feed. We've had a bit of trouble getting her to latch on.'

Josefine wriggled as close as she could and stared. The baby's eyes were tightly closed, and her mouth was moving, making soft, sucking sounds.

'What's her name?'

Dad was clutching the flowers. 'I told you. George.'

'Victor, we can't call her George. How about Georgina?'

'George for short.'

Mum used her fingers to release the baby's mouth from her nipple, and Josefine reached out to touch her cheek. 'George is all crinkled, just like a Cabbage Patch doll, except her skin is all blotchy.'

'Josefine.' Mum sounded hurt.

When Josefine held her sister for the first time, it felt nothing like holding Adele Rose. The baby had a special smell, her eyes drifted, her head was a bit flat on one side, and her fingers were curled tight around Josefine's.

'Please, can I look after her? Can she be mine?'

Mum smiled again. 'I'll be grateful for all the help I can get.'

When Josefine turned to look for Dad, she realised he was peering over her shoulder, his eyes wide and dewy.

'Barb, love, I'm taking you home now. I don't trust these bloody hospitals full of sick people.'

Josefine held George while Mum slid off the bed, wincing as Dad shoved her things into a bag.

~

George was only a few weeks old when the first shipment of timber arrived. Mum hurried outside, her top two buttons still undone and George wailing in her arms while Victor stood next to the pallet. 'I plan to create a home befitting my growing family.' He draped an arm around Mum. 'Number seven will become the grandest home in Hope Street.'

Within days, the walls of the house Josefine had grown up in became gaping holes where Josefine peered into the anatomy of the house and shuddered at its cobwebbed innards, tangles of wires, and insulation. When anyone had a shower, the pipes wailed, and Josefine whispered to baby George that the house was embarrassed to stand half naked in the street with all its bits showing. The weathered old Queenslander sagged under Victor's strenuous efforts and shuddered as he cursed his way through weekends of home improvements. Their place degenerated into a draughty shambles of tarpaulins, rotting timbers, and eroding aspirations.

Josefine peered from behind the half-closed door when she heard the *tap, tap* of Mum's shoes on the tired wooden floor after a long day of trying to keep what was left of the house in order with George in her arms.

'Do you think we should get some help?' Barb's smile was strained, her eyes pleading. Josefine slid further behind the door and held her breath, careful not to make a sound.

Victor lunged at Barb, wielding a mallet in one hand. 'Are you suggesting I'm not doing a good job? If you stopped talking and gave me a hand, the place would be finished by now.'

Josefine watched Mum move furniture away so Dad could demolish another wall to make room for the archway he envisaged. Josefine stroked the wall near the doorframe and whispered reassurance to the house after this latest gutting. She heard her mother's anxious voice. 'Victor, it will look wonderful, but I find it hard to imagine.' She shrugged and gazed at the fresh detritus.

He kissed her. 'That, my dear, is why you married me. You lack imagination. How about you go make us a coffee, bring me some of that *gugelhupf* you made?'

In the year that followed, the house continued to deteriorate, its innards spilling, wind rattling through gaps in walls, rain trickling past cracks in the roof. Josefine barely noticed the accumulated debris anymore. Still, she worked hard to keep George safe from stray nails, splintered timber, and fraying insulation once the baby became mobile. She was demanding, but adorable. George followed her big sister everywhere and cuddled up close while she read picture books. Sometimes, Josefine built cubby houses using blankets and chairs. They felt more solid than the floundering walls of 7 Hope Street.

While the promised new bedrooms awaited construction, George shared a mattress with Josefine on a closed-off part of the veranda. It was a hot box in summer and freezing during the brief, sharp winter. At night, Josefine buried her nose in the soft tangle of George's shampooed hair and held her close, skin sticky with sleeping sweat. Josefine was the only person who could soothe George and get her to sleep.

It was not long after George's first birthday when she appeared from under the table, rattling one of the boxes of screws.

Josefine held out her hand, 'George, give it to me.'

Josefine reached in and tried to grab the box, but George threw it across the room, where it hit the table and opened, pieces flying everywhere. George flung herself on the floor, beating her fists, screaming. Mum came running out and picked George up to console her while Josefine scrambled to find all the screws.

Victor laughed. 'She is just like her old dad. Doesn't give a shit what anyone thinks.'

Mum covered George's ears. 'Be careful of your language. We don't want her first words to be swear words.'

It turned out her first word was not *Mum* or *Dad* or a swear word, but *Fin*. It stuck. No one ever used the name Josefine again.

3

Four years earlier

ANTHONY turned the car into what George and Fin called the never-ending driveway. Not in front of Dad, of course. Even Mum smiled when she heard it for the first time. For years, Victor had plans to have it graded, determined to convince the local council that the dirt road on his property was their responsibility. Like most of his grand projects, though, the road was never completed.

With adroit manoeuvring, Anthony slowed Fin's old Corolla to a crawl. The corrugations vibrated up Fin's spine, and she clenched her teeth to keep them from jarring. The road had deteriorated even further since her last visit.

'With a bit of luck, we'll beat my sister, George.' Fin's voice juddered as Anthony veered around an uneven mound larger than a speed hump. 'She's always late for everything.'

'Is her name really George?'

'Georgina. Dad was convinced she was a boy, so the nickname stuck.' Fin's mouth was thick with dust, even though all the windows were wound up. She squinted into the sunlight, gut clenched, waiting for the first view of The Estate, a half-finished Besser brick structure perched like a wart on a barely accessible hill. It was so dry she could hear the grass snap under the tyres in the heat. One of the first things Dad did to the property was dam the creek, and soon afterwards the water dried to a trickle and then to a dusty gash in the landscape.

Fin shuddered.

'You okay?' Anthony glanced her way while keeping one eye on the road, careful to avoid potholes. The final stretch curved treacherously up

10

the steep hill. She forced her thoughts away from the past. Pressing her palms to her eyes, Fin slowed her breathing.

Anthony swerved to avoid another ditch and Fin's head banged against the window. Just then, they drove around the final bend and saw the dilapidated outline of her parents' home.

Anthony pulled up sharply at the curve and stopped the car. Sweat glistened on his forearms.

'Is that it?'

From this distance, the house seemed to sag from the effort of not slipping down one side of the hill, the foundations scrambling for purchase.

'Yeah.'

Fin could make out two silhouettes and knew it was Victor and Barb, waiting next to the lopsided sign that proclaimed, "The Estate". They would have spent the last twenty-four hours in preparation, polishing silver and glasses, setting out their fine Arzberg dinner set, and preparing an elaborate meal. The good thing about seeing them waiting was that George was, as expected, late.

From there, Fin felt it. Victor was reeling them along the final stretch of winding road, drawing them closer. The car shuddered over the final mound, the house rising large and lopsided in front of them. Anthony eased the car onto the flat expanse of the driveway and stopped. Barb smiled, her hands folded over the red hearts on her apron. Victor moved to open the car door.

'Welcome,' her father said, his large frame bending to lean into the car. 'It's been too long.'

He half dragged her out, kissed her on her left cheek, her right, and then her left one again before turning to Anthony, who stepped out from his side.

'So, at last, a man game to take on Fin.'

Fin clenched her jaw, folded her arms across her chest, and ignored Barb's warning look. *Just let it go, Fin.* Barb had always flashed it to divert confrontation. Anthony stepped forward into the scant shade of the half-finished stone wall with weeds and daisies thriving in the cracks.

'I'm Anthony. Lovely to meet you. I consider myself a very fortunate man to have Fin in my life.'

Fin unfolded her arms. Barb's face relaxed. She retreated to the shadow of the wrap-around veranda and waited near the door. Victor pumped Anthony's hand up and down like he was drawing water from the bore. 'Well then, Tony, come in, come in and I'll show you around.'

'It's actually *Anthony*.'

Victor turned. 'I built all this myself, Tony. With my own bare hands.' He held them up for emphasis and walked toward the house.

Fin had forgotten how exaggerated her father's accent was. He sounded like a caricature of Arnold Schwarzenegger. Her eyes sent Anthony an apology as they followed Victor inside.

Fin paused before walking past Barb. 'Mum, I'd like you to meet *Anthony*. Anthony, my mum, Barb.'

'Delighted, Barb.'

He shook her flour-coated hand while she apologised, her cheeks flushed. Afterwards, she wiped her hands on her apron and knotted the fabric in her fingers, tugging at the loose thread unravelling from one of the embroidered hearts.

Victor's voice boomed from inside the house. 'I thought you were all following me. I wanted to show you around The Estate.' He appeared again. His dark hair glistened. Rings of sweat stained his white shirt.

The three of them traipsed behind him. He gestured to the half-open door on the right. 'My workshop.' He tapped his head and looked at Anthony. 'This is where I use my engineering knowledge to design each stage of this exclusive resort we are developing. It's all rather top secret, I'm afraid.'

He pulled the door shut and gestured to the left. 'My personal library. Maybe after lunch we boys can retreat there a while and I'll tell you all about Fin.' He winked at Anthony. 'It's always good to know what you are getting yourself into. No one warned me.' He laughed and patted Barb on the bottom. She twittered and snapped the broken red thread dangling on her apron.

Victor lowered his voice to a loud whisper. 'Fin works wiping bums for people with one foot in the grave.'

Fin clenched her jaw. 'It's called palliative care nursing, Dad. You might just need it yourself one day.'

Victor turned to Anthony. 'And what do you do, Tony?'

'I own a bookshop.'

Victor thumped him hard on the shoulder and laughed. 'Never trust a salesman.'

The others stayed silent.

The final stage of the tour led them up the tight coil of prefab metal stairs to a ledge with a large skylight. Barb was downstairs putting finishing touches to the soup, the scent of freshly chopped dill pungent. The heat from the wood-fired Aga stove filled the cramped space. Sweat trickled between Fin's breasts, and she wondered how she could interrupt her father and suggest they head back to the dining room, where they could open a couple of windows and enjoy a cold glass of water.

Victor looked even taller in the tight space. 'This is where I plan to install my telescope. I will import one of the best and have it assembled by a friend of mine who is an astronomer. No light pollution out here. We will run tours, bring schools up to see the stars, and learn about the beauty of the night sky.'

He had his arms splayed wide. He fumbled for his handkerchief and mopped the dampness from his neck and forehead. Anthony waited politely, hands limp by his sides. Victor sidled up to him and put an arm around his shoulders, emphasising that he was taller.

'I like you. I can see the two of us getting along just fine. We will become, what do you Australians say again? Mates. When you need a break from Fin, just give me a tingle.'

Without waiting for a response, he waved his free arm around the cramped space. 'Well, Tony, what do you think of my plans? I suspect we will be booked up a year ahead.'

Fin calculated that her father could fit at most six small people up here at a time and wanted to point out that there were no safety rails. A child could easily plunge down and wind up with fractured limbs or a head injury. She bit her tongue.

'The views would be excellent,' Anthony managed, shifting away from Victor and closer to Fin. Anthony took her hand and gave it a squeeze while he stared up at the skylight and the intense blue it framed. 'Perhaps we should head down and give Barb a hand.'

Victor reached up to a shelf and pulled down a small brass solar system orrery. 'Look at this little beauty. Just imagine the two of us up here looking at the sky like the ancients.'

A loud clatter downstairs startled them.

Victor frowned. 'Barb must have dropped something again. She can be quite careless with things.'

To Fin's relief, they made their way down the spiral staircase, the three of them causing it to creak and sway. She was hoping it would hold up until they made it to the bottom when she heard voices in the passageway leading from the kitchen to the front door. George must have arrived. Only forty-five minutes late. Fin sidled closer to Anthony.

The excited chattering of voices drew closer until Fin saw George emerge, giggling. Fin looked beyond her sister to the figure behind her, a lanky, dark-haired fellow wearing ripped jeans, a black tee, and unlaced Converse sneakers. Anthony stepped forward with his hand outstretched to George. 'Didn't I see you at Books at Stones the other day?'

Then he stiffened as the dark-haired man stepped up to George's side. Anthony cleared his throat. Fin felt a tremble of premonition.

'Damon.' Anthony's voice cut through the air and there was a moment of complete silence.

'Dad? What the...'

George gave a knowing laugh directed at Fin. 'I'd like you to meet my new beau, Damon.'

$$4$$

Childhood

ON Mum's thirty-first birthday, Dad didn't come home. George, who was nearly four years old, was excited because Mum had made a special dinner: schnitzel with mashed potatoes, beans, and carrots in parsley sauce. The three of them waited for him until eventually, Mum opened the two presents Fin had wrapped with help from Mrs Peterson: a white photo frame shaped like a heart with *MUM* written underneath and a small red box with stars stuck on it. When Mum opened the box, George scrambled up and peered inside, her eyes wide. 'Careful, Mum. Fin put one of my kisses inside.'

Mum put the lid on very fast and hugged Fin and George hard. 'That was the best birthday ever.'

They ate dinner at nine o'clock when the food was cold. George kept drooping sideways. Josefine sang *happy birthday to you* and watched Mum blow out the candles before she cut the *nusstorte*, Victor's favourite. Fin wondered where Dad was but knew not to ask. Mum fiddled with her piece of cake until it was all crumbly on the plate, and when she heard a noise outside, she dropped her fork with a clatter.

Mum stood up to let Dad in, then realised it was the neighbour unlatching his gate, and slumped back into her chair. Fin took Mum's piece while she was distracted and shared it with George.

In the middle of the night, Barb got them out of bed and rugged them up. 'Quickly, girls. Dad needs me to pick him up.'

They stumbled out to the car and drove to the city, where Dad worked during the day. When Mum pulled up, Fin saw him in the headlights, holding up a lamppost. He staggered into the front seat. His words sounded blurry, and Mum wound down the windows to let a fresh breeze through the car.

When they got home, Mum ordered Fin to take George back into bed, then heated up Dad's dinner.

In bed, Fin listened to her father's raised voice. 'The bastards restructured and let me go. Can you believe it? I came to this country, learnt their stupid language, studied engineering at their university, and now they choose some young idiot over me.'

Fin strained to hear Mum and wondered what Dad had bought for her birthday. Mum made soothing noises between the clink of cutlery and thumps of a fist on the table.

Victor's chair scraped across the floor. 'What's with the potatoes? They taste bloody awful.'

There was the screech of a chair and the dull, uneven thud of Dad's tread, followed by a loud crash that vibrated the floor under Fin's mattress. She couldn't move because George was fast asleep, huddled close beside her. There was a moan, followed by Mum's hushed voice and the sound of dragging. After a while, the light went off and the house retreated to its familiar creaks and sighs as it contracted back into the stillness of early morning.

Mum went back to part-time teaching, entrusted with the children who struggled to learn. On workdays, Fin watched Mum hum to herself, lips painted pink. Her feet glided across the floor and her skirts swished like the ballerina she had once been.

They all piled into the car, with Mum coaxing them along. 'Hurry girls, I can't be late.'

Mum dropped George to Myrtle, the babysitter, and Fin to school. In the afternoon, Mum picked them up again in reverse order and headed home, where she started her second shift.

After a few false starts with jobs that didn't work out, Dad came home wearing a suit, his chest puffed out. 'I have a new job, working on the cutting edge of technology, spending my days involved with today's fastest-growing area of office automation and business communication.'

Fin paused in the shadow of the hallway to listen.

'I'll be travelling all over the country selling fax machines.'

The tight clench in Mum's stance softened. 'When do you start?'

'Tomorrow.'

The next morning, Fin poured cereal for George's breakfast and watched while Victor ironed his own shirt. He chose one of his sharply creased suits and polished his shiny black shoes. Mum prepared a soft-boiled egg and buttered rye bread for him. She used the coffee percolator to make his bitter morning brew.

It was a steaming summer day and Mum's skin glistened in a light cotton dress. 'Won't you be too hot wearing all that?'

He pulled himself to full height, suddenly filling the kitchen with his presence. 'I'm the only one at that place who dresses properly. It's why they want me to do this job. Customers will see I have standards and trust me. I'll be running that place soon.'

That evening, he brought one of the fax machines home. Mum stared at it. 'What do we need that thing for?'

'Barb, you must leave these things to me. You'll see, everyone will have a fax one day. We are just miles ahead.'

The fax sat unused in pride of place on a special table, and Barb dusted it carefully each week.

One Saturday, Victor packed up and headed off on one of his weekend sales trips. Barb waited until his car disappeared around the corner and winked at Fin. 'Let's rearrange things a bit and then go and have some fun.'

Mum simplified their living space across the usable rooms. The kitchen was half dismantled, so Fin helped move essentials to the remaining two cupboards. They dragged a bookshelf to where the new pantry would be and used it for tins, bags of sugar, and flour. In the living area, they pulled the old rust-coloured lounge across a bare section of timber floor.

Mum smiled at Fin and George. 'I have a surprise, girls. Myrtle gave us her old television.'

She hauled it up the stairs from the car boot using an old blanket, with Fin helping. They set it up in one corner on the spindly-legged coffee table. Mum's hair stuck to her scalp and her dress was damp. 'Let's pack up and cool off with a swim.'

In Wynnum, they lazed in the giant wading pool with its sandy bottom. The tide was a long way out, with mudflats extending for miles from the concrete sea barrier. When their skin wrinkled, they got out, shared fish and chips, and stayed late until the sun dissolved red and gold behind the horizon. By the time they drove back, excited to watch the new television, George was fast asleep, gritted with sand and dirt.

They turned into Hope Street and saw Victor's van blocking the driveway. His silhouette was a dark cloud at the door. Fin watched Mum's fingers tighten around the steering wheel, and with the salt tang of fish and chips still on her lips, her belly curdled.

'Victor, darling. You're home early.' Mum's voice was brittle, her smile watery.

He loomed large in front of them, his quiet anger simmering. 'Where the hell have you been?'

His voice was low, and Fin clung to George, who stood damp and dirty beside her.

Hands trembling, Barb fumbled the key until Victor snatched it off her. 'This must be mine. No wonder I couldn't find it.'

'Yours is inside somewhere. I'll help you look for it.'

He slid hers off her keyring, unlocked the door and pocketed the key. He kicked the door open and took in the surrounds. His eyes landed on the television and narrowed to slits. Without speaking, he walked over, picked it up, walked through the makeshift room on the veranda, and threw it out the window. It landed with a loud thud and sharp crack in the darkness below.

Mum busied herself with the picnic rug and wet towels. Fin waited until he left her room and placed George, now wide-eyed, onto the shared mattress. 'Shh, George. It's all fine. I'm right here.'

Fin listened to them in the lounge room.

'Where the fuck did that piece of shit come from? I work the arse off to earn an income to give us a good life and you rot their brains with that idiot box.'

'It was Myrtle's, the babysitter. She bought herself a new one and gave it to us. Where's the harm?'

His voice lowered, which Fin always found more terrifying. 'I don't ever want to see my family exposed to the crap they have on television again. We are better than that. I want them reading and using their time to study. I want them to think for themselves.'

The silence hung in the darkness. Fin didn't risk going to the bathroom in case she saw him. She held George close till she was asleep and waited a bit longer. Without making a sound, Fin found the bucket used to catch the drips when it rained and peed in there.

The next morning was subdued. Mum enrolled George in ballet classes and piano lessons. The same day, Victor purchased a second-hand Yamaha upright piano and stood it where the television had once been. George's feet dangled like loose ends, her fingers tapping out *Three Blind Mice* after her first lesson.

Victor winked at Barb, slid an arm over her shoulder and whispered loud enough for Fin to hear. 'The child is a prodigy. We must cultivate her mind.'

At school, Fin joined the swim club. Miss Batch pulled her aside after swimming and told her she had promise. It made Fin warm inside. She imagined standing on the podium, a ribbon pinned to her chest, Mum and Dad proudly watching. She came home with the permission slip and handed it to Mum.

'Can you sign the form, please?'

Victor peered over and frowned. 'What a waste of time and money.'

Barb shooed him away. 'Go and put your feet up. It will be good for Fin.'

Fin swam with the club every afternoon and then stayed on longer to swim laps and push herself further. She grew to love the still quiet of the water as she stroked her way up and down the pool. She focused on her breathing and the rhythmic movement of her arms, her world temporarily reduced to the small pocket of air when she turned her head to inhale, bubbles rising to the surface when she exhaled.

Stroke, stroke, breathe. Stroke, stroke, breathe.

There was a pure simplicity to it.

A harmony.

It was the one place where everything made sense.

Victor's endless drilling and hammering slowly progressed the extensions and renovations at home. He was determined for George to have her own room.

'Fin!' he shouted. 'Come and help me with this shelf.'

She stood on a ladder and held the shelf using both hands while he measured where to place the brackets. After he screwed them into place, he realised it wasn't straight. 'Jesus, Fin. How hard is it to hold a bloody shelf straight? You are as useless as your mother.'

After working non-stop for three weekends in a row, George's bedroom was complete. Barb helped to paint the walls and windowsill, then added baby blue curtains and a quilt. George played in her room during the day but crept onto the veranda to cuddle up with Fin at night.

One Friday at squad, the coach, Miss Batch, pulled Fin aside. 'You're good. Keep up your training and you'll win your age championship and represent the school.'

Fin hummed inside and imagined telling the family. She ran but missed the bus and was late home.

Dinner was ready and everyone was waiting for her.

Victor looked at his watch. 'You are spending too much time at that swimming pool. Look at the time.'

'Sorry I'm late.' Fin slid into her chair.

He reached over and patted her arm. 'You are smart, and it is important you study hard so you can be successful like me. My family are everything to me and I don't like to see you wasting time.'

He glanced at Barb, a silent communication, like she knew what was coming next.

'And I think it is time George stayed in her own room at night. It is ridiculous the two of them sleeping together still.'

Mum left and came back with a bag. She reached inside and pulled out a Care Bear Bedtime Bear, its belly decorated with a smiling half-moon and golden star. She handed it to George and glanced at Fin, apologetic. 'It's something for George to cuddle now she's getting too big to sleep with you.'

George held the bear by one of its legs and let it dangle a moment before dropping it on the floor, where it lay on its back and stared with unblinking eyes, an embroidered smile below a heart button nose.

That night, Fin pulled her knees up to her chest and stared outside. She missed George's tangled limbs sprawling across the mattress, her breath damp on the pillow.

Fin had the veranda room all to herself now and felt very alone.

5

Four years earlier

DAMON and Anthony stood facing each other, the air between them taut. Damon shoved his hands into his pockets, his dark eyes unblinking. 'You keeping tabs on me or something?'

Fin watched Anthony's neck muscles tense. His voice trembled. 'Believe me, it's a surprise to see you too, son.'

Damon shook George off and took a step towards Anthony, one hand raised. For a moment, Fin thought Damon was going to punch his father. Instead, he shook his fist, his voice guttural. 'I don't know why you're here, but don't bloody mess with things.'

George moved in close to Damon and put her arm around him. She leaned her head against his shoulder and seemed to have as much of her body in contact with his as possible. Fin realised she was standing apart from Anthony but felt too awkward to close the gap between them.

Barb hurried out from the kitchen, flustered. 'Why don't we all sit down and have lunch? The soup is ready.'

There was a weighted pause in the room with no one game to take the first step towards the dining table with its candelabra, stark white plates, and enough polished cutlery to remind them that this was no quick, casual lunch. Fin wondered if Victor had known and deliberately set out to humiliate her. How on earth had George worked out that Damon was Anthony's son? Fury swirled in dark, angry clouds in Fin's head.

George's eyes were wide, one hand clutching Damon's again. Barb stood frozen at the kitchen door, the whole wretched scene a theatre piece where someone had forgotten their lines and was waiting for a

21

prompt. Victor's lips curled upwards, visibly enjoying the drama.

Anthony's gaze dropped first. 'I promise, I had no idea you would be here.' He stepped forward, his polo-neck shirt damp in places. The house was a sauna. Fin noticed the pulse in his neck was pounding, but his voice sounded like it always did – calm and considered.

Anthony turned away from his son to Victor. 'Let's open a few of these windows, let a breeze through.'

Victor cleared his throat, or maybe it was his attempt at laughter. He had been wearing a suit, but in deference to the heat, had removed his jacket.

'These windows are special. I designed them myself. They don't open, but instead have a tiny permanent space around the base to allow air to circulate all the time.'

Everyone stared at the tightly shut windows in dismay. Fin noticed the silver edges of insulation still poking along the edges. Why did that surprise her?

Barb appeared with a jug of water, ice cubes clinking. 'How about a cool glass of water?'

Victor shot her one of his disapproving looks.

She ignored it, smiled at the clutch of guests, standing and awaiting the next cue.

'Victor, dear. Go and get some water glasses, please.'

He was about to mutter a complaint when George spoke up. 'Yes, please. I could drink a jugful of the stuff.'

She dragged Damon towards the table, sat him down, then shifted her chair closer to him before sitting herself, her hand in his lap. Fin panicked and calculated the least challenging place to sit. She worried about Anthony being next to Victor but was anxious about sitting him close to his son. She decided to risk Damon. Inflicting Victor on Anthony on their first meeting was too much.

Victor materialised with glasses the size of thimbles and made a big show of polishing each one, holding it up to the light. Fin noticed enlarging rings of sweat under his arms but was careful not to roll her eyes. She wanted to take Anthony's hand and give it a squeeze, but kept her own hands firmly in her lap, unwilling to chance it.

Victor poured everyone a tiny glass of chilled water.

Barb appeared with a white tureen of steaming soup. *'Griessnockerlsuppe.'* She beamed. 'Semolina dumpling soup. Victor insisted. It's his favourite.'

Fin's legs stuck to the chair. Why couldn't Barb just have made some salads and dragged a few chairs out onto the veranda where they might catch a passing breeze?

Barb served everyone two dumplings and a few ladles of broth. The steam rose like an omen.

Victor rubbed his hands together, his nose red like that of an alcoholic. 'This is perfect. All my family together around the table again.'

There was the clinking of spoons against plates.

George whispered something in Damon's ear.

Victor stood up suddenly. 'My apologies. The wine, I forgot the wine.'

He disappeared, leaving a momentary softening of the mood. Anthony refilled the water glasses while Barb flapped her napkin to cool off. Wisps of hair clung to her forehead and neck. In a moment of inspiration, she looked over at Anthony. 'Let's pull out the old fan. It might just move the air a bit.'

The two of them rose simultaneously, and Anthony followed Barb down the corridor.

Fin wanted to say something to George. *Did you know?*

The silence was thick in the still, hot air. Damon had ceased to eat, one hand draped behind George's chair. Just before Fin turned her head to stare down at her uneaten dumplings, he nuzzled George's ear and she giggled again. She looked radiant and was the only one of them apparently unaffected by the heat. Being in love was George's specialty. She glowed, sparkling like sunshine on water whenever she met someone new. The thing was, she was always meeting someone, falling desperately in love, certain that this time it was forever.

Victor's voice shouted from somewhere. 'Barb! You pulled the Riesling out of the fridge, and it's warm as bloody piss. What the hell were you thinking?'

Wide-eyed, Barb hurried down the hallway to the alcove where Victor had temporarily installed the fridge. He hadn't gotten around to creating a slot for it in the kitchen. Anthony came up from behind her with a dusty pedestal fan. Relieved to have an excuse to stand up, Fin pushed away from the table.

'Here, let me give it a wipe down.'

She headed to the kitchen, found a cloth, and busied herself cleaning off the worst of the dust before plugging it in and turning it on high. The welcome breeze was accompanied by a death rattle as the caged blades shifted slowly back and forth, rippling the flap of tablecloth where it folded over the corner.

Victor appeared with a bottle. Barb hurried behind him carrying a small bucket of ice.

'This stupid woman took the wine out of the fridge, so I'm afraid we have to chill it.'

Barb hung her head and used tongs to drop an ice cube in each of the wine glasses. Victor poured with a flourish, the genial host once again. Damon drank half of it in one swallow. George joined him, her feigned innocence getting under Fin's skin.

Anthony and Victor were the only ones who finished their dumplings. Fin managed one. George and Damon drank two glasses of wine each and didn't touch the soup, but Victor leant in to take Fin's bowl and frowned. 'Didn't you like the dumplings?'

The main course was pork chops in caper sauce with mashed potato and a green bean salad swimming in vinaigrette. Victor opened a rosé this time. He refilled George and Damon's glasses. Barb held hers up.

'My wife is a bit of a lush.' Victor winked at Damon as he filled Barb's glass. Anthony and Fin had barely touched theirs.

Everyone studiously bent over their plates, knives and forks clinking. Victor leant back in his chair and placed one hand on the back of Barb's. He looked over at the two lovebirds with approval. 'I just want to say, family is everything. Barb and I have been married nearly 40 years now. I am her first love. Thick as thieves we are. I hope you young ones find the same happiness.'

Barb finished her rosé and poured herself another while he continued talking. He turned to Anthony. 'Well, Tony. What do you think? We might become grandparents together, you and I.'

Fin stopped, her fork poised mid-air, the dreadfulness of it all culminating in the horror of that moment. Immobilised, all she wanted to do was get up and run, keep running until she disappeared.

Anthony paused with the tines of his fork impaled in his pork chop. He lay his cutlery down, and wiped his mouth with his napkin. The pulse in his neck bulged.

Fin half stood, hands on the table and glared at George. 'Are you pregnant? Is that why you came today?'

The thought of George pregnant again sucked the anger out of Fin. She slid back into the seat and dropped her head into her hands. She had an urge to tell Victor about all the grandchildren George paid to have removed from her womb. They would have a bloody kindergarten by now, all to different fathers. Of course, no one else knew that.

George sat, head drooping, her body curved over the food congealing on her plate. She shook her head. Damon reached over for another bottle and made a show of reading the label.

The lunch dragged on while Damon and George drank their way through the wine. Barb's awkward efforts at conversation were interrupted by Victor. The fan, on its last wheezing breath, offered only the slightest relief while it swayed back and forth. Finally, Barb brought out her *pièce de resistance*, her famous Black Forest Torte, with its *kirsche*-soaked sponge, dissolving cream and melting chocolate curls rapidly becoming brown puddles as they dripped down the sides. She cut everyone generous slabs, and asked if anyone wanted coffee.

The table was in disarray, shirts unbuttoned, the conversation a discordant flow of words. Fin stopped listening. She shovelled cake into her mouth instead. Anthony sat quiet and polite beside her. Damn him. She wanted him to rail, to tell Victor to fuck off and make a show of leaving.

Late afternoon shadows stretched across the room when George looked over at Fin with beseeching eyes, a dob of cream on her chin.

'Do you think we could catch a lift home with you guys? We'll come back and pick Damon's car up tomorrow.'

Just as Fin was about to tell George she should have thought about that before downing two bottles of wine, Anthony intervened.

'No problem. We'll be happy to drop the two of you home.'

He stood, his arm brushing lightly against Fin's.

Turning to Victor and Barb, he gave a nod. 'Thank you for the lunch. We might just head off.'

6

Early Teenagerhood

POISED on the block, Fin gripped the edge with her toes, ready to slice the water with her dive. A momentary hush fell before the four houses erupted into their war cries.

The whistle shrieked and Fin made a perfect entry into the water. Her legs pushed in a powerful frog kick. She pulled ahead of the competition on an adrenaline rush, the urge to win propelling her through the pool. After the final turn, executed with barely a ripple, she stretched for the home lap. The minute her hand touched the tiles, her house erupted in a cheer buoyed by golden pom-poms and banners. She pumped the air like an Olympic champion.

Later, on the podium, she scanned the bleachers for her parents as her blue ribbon was pinned to her chest, but she knew they had missed her record-breaking swim. Careful to keep a smile pasted on her face, she heard the chant from her peers. 'Fin, Fin, champion swim!'

Miranda, still her bestie, came up for a hug. She was tiny next to Fin and barely reached her armpit.

'Wow, that was incredible! You smashed it!'

Fin's arms ached. She suddenly felt ravenous and very tired. 'Let's grab something to eat.'

A towel draped over her shoulders, she walked back to the bleachers and ferreted through her bag. Mum had given her liverwurst on dark rye again. She stared enviously at Miranda's two rounds of sandwiches. One Vegemite, one peanut butter on neat white slices.

'Would you like one?'

'Are you sure?'

Fin loved peanut butter, and had learned to like Vegemite.

Bloody shoeshine, Dad called it. *Can't believe Australians eat this shit.*

It made Fin determined to love it. She bit into the Vegemite half first and let the sharp saltiness stay on her tongue.

'Are you okay?' Miranda paused, her long blonde hair catching the sun, most of her sandwich untouched on the greaseproof.

'Yeah, just tired.'

Fin stared with longing at Miranda's leftovers.

'Hey, I'm not hungry. You must be starving. Help yourself.'

Fin shovelled the neat triangle into her mouth.

Later that afternoon, Fin caught the bus home. 7 Hope Street was still a disaster of tarpaulins and warped timbers with the guttering hanging loose. She pushed open the back door and called out, 'Anyone home?'

The place was quiet and still, and felt like any other day, not one where she had broken the school record for 200-metre breaststroke and won the age championship for under-thirteens. Then she remembered. It was Wednesday, Mum's shopping day. Her grocery shop was a sacred ritual where she liked to linger, and she'd be back late.

Fin calculated the time in her head. She had just under an hour to herself. She was always hungry these days since her breasts had started to sprout and her hips had grown wider. When Mum was home, she kept a tight rein on the pantry.

Fin dumped her school bag, still filled with her wet towel and togs, and went for a forage. She poured herself a huge bowl of muesli flakes, added milk, and topped the milk carton up with water so it looked less empty.

Mum came home later than usual. George was irritable, clutching the remains of a jam *kipfel,* crumbs in her blonde hair and dotted around her mouth with jam splotches on her dress.

'Have you done your homework?'

Mum walked back and forth from the carport, laden with bags.

'We had the swimming carnival today.'

'Well, go and have a shower then get ready for dinner. A cold collation tonight.'

Fin hated these dinners. Mum sliced salami, cheese, and brought out an array of Dad's favourite pickles, but Fin longed for something hot;

sausages and mash, or chops and vegetables like Miranda's mum made. 'I won my age championship and broke the 200-metre breaststroke record.'

Without pausing in her methodical unpacking, Mum murmured, 'That's nice. Now please go and have a shower and make sure you hang up your wet things.'

George started to cry, and Fin thought she might as well.

Dad came home late, so dinner wasn't until after eight. 'I have an important announcement to make,' Victor proclaimed at the table.

He looked pleased with himself. He reached for some bread and speared salami, speck, and a few slices of Jarlsberg on his fork. George was falling into her plate, half asleep. Mum pulled her out of the chair into her lap.

'I resigned from work today. Those bastards don't recognise talent when it's right under their noses. They just think I'm a dumb new Australian and are intimidated by my intellect and my engineering degree.'

He took an aggressive bite of bread and cheese with a gherkin slice on top. It was impossible to know if Mum already knew or if this was a surprise to her also. Her face remained impassive while she stroked George's hair.

'I've decided to become my own boss and have bought a property out of town near a tiny place called Yowie, forty minutes from Ipswich. My plan is to build a series of rustic cabins for tourists, maybe include a hot tub, breakfast, and walking trips. It will give people the opportunity to get out of the city and away from it all. I will make it an exclusive place to stay. We move at the end of the month.'

The shock of his announcement hit Fin with such force that it winded her. She stood up so quickly that her chair fell over with a crash. 'I don't want to move away from Hope Street. What about my swimming? What about Miranda?'

Dad raised his eyebrows. 'It will be good for you. Forget this swimming and focus on your studies. You are in high school now. I migrated to this godforsaken country and worked the arse off to give my family opportunities. Do you even appreciate that? Anyway, there is a creek on the property. You'll be able to swim as much as you like on the weekends.'

Not wanting to cry in front of him, Fin fled from the room, just in time to hear him say to Mum, 'And you better keep an eye on what she eats. Her bum is the size of a draught horse.'

~

Fin delayed telling Miranda and attended swim club every afternoon as if everything were still normal.

One afternoon, Victor arrived home just as Fin got back from school. Barb blanched. Victor was driving a second-hand truck.

Barb's voice was a squeak. 'What happened to the car?'

'We won't be needing it on the property. I traded it in for this beauty. What do you think?'

Barb stared at it with George hiding behind her skirts. 'I don't think I can drive that thing. How will I get to work? Get into town to shop?'

Fin stopped, dropped her school satchel on the ground, and stared from Barb to Victor. His face was red. 'Don't be so negative. You always focus on the problems.'

Barb snatched the keys off him and hauled herself up into the driver's seat. She called out to Fin, 'Go inside with George and start your homework while I learn to drive this beast.'

Fin watched Mum crunch the gears and bunny hop out of the driveway. Half an hour later, she parked it crooked with one wheel up on the kerb. She stomped into the kitchen and banged saucepans about.

The truck was christened The Beast. Over the following weeks, it made endless trips out to the dilapidated settler's shack, where boxes and furniture were either dumped on the floor or piled into the rapidly filling shipping container perched under the gnarled forest of turpentine mangoes close by.

~

On Fin's last day at school, she wondered if she could just not come home. Instead, she would go to Miranda's and ask Mrs Peterson to call Barb and explain that, as Fin was part of the swim squad representing the school, she had to stay.

Miranda stepped out of her mother's sparkling Holden Commodore. She saw Fin and her face cracked into a smile, her hair in perfect braids down her back. 'Fin, do you want to come over to my place for a video night and a sleepover tomorrow?'

Fin looked away, her eyes welling with tears. She would have to tell Miranda today. Mrs Peterson drove off, leaving the two of them standing outside the school gate.

'Are you all right?'

Fin shook her head, the words stuck on the stone in her throat.

'Should we head to sickbay?'

Fin let a sob escape. 'No, nothing like that.'

Miranda dropped her satchel, stepped forward and gave Fin a hug. 'What's going on? You're scaring me.'

'I'm leaving.'

They sat under the drooping fig, with only minutes left until the warning bell. There was nothing to say. Fin knew her life had ended. Miranda pulled her pencil case out of her bag and dug around. Triumphant, she pulled out her compass. 'Give me your finger.'

Fin turned her hand over, her right index finger facing the sky. Miranda pressed the point into the flesh until a bright red drop hovered. Then she handed the compass to Fin, who did the same to Miranda.

The bell sounded shrill in the distance. Light shifted through the canopy and lay scattered in shards at their feet. The two of them pressed their throbbing pads together, their bleeding fingers steepled in a potent symbol of eternal sisterhood.

7

Four years earlier

THE drive back to Brisbane felt like an eternity. Fin stared straight ahead, hands tight on the steering wheel, lips pressed into a thin line. George and Damon were visible in the rear-vision mirror, talking in low voices, their bodies pressed close together. The Corolla's engine was so loud Fin couldn't hear what they were saying. Anthony had one elbow leaning against the window, his other hand drumming his knee. Fin wanted to apologise on behalf of her family, but fury gripped her vocal cords. She punched the radio on and turned the volume so loud it ricocheted around the small cabin and startled the lovebirds apart.

When Brisbane finally shimmered on the horizon, Fin turned the sound down a notch, but Damon still had to shout the directions to his unit in West End. Just before he and George got out, he thanked her for the lift. His liquored breath lingered stale inside the car even after Fin pulled away, her foot hard on the accelerator. Anthony's head slammed into the headrest. 'Hey, steady up. It's a fifty zone.'

'Back seat driving now.'

Anthony hung onto the grab handle. 'Just keen to get home in one piece.'

He turned to look at her and she could feel his cautious smile. Her fury uncoiled a little. Then someone cut into her lane without indicating and Fin sat on her horn, her rage exploding afresh.

Anthony leant towards her. 'Do you want me to drive?'

'Are you criticising my driving now? You don't think I've had enough criticism for one day?'

'It was a shock for me too. I didn't expect to see Damon there. He barely speaks to me.'

Fin punched one hand on the steering wheel, indicated, and pulled over into a vacant spot. 'George bloody knew. She set me up.'

'How would she even know my son? Could it have been an unfortunate coincidence?'

Fin rested her head in her hands, elbows on the steering wheel. 'I told her I was going out with you. I shouldn't have said anything. Nothing is a coincidence with George. She *knew.*'

'That day in the bookshop.' Anthony reached for a memory. 'You introduced her to me.'

'Oh my god, I saw her grab one of the fliers for Damon's next gig.'

The air sat hot and tense between them.

Fin leaned back against the seat again and spoke through gritted teeth. 'George spoils everything. Today was so awful. I wish we'd never gone.'

Anthony sounded terse. 'Damon can be difficult. I am trying to reach out to him. I want to rectify our relationship. Maybe something good can come out of it all. Why don't the four of us go out for a meal sometime?'

'No.'

Anthony flinched like she had struck him. He changed tack. 'I doubt your old man knew his daughters were bringing home partners who were related. He seemed as surprised as we were.'

'Don't you defend him. Dad was so rude. Worse than usual.'

'Look,' Anthony said, 'the lunch is over. Who knows if Damon will even stick around? He's hardly reliable. Your folks live a long way away and we don't have to see them often. Why not just get on with our lives, and let the others get on with theirs?'

Fin indicated and slipped back into the traffic. She knew that this would not be the last of it. Victor would be revelling in her humiliation. George would pretend nothing had happened and ring up tearful next time she needed something. The whole saga would be yet another shadow looming over Fin, waiting to swallow her up.

They drove in silence the rest of the way home, all the unspoken words hovering murky between them. Fin turned into the driveway and crunched the back fender on the gutter. She swore under her breath, reached for her bag in the back and got out, slamming the door behind her.

Anthony stood on the porch and fumbled for his keys in the dark, unlocked the door, and switched on the light.

'Let me make you a cup of tea. Why don't we just relax in the lounge room and read our books?'

Fin stood, arms crossed. Anthony's solution to every problem was to make a cup of tea and read a book. She wanted to make a sarcastic comment about it, but he was already in the kitchen filling up the kettle.

Jaw clenched, Fin moved to the lounge room and sank into the sofa, frowning at the to-be-read pile waiting on Anthony's coffee table. Several had their spines bent open. She slammed them shut without bookmarking his pages and braced herself to confront his dismay.

Anthony pushed the books aside without comment and made room for the tray of tea things. He poured her a mug before pouring one for himself, then eased himself next to her, leaving a small gap. Fin thought about the way George and Damon were entangled all afternoon, pawing each other and stealing kisses. She clutched the mug with both hands and took a sip. Anthony put his own mug back onto the tray.

Fin gritted her teeth. 'Does it bother you she's a lot older than him?'

'Now, that's a bit sexist of you. Here I am, nine years older than you. How old is George?'

'Thirty-two.'

'Well, that's only a difference of seven years.'

She thought about all of George's relationships, the way they started off with passionate enthusiasm and breathless phone calls only to end up in tears and regret. Only this time would be different. Fin balled her hand into a fist. The rosy future she imagined was now vulnerable, tainted by George's reckless disregard for Fin's happiness. Victor's barb about grandchildren needled her and made her fiercely protective towards Anthony. With a sudden clarity, Fin knew how they could find redemption and move beyond the shadow cast by George's unpredictable behaviour.

Fin's voice was passionate with suppressed desire. 'I really want to have a baby.'

He gazed at her, the corner of his lips twitching. 'Are you proposing?'

She refused to meet his eye but glimpsed the crinkle of a smile on his face. She suddenly wished she could take it back. Hand trembling, she put her mug back onto the tray, took a risk and gave voice to her fears. 'I'm getting on. I'll be forty in a few months.'

He leaned forward for his mug and had another sip of tea. He didn't say anything for what seemed like a long time. Fin worried she had scared him away, when at last he spoke.

'It might be an opportunity to redeem myself, a chance to become the father I imagine I would like to be.'

Anthony reached over and placed two fingers on her cheek. With reluctance, she turned to face him. His eyes were a soft grey, crinkled at the edges. His voice was gentle. 'I was so bloody angry when Pip told me she wanted a divorce. I made the whole separation as difficult as possible and barely saw Damon for a few years after that. I was that terrible absent father you hear about.'

He stared down at his hands. 'I haven't been in a relationship since then. Just a few dates that fizzled.'

He looked up at Fin. 'I love you, Fin. But I'm also scared I'll disappoint you. Like today.'

Fin hunched over, hands locked together. 'I'm sorry Dad was so rude.'

'It's okay. It's not up to you how he behaves. Anyway, I'm not interested in him. I'm interested in you.'

Fin's eyes were moist. A sob escaped from her lips. She felt Anthony move closer on the sofa. He gently prised her hands away from her face, used his hanky to wipe the tears away, and held her. He had a way of making her feel strong and valued, despite everything. It was a relief to press into his shoulder and weep, to let the tensions of the day pour away.

The tea cooled.

Sounds from outside started to filter in. The distant hum of traffic, the local bat colony screeching overhead. They held each other until there was no light left.

Anthony handed her his hanky, moist with her tears. 'I'm thinking about your proposal.'

Fin sat very still, aware of her galloping pulse. She didn't dare move in case the moment evaporated.

Anthony slipped down off the sofa and kept his hands on her thighs. He went down on bended knee. 'After giving it due consideration, I would like to accept.'

He reached up and his lips brushed hers, light as a butterfly's wing. He whispered, 'I would like to propose getting started right now.'

8

Teenagerhood

THE first week on the property was chaos. Today was yet another morning of unpacking and Barb trying to create some semblance of order. Fin realised that most of the boxes were a jumble of miscellaneous goods still being used during their last days in Brisbane. In the final frenzy to vacate the house, kitchen drawers were emptied onto toys, family photographs, and linen. The toaster and kettle were yet to be found.

Victor stood in the small kitchen nook and fumed. 'Jesus, you can't even manage to put a few items into boxes in such a way that we can find them again.'

Barb shrank from his words and concentrated on setting up a makeshift kitchen. She unfolded a card table and used a single patterned sheet doubled over as a tablecloth. 'Fin, see if you can find some cutlery and arrange it in the plastic rack. I stacked some plates on the overhead shelf.'

Victor sat at the table drawing up grandiose plans for a large home, several cabins, and a hanging garden of exotic plants where clients could sit and relax. 'Come and look at this. We will have such a great life, out in the bush away from the stress of city life.'

Across the top, Victor wrote "The Estate" in bold letters. Fin stared at the drawings as Barb appeared, her hands full of oddments. Half-unpacked boxes were scattered shambolically around them. Victor traced the boundary with his finger. 'And I plan to construct a wall to keep the curious bastards out.'

Soon, every surface of the settler's hut was covered with butcher's paper sketched with Victor's plans. He stood back, hands on his hips,

37

feet apart, and stared at his scattered handywork. 'This is why I came to this country. To build my own place and get away from people who live by the rules.' He turned to Barb, whose hair was coming unpinned, her face slack with fatigue. 'You are a lucky woman.'

He waved his arm in a grandiose gesture. 'Now, if we just put a new window in here, you will get the perfect view of the site for our new home.'

Victor burrowed inside upturned boxes, spilling their innards onto the cracked floor, sweat trapped between folds on his neck.

'Where the fuck are my tools?'

Barb hurried over. 'Victor, darling, we'll find them.'

Another box erupted, scattering an assortment of cutlery, photographs, baby clothes, and a screwdriver onto the limited space on the floor.

Fin gathered up the knives and forks and tipped them into a tray. She gathered the photographs but paused over one of them. Her mother looked so young and fresh that Fin's breath cut glass in her lungs.

She glanced at Barb, who was still tearing into boxes, leaving an eruption of chaos in her wake. Fin slipped outside, the fresh morning air welcome on her skin. Something clattered and Victor shouted. Fin hurried down the long dirt drive, the river a sinuous brown in the valley below.

Fin pulled the photograph from her pocket when the shack was no longer visible and studied every detail. Barb looked so different. Younger and unconstrained, smiling in a way that made her eyes dance. Her gaze was fixed on a man who was not Victor. Fin slid the photograph back into her pocket, confused. Victor had always boasted that he was Barb's first love and that they married within a week of meeting.

Fin touched her pocket, breathless, and pushed uphill, heart pounding. She would hide the picture and keep Barb's secret safe.

At the junction in the road, an old Land Rover stirred up a cloud of dust. Putting her arm up to shield her face, Fin stepped backwards onto the grassy verge, surprised to find another person nearby.

A young bloke poked his head out. 'Are you right? Can I give you a lift?'

Fin let the dust settle, coughed, then looked up at the face peering down at her from the driver's seat. He was maybe a few years older than her, seventeen or so, wearing a battered hat, his skin as sun-kissed brown as the river.

'Arch, by the way. You must be the new folk living down at Yowie's shack.'

'I'm Fin. I might just take up your offer and grab a lift.'

She hauled herself into the cabin and screwed up her nose at the pungent smell. He grinned. 'Sorry about the pong. We run Liberty Chicks and produce fresh eggs on the farm up the road. You get kinda used to it.'

Fin nodded, breathing through her mouth.

'I'm heading to Yowie. Where can I drop you off?'

'Yowie is fine.'

Arch drove in silence, focusing on the rutted road. It was a relief he didn't expect Fin to speak, as the only way to be heard was to shout over the engine. Even when they hit the tarmac, Fin's ears buzzed. Before too long, he pulled up and parked in front of the Yowie General Store. It was one of those places with everything from groceries to tools to kitchenware.

Arch looked at her and shrugged. 'I'm just getting a few bits and pieces. I won't be long. I'm happy to give you a lift back. It's a bloody long walk.'

Fin stared down at her feet, suddenly very aware of the dimple dancing in his cheek, certain her face was red. 'Sure.'

She looked up, absorbed the quiet main street that consisted of half a dozen shop fronts, and made up an excuse to be there. 'I'll be in the bakery. Shouldn't be too long.'

The slamming of the car's doors echoed down the empty road. Arch disappeared into the darkness of the store and left Fin standing in the blistering heat. She made her way over to the bakery, squinted, and looked up at its shingle.

The Sweetest Spot in Yowie — Life is short, eat dessert first.

Fin walked through the plastic strip door into a blast of cool air and set the customer bell jangling while she inhaled the scent of freshly baked bread, cakes, slices, and hot pies. There was an enormous array of inviting goods under the curved glass counters. Old-fashioned vanilla slices, caramel and hedgehog slices, biscuits decorated with funny faces, cream buns, finger buns… the list went on.

Fin looked up to see a stout woman appear from the bowels of the shop. She stood in front of racks of bread and rolls, behind the wicked selection of temptations. 'Can I help you?'

Fin made a quick calculation, fingering the money in her pocket – the only place it was safe from George. It would surely be enough to get everyone a sweet to soften the mood at home. She pulled out a couple of crumpled notes and some coins. There had been nothing to spend her pocket money on since moving here. Mum adored cakes, and even though he denied it, Dad had a very sweet tooth. He was the only person she knew who added four spoons of sugar to their coffee. As for George, she was a total sucker for anything iced or sprinkled with hundreds and thousands.

Fin's eyes swept across the array of options. She settled for a vanilla slice for Mum, a knotted meringue for Dad, a happy-face biscuit for George, and caramel slice for herself. She added it all up in her head then added a second caramel slice for Arch to say thanks for the lift.

The woman used tongs to pick everything up, then placed each item into a box before lowering it into a plastic bag.

'Thank you. It's a great shop you have here.'

The woman's face beamed.

Arch was already in the dusty four-wheel drive, waiting. Fin hauled herself up, careful not to tip the box.

'So, you've discovered Yowie's number one tourist attraction. Doug and Sheila make the best stuff.'

'I bought you something.'

Arch looked away.

'I hope you like caramel slice.'

He fiddled with his keys. 'It's my favourite.'

She reached into the box and handed it to him. They ate in silence, the body of the car shuddering when a truck thundered past.

Arch steered onto the road home, the silence awkward this time. He drove to the junction where he had picked her up. 'How about I drop ya home?'

The thought of Dad meeting scrawny, dishevelled Arch made Fin shrink. 'No, please don't go to any trouble. Here is just fine.'

She unbuckled her seatbelt and opened the door.

Just as she was about to get out, Arch cleared his throat. His words came out in a rush. 'Would you like to go for a swim in the river? I could pick you up Saturday, around eight, before it gets too hot. I know a great spot.'

'Sure, that would be great. How about I meet you right here?'

Arch swallowed. As if to delay her for another moment, he reached across and burrowed in the glove box.

'Just so you know, there's a bus comes up a couple of times a day. Only once on Sundays.'

He handed her a timetable stained with coffee rings, the edges frayed and curled over.

'Thanks. And I really appreciated the lift.'

She stood in the cloud of dust his truck left behind and watched until he disappeared over the rise and the dirt settled.

9

Three years earlier

FIN tried not to focus on the calendar, but Dr Prasad said she'd refer Fin to a fertility specialist after six months of trying. After nothing but disappointment for five months, Fin promised herself she would not check until she was one whole week overdue. When she woke in the still, dark hours on day seven and the elusive second line emerged, she stared at it in joyful disbelief.

Heart pounding, Fin reached into the vanity, pulled out a second test kit, and managed to squeeze out a few more drops of wee. It was absurd, she knew how accurate they were, but needed reassurance. This time she closed her eyes for a full three minutes before she peered down to see the pink line, distinct and certain.

Her first instinct was to snuggle back into Anthony's warmth and whisper the news to him, his breath in her hair, but she had the early shift at the hospital this morning and was already late. She gazed down at the way his hair stuck up when he was in bed and reached in and smoothed it down. He sighed in his sleep and rolled over.

Fin made up her mind. This news was too immense to share on the run. Instead, she would delay gratification and spend the day savouring the sweet secret of their success before announcing it over a special shared dinner this evening.

Jubilant, she dressed for work, aware her breasts were full and tender. She imagined one brave tadpole burrowing its way into an egg, her womb a welcoming warmth nurturing this new life and enveloping its rapidly dividing cells with a nourishing placenta. Fin leaned in and kissed Anthony goodbye once on his lips, then gently on each closed

42

eyelid. They fluttered awake and, half asleep, he reached up and pulled her back down into a hug.

'I've got to go,' she whispered, disengaging his arms, anticipating the moment she would share her news.

The air was chilled, the headlights white cones probing the morning darkness. Fin defrosted the gathering fog on her windscreen. She sang out loud to early morning radio. The city seemed reluctant to turn away from night, her eyes bleary with sleep while fog hovered in clouds along loops of the river.

Inside the hospital, Fin called out a cheery *hello* to Martha who was waiting to hand over.

'Kettle has just boiled, Fin.'

'Ta.'

She pulled out her favourite mug, added a teabag, and dropped two slices of bread into the toaster before getting herself up to speed with Martha, who had been the palliative nurse on call overnight.

'Is Rob still with us?'

'Yeah. I think he's hanging on till his grandson flies in from Sydney.'

Fin reached for the butter and the Vegemite. *Bloody shoeshine*, she remembered as she spread it thinly on hot toast.

She sat down and scanned the sheet of names Martha had printed out. 'Thanks. You head off, get some sleep.'

Dr Janssen was on call today. Fin liked working with her. She spent a lot of time with each patient and listened when the nurses made suggestions about care. Fin never tired of sitting with the dying and kept a scrapbook of their names and often a photograph or some memento they gifted her in their final days. She remembered details of every single person she had nursed through to their final passage, even without these prompts.

Fin checked the drugs and the equipment in the bag she took on home visits. Only one new assessment today, following a call from one of the local general practitioners who was happy to do shared palliative care.

Suddenly a familiar pain shot through her pelvis. It was sharp and sudden and nearly doubled her over. She hunched over in the plastic chair, realisation flooding her, even as she felt the warm trickle of blood.

'Are you alright?'

Dr Janssen walked in and looked down at Fin, her brow creased.

'I'll be fine in a minute.' Fin clutched her belly, still folded in half.

'You don't look fine. How about we get you home and get someone else in?'

'No!'

Dr Janssen handed Fin a glass of water and crouched beside her. 'You look awfully pale. Why not take the day off?'

'Thank you, but I'll stay on. The pain is easing off.'

Fin stood up, fighting off tears. She hurried to the door and went to the staff toilets. Blood and lots of it. One month off forty and she had been so certain he had planted a baby there for her big birthday. She had felt it.

Another cramp stabbed her hard. She bit her lip and tried to pull herself together. Blood stained the ceramic bowl, clotted and dark. She rocked back and forth, tears streaming down her face, very alone. Another cramp squeezed her hard. She balled a fist into her lower abdomen and pushed.

When it eased, she used toilet paper to wipe her eyes and blow her nose. She splashed water on her face and smoothed her hair back.

The pain in her pelvis gripped her like a fist. Fin was used to painful periods, but this was so much worse, the cramp twisting not only her womb but her heart, squeezing all hope from its ventricles. She clenched her teeth, smoothed down her uniform, and pushed her shoulders back. Rob needed someone beside his bed this morning before his grandson arrived later today.

Fin punched out a couple of ibuprofen and swallowed them without water. She gritted her teeth and opted to assess her new patient before spending the rest of her shift with Rob.

The new patient, Neve, was the same age as Fin. A tall, clean-shaven man wearing jeans and a white t-shirt opened the door and invited Fin inside. There were photographs of young children on the mantle, colouring books and pencils on the floor in the living area, and a half-complete Lego castle pushed to the side of a dining table.

'I'm Fin, one of the nurses who'll be looking after you.' She pulled up one of the dining chairs and sat beside this young woman who would not see her children grow up. 'Today, I just want to learn all about you and your family.'

A cramp gripped Fin so hard she nearly cried out, but when Neve looked up at her, eyes large with fear, Fin turned away from her own losses, reached over and took Neve's hands between her own.

~

'Fin?'

There was a voice calling her from someplace. Disorientated, she sat up and realised it was dark. She must have fallen asleep.

'Fin? Are you home?'

She crawled out from under the doona and glanced at her dishevelled self in the mirror. The pain had settled to a dull throb now.

'I'm up here. I planned to make dinner but fell asleep.'

She heard Anthony treading closer. He peered into the semi-darkness of the bedroom, concern on his face.

'You okay? I've never seen you asleep during the day. Tough shift?'

Fin shook her head, feeling ugly and unlovable. If only she had managed to have a shower to freshen up and had prepared dinner. The thought of discussing fertility treatment with him made her shiver. It seemed so clinical and unromantic and would confirm just how useless she was. She wished Anthony would just leave her alone. Her voice was curt. 'Can't I just feel unwell and have a minute to myself?'

She saw him flinch and hoped he wouldn't touch her. Her skin was sensitive, her womb empty.

The bed dipped where Anthony sat, and she had to stop herself from rolling towards him. She shifted just far enough away that he couldn't reach her and pretended not to see his hurt. His silhouette was hunched, elbows planted on his knees.

'How about I grab us some Thai?' His voice sounded hopeful. 'We can enjoy it on the back deck with the patio heater on.'

She didn't respond, willed him to go away, when he continued. 'I wanted to discuss something with you tonight.'

She moved further away from him and slipped off the bed. 'I need a shower.'

He had already worked it out. He must have realised that she was a barren failure.

'I'm not sure I'm up for any discussion tonight. I might turn in early. Let's just have eggs on toast.'

10

Teenagerhood

FIN woke early, slipped into her Speedos, shorts and tee, and stuffed her towel into her bag. It was Saturday and Arch was taking her swimming. Excitement bubbled inside her, but now, at fourteen, when she wanted privacy, she was forced to share a room with George again. Fin stepped around George's mattress, crept out of the room, and pulled the door shut, determined to keep Arch a secret.

Dawn found its way into the kitchen, a soft, pink light promising heat and sunshine. Perfect for a swim. Quietly in the sleeping household, Fin foraged the open shelves for food she could share with Arch. A couple of apples and some smoked almonds. The household still silent, Fin poured herself a bowl of muesli, then stepped outside where the noisy fridge rattled on timber slats on the covered deck. The minute she opened the fridge door, cold hair hit her face, a welcome relief from the heat already rising from the ground. Fin pulled out the milk and sloshed it over the muesli. Just as she settled in one of the chairs with her bowl, she heard a scream.

George, hysterical.

Victor's voice roared, 'Keep the kids quiet when I'm trying to sleep!'

The floor creaked and the kitchen door banged.

Mum's voice called out, 'Coming, give me a minute!'

A pause, followed by an irritated tone. 'Fin, please do something. Can't you hear George is upset?'

Sighing, Fin left her breakfast and stepped back inside, the door shutting with a thud then slowly swinging open again and slamming into the wall. 'Coming.'

George was hysterical. 'Fin's gone!'

'Shh. I'm right here. I just got up early, that's all.'

Fin crouched and pulled George's dishevelled blonde head against her shoulder. 'Why don't you lie down, go back to sleep? It's Saturday and early.'

George's sobs subsided. She clutched her woollen pet Lucky, a mangy dog Fin won at a vending machine in the mall back in Brisbane over a year ago. His tail hung by a thread, and he was missing an eye, but George, even at seven, was devoted to him.

Now Mum was up, her summer dressing gown knotted around her waist, her posture like a dancer, feet turned out, shoulders back, spine straight as a die. 'What happened? Is everything all right?'

Fin nodded while George ran to Mum, Lucky dragging behind her. 'Fin was gone. I couldn't find her anywhere.'

Mum raised an eyebrow.

Fin shrugged. 'I just got up early, made some breakfast and was sitting outside.'

'Can I have breakfast outside too?' George stared up at Fin, her eyes pleading.

Mum ruffled George's curls. 'Of course. Fin will get you something.'

Fin clenched her teeth. Mum turned to go back to bed, then stopped. 'We'll need your help today. Dad plans to peg out the gardens and clear the site where the cabins will go.'

'But I'm going out. I won't be here.'

'Where are you going?'

'Just meeting a friend to have a swim.' Fin bit her lip and wished she hadn't mentioned the swim.

George dropped Lucky and tugged Mum's gown. 'Can I go too, please?'

'No, she can't come. She wasn't invited.'

Mum loosened George's fingers. 'I think it would be lovely to take your little sister along. I'll help Dad and you girls go and have some fun.'

Mum disappeared. Lucky's one good eye stared up at Fin and it was all she could do to stop herself from kicking him across the room.

'I want pancakes.'

'Well, you're dreaming. It's muesli or toast.'

George stamped her foot. 'I *hate* muesli and I don't want toast.'

'I'm not making pancakes.'

George's face went red, and she started shrieking again.

Victor poked his sleep-crumpled face through the half-open door. 'Can't a man get some sleep around here? Stop bloody fighting.'

Fin cracked some eggs into a bowl, went outside for the milk, then added some flour and sugar.

Ten minutes later, she was melting butter and dropping sizzling blobs of batter into the pan without looking at George.

Fin spooned cereal. George poured far too much maple syrup onto her pancakes. They ate in silence.

Later, lathered in sunscreen, Fin walked to the fork in the road with George panting behind her. 'Why do we have to walk so far?'

'Quit complaining. You shouldn't have come.'

'Wait… wait for me.'

Fin picked up the pace. Sweat trickled down her face while anger smouldered just beneath her skin.

Just before the final ridge, she could see Arch's Land Rover. She waved. He waved back.

'Hi, Arch.'

Fin heard George scramble up behind her, breathing heavily.

Arch fidgeted with his weather-beaten hat, a half-smile on his lips.

Fin sighed. 'My younger sister, George. She insisted on coming.'

'No worries. The more the merrier. Let's get going.'

He lifted George into the back seat and dug out the seatbelt with difficulty. 'No one sits in the back. It hasn't been used for ages.'

Soon they bounced along the rutted road, Fin once again grateful that talking was impossible. Arch turned off into a paddock of dry, waist-high grass. Fin clung to the side of the car and thought it was about to roll when Arch deftly spun the steering wheel around and they righted again. She felt George's fingers clinging to the back of the seat, heard her squeals of excitement as they made slow, bumpy progress.

Fin's teeth rattled in their sockets and the seat sucked her thighs. Over the final hill they stared down at a wide, brown body of water sliding sinuously through the dry landscape.

'We might walk from here.'

Arch reached behind his seat and pulled out an esky and an old, frayed towel that might have been white once but was reduced to a worn grey. The three of them half ran, and half stumbled down to the water. Without waiting for George or Arch, Fin slid into the water, still wearing board shorts and a tee over her Speedos.

She dissolved into the muddy cool. Her arms sliced through the water. The stillness beneath the surface silenced the whirling, loud thoughts hammering inside her head. She emerged, powerful after swimming to the other side then back, water sluicing off her skin, her hair clinging to her head.

'Swim with me, Fin. *Please.*'

George stood calf-deep at the edge, arms stretched out.

Arch stared at Fin with undisguised amazement. 'Jeez, you aced it in there. You in training for the Olympics or something?'

Fin felt the way the tee clung to her curves and suddenly was shy in front of him. She crossed her arms. 'Nah. Just always loved swimming. I used to train and was part of a swim club.'

George was coming in deeper, holding her arms out to Fin, who called out to Arch.

'Toss me the swim ring in the bag.'

George never seemed to get the hang of swimming. Despite weekly lessons and a block of classes one summer, she flailed and sank like a stone. It was hard to believe she was so graceful in her ballet class.

The morning passed in a blur. They swam, relaxed in the shade, and enjoyed a picnic. Fin pulled out the apples and smoked almonds while Arch unpacked boiled eggs, buttered white slices of bread, and a couple of caramel slices from Yowie's sweet spot.

'I only brought two, so you have them,' he said.

Fin handed one to George, then broke the other in half and handed Arch the bigger piece. Her hand brushed his and he looked away, a rising tide of red on his neck.

'Hey, thanks.'

They sat in silence for a while and watched George sit on a rock in the shallows.

'It's a great spot. Thanks for bringing us along.'

'We'll have to come again. On days where I'm not helping the old man and Mum's all right.'

'Is your mum sick?'

Arch chewed on a piece of grass and stared into the distance. 'Kind of.'

He rolled off his towel and packed up the rubbish. 'We might need to head off. Dad will need me soon.'

Fin longed to ask him more but instead helped pack up.

They drove back through the paddock and turned onto the dirt road. 'I'll drop you at the front door this time.'

'No, it's okay, we can walk.'

George piped up from the back. 'No. I'm too tired.'

Arch raised an eyebrow. 'Sounds like that's sorted then.'

Fin hunched back into her seat and hoped Dad wouldn't be home.

Mum was hanging up clothes on a line strung up between two posts. Dad saw them coming and walked over. George leapt out of the car, damp hair plastered on her cheeks, eyes sparkling. 'This is Arch. He took us swimming and we had a picnic. It was the best day ever.'

Fin gathered their towels, bags, and George's flotation device. She longed to speak to Arch alone, but he was already out of the car, shaking hands with Victor and nodding a greeting to Mum.

Victor looked him up and down. 'So, you're our neighbour then. Well, we are planning to have a party to say hello to everyone. You'll have to come along. Bring your parents, of course.'

Fin chewed the inside of her lip. A party? It was the first she'd heard of it.

Arch's arms hung down by his sides, his thongs scuffing the dirt. 'I'll ask them. They aren't really party people.'

Victor slapped Arch on the back so hard he nearly stumbled.

'Well, we might keep it simple then. Just your family. Next Friday night? That's settled.'

Arch turned to his truck, backed out, and drove away while George spoke excitedly to Mum and Dad about the swim and Arch – how much she liked him. Fin walked past them and let the door slam hard behind her.

11

Three years earlier

FIN ground through the days, even working overtime while she miscarried. It was just over a week before the cramping finally eased, leaving her body weakened by exhaustion and disappointment. She pushed open the front door, relieved to get home and have a few days off. This evening, she promised herself she would sit down and tell Anthony about losing the baby.

'Are you sure everything's okay?' His brow crinkled with concern.

'I've had a huge week.'

Fin dumped her bag on the floor and was about to suggest retreating to the lounge when The Beach Boy's *God Only Knows* started on Anthony's phone, alerting him that Damon was calling. He hardly ever rang. Anthony sent texts regularly, and sometimes Damon responded. Fin ignored the guilt prodding her conscience. She had not made any effort to get to know Damon. His surprise appearance at the family lunch with George still felt raw and unresolved.

Anthony's voice was curt. 'Hello.'

Fin slumped onto one of the bar stools, annoyed at the interruption to their evening. She reached for the bowl of macadamia nuts, then for the nutcracker. It was the first thing she and Anthony had purchased together. Having this shared thing with its smooth timber and shiny metal made her happy in a way that was hard to put into words. It felt secure and permanent to buy something practical yet indulgent with a person you loved.

Anthony started to pace, and his eyes narrowed to a frown. His voice went up a notch. 'Why not wait till you can save up the money? I told you

I'm happy to employ you at the bookshop.'

Fin positioned one of the nuts under the corkscrew and twisted the handle until the hard shell cracked, startling Anthony who pressed the phone harder to his ear and walked away. 'No, I'm not telling you how to live your life, I'm providing an opportunity…'

Damon must have hung up. Fin was poised with a fresh macadamia. She raised an eyebrow, her own grief momentarily shelved. 'Is everything okay?'

Anthony tossed the phone onto the bench and ran his hand through his hair. 'He can be so exasperating. I want to do the right thing, I really do, and I just stuff up every time.'

He walked over to the kettle, filled it up and jammed it onto the cradle. 'I was such a bloody awful father and I guess this is the result.'

Fin left the scattered shell on the bench and walked over to him. 'Maybe it's not just you.'

He leant over the sink as the kettle wailed to a crescendo. 'He's obsessed with his music, but he's never earned enough with his gigs. Pip kicked him out and I help him financially from time to time. We both think it would be good for him to get a job and earn his way.'

Fin hugged Anthony from behind, but he didn't respond. She felt another twinge in her pelvis, a reminder she had not told him about the miscarriage.

'How about a cuppa?' Anthony suggested.

'Do you want me to make it?' Fin let go of him.

Anthony continued his tea-making ritual without responding, without even looking at Fin.

He set the tea things on the tray with two of the fancy cups and saucers, his movements terse. 'When Pip fell pregnant with Damon, I was travelling all the time with a wine distributing company. I earned a lot of money and was never there for her or my son. When Damon was seven, she fell in love with someone else and that was it. It was a year before we came to some sort of arrangement where I could see Damon. I indulged him, hoping to win his favour, but it backfired, of course.'

Anthony picked the tray up and carried it rattling to the lounge room.

He swirled the tea in the kettle and poured them each a dark brew, then added a slosh of milk. Holding his cup and saucer in one hand, he sat forward on the edge of the sofa, a short distance away from her.

He took a sip, then placed the cup down again. Fin's mobile rang and he winced. 'Just leave it for a minute.'

She had already answered, 'Hello?'

George's voice gushed down the phone. 'We're flying out next weekend. To New York. Can you believe it?'

Fin scrambled to make sense of what George was saying. When she was excited about things, it could take a few moments to find a foothold in the conversation and to work out if she was on a high or a low.

'With Damon?'

Fin sensed Anthony holding his breath.

'I was ringing to see if you would like to come out with us to celebrate.'

A high.

Fin turned around to face Anthony, who looked worried. He mouthed, 'George?'

Fin nodded. 'When? I've got a couple of late shifts coming up.'

Anthony folded his arms.

Fin sighed. 'Wednesday sounds good. I'll check with Anthony.'

She dropped her phone near the tray and looked at him. He was rubbing one thumb over the knuckles of his other hand. When he looked up, expectant, Fin saw he had dark bags under his eyes. She sagged into the cushions, leaving a gap between the two of them. 'It was George. She's moving to America with Damon.'

Anthony's shoulders slumped. 'I'm sorry, Fin. I have been trying to talk to you about this trip for the last week but haven't found the right moment. You seemed distracted and not yourself.'

The quiet was uncomfortable. Anthony sat with his elbows on his knees, leaning forward, his fingertips pressed together as if in prayer.

'Damon has had a few problems. I'm a bit concerned about him moving so far away from support.'

'I guess he's an adult now. We'll keep in regular contact with them.' Fin sighed. 'To be honest, I'm worried about George. She doesn't have a great track record when it comes to relationships or holding down a job. New York is a long way away if things turn to custard.'

Anthony stared at the floor and didn't respond. Fin squared her jaw when she thought about George bringing Damon to that lunch. They hadn't spoken since.

Anthony cut across her thoughts. 'Damon rang me recently and asked to borrow money to pay for the trip. I suggested he delay until he had enough funds and offered him a job working at the bookshop.'

Anthony sank deeper into the couch and left his tea untouched. 'We argued. He accused me of never being there when he really needed me.'

'How are they paying for the trip or arranging green cards and somewhere to live? George struggles to get to a job interview on time. She has a sales job at Dance Revolution but barely makes it from one pay to the next.'

'Your parents paid the airfares and some indie music label, Back Alley Sounds, is putting them up in Brooklyn, organising the paperwork needed for Damon to do gigs.'

Fin tried hard not to resent her parents funding this trip. Surely if she ever needed help, they would do the same for her.

Anthony sighed and held his head in his hands. 'I just hope this big break turns out to be what he imagined.'

He was drumming his fingers on his thigh now. Fin shifted sideways and closed the gap between them. She felt the warmth of his thigh near hers.

They continued to sit side by side on the sofa, neither of them moving, the stillness thick with words unspoken. It had grown dark outside, the hum of traffic distant. A door banged next door. They both startled. Fin nuzzled into Anthony's warmth and felt the tight ball in his neck and shoulders soften. The throb in her lower belly slowed to a dull beat. She pressed her face into the weave of his sweater and inhaled his familiar scent. It loosened something inside her. She whispered, 'I miscarried this week. It was awful.'

His arm wrapped around her and pulled her so close she could feel his heartbeat against her own, aware of the silence where the baby's flutter should be.

'I'm so sorry.'

He kissed the top of her head, then brushed her lips with his own. 'Why didn't you tell me? I want to be there for you, to mourn the loss of this baby together.'

The teas grew cold and neither of them let go of the other, both leaning into the other's need. Then Fin felt Anthony's lips near her ear, his voice soft with understanding.

'It's been close to six months, hasn't it? I remember that doctor mentioning we should get another opinion if we were not pregnant. What do you think?'

12

Teenagerhood

FRIDAY was hot and still. Leaves hung vertical and motionless. The day held its breath, foreshadowing ruin. Fin longed to warn Arch.

Victor hung lights up in the trees, unrolled some rugs, and placed them on the deck. He spruced up the garden and gave orders for Mum to cook all sorts of impossible dishes that required an oven.

'Darling, I just can't bake any sort of cakes now,' Mum said, standing next to the fridge, which was propped up on old sleepers on the deck. 'We might have to keep things simple until I have a kitchen.'

'We don't do simple when we have guests. Use your imagination for fuck's sake.'

He stomped off, leaving Barb wringing her hands and the old fridge rattling to life behind her. Fin wondered whether Mum ever longed to pack up and snatch back her old life, where she smiled like in that hidden photo.

Fin was tempted to suggest it when her thoughts returned to Arch; his soft, hazel eyes, his lanky arms and legs, and the way water droplets glistened on his sun-browned skin when he lay with arms folded behind his head after their swim. Mum walked back into the tiny kitchen nook, mangling her apron like a washcloth.

Fin followed. She bit her lip, then asked, 'How about I head down to the bakery and get a few sweet things? They have a huge selection, and we could arrange it all on a platter?'

Mum turned from the twin-burner gas hotplate. 'Fin, would you? That sounds marvellous. I might make some schnitzels and salads and have some nice cheeses and crackers for entrée. What do you think?'

'It sounds great. Everyone loves your schnitzels.'

The day crawled past, and Fin prayed for some miracle like a phone call from Arch's family, apologising that they wouldn't make it. At five o'clock, a battered Land Rover pulled up on the flat gravelled area near Victor's truck. The sun still burnt a white hole in the sky and Fin felt a ring of perspiration blooming in her armpits. Victor had insisted they all dress up. The striped cotton dress he wanted her to wear was much too small and clung to her curves, her breasts straining against the buttons at the front. If it hadn't been so hot, she would have hidden behind a cardigan. She was grateful her parents were so busy with preparations that they hadn't heard the car pull up.

A rugged fellow with grey-speckled hair stepped out of the car wearing worn jeans, a checked shirt rolled up to his elbows, and scuffed boots. He walked around to the car boot and pulled out an esky while a slender woman in a long, white sundress and large straw hat alighted from the passenger seat. Fin tried not to stare. The woman stood with the sun behind her. She was strangely beautiful: tall and pale, the shape of her legs visible through the fabric. Her hair was very long and straight, and swished across her back whenever she moved. Arch waved with one hand and balanced a box in the other.

Fin was about to go and greet them when George ran out. 'Arch, can we go swimming again, please?' She stood staring up at him and tugged his shirt, her soft curls golden in the glare of the sun.

'Careful,' he said, holding the box with two hands now. 'I've brought you some fresh eggs. Maybe you could have some for breakfast?'

George reached for the box. 'Yes, please'.

Fin stood back with her arms crossed over the bulging buttons on her chest.

Arch kicked the car door shut with his foot and smiled at Fin, still holding the box of eggs. 'I'd like you to meet my mum, Joy, and my dad, Cliff.'

Joy's face was barely visible under her hat, the skin on her pale arms dusted with freckles. Only her wide smile peeked out from under the broad brim, revealing a gap between her front teeth. She smelt like those shops that sold new-age stuff. Unlike Fin, Joy appeared unaffected by the heat.

'Thanks for having us over.' Joy's voice was throaty and deep. 'We were wondering who bought Yowie's place, it's been for sale so long.'

Fin remembered Dad saying how lucky he was to get in first and what an incredible bargain the place had been. Staring at the drought-packed earth in the distance, she couldn't help wondering if he'd been had. Then she remembered her manners. 'Thanks for coming. Lovely to meet you both.'

Fin went over to Arch and peered into the box filled with eggs layered in blue cardboard packing cases. 'That's so generous of you. Let me take them inside.' She eased the large box from his grasp.

Joy bent towards her. 'Arch has been talking about you non-stop. I was really looking forward to meeting you.'

Fin felt a small thrill inside and saw him look away. Maybe things would work out and she would have a friend here. She would have to write to Miranda and tell her.

George ran inside through to the back deck. Fin heard her high-pitched voice. 'Mum, Dad, they're here!'

Victor came out red-faced, mopping his brow and neck with a sweaty handkerchief. He was dressed in a suit with braces minus the jacket, his tie patterned with brown and beige stripes. Overdressed, he hurried out to his guests. 'Delighted you could make it.'

He pumped Cliff's hand and kissed Joy on both cheeks, bumping her hat.

'Please come around to our entertainment deck. We are, of course, in the process of building a substantial home up on the hilltop with incredible views. We have big plans for the place.' He gave an exaggerated wink. 'But it's all a bit *hush, hush* at this stage.'

Cliff nodded. 'Well, mate, if you need fresh eggs, we're a short drive away.'

They followed him to the back, all set up for the party. Barb stood in front of the table – Victor had used two trestles and an old door – draped with a white cloth and set up with an oddment of cutlery and mismatched wine glasses. The chairs were a motley collection foraged from the shipping container and inside the shack.

Barb fiddled with her apron. She was dressed in her traditional *dirndl*, looking like a character from *The Sound of Music*. She half smiled, fingers twitching between fabric. 'I'm Barb. Do have a seat and I'll bring out some food.'

She looked grateful to escape inside. Fin followed with the eggs and listened to Victor's booming voice. 'Now, don't be shy. Can I get you a glass of wine?'

Cliff's voice sounded a bit rough at the edges. 'Nah, mate, I've brought some beers. That'll do me.'

Fin heard melting ice shifting in the esky and the hiss as the top was screwed off his stubby.

Joy had taken off her hat and found a shaded spot on the deck. She pulled a chair out from the table. 'I'd love a glass, hon.'

Arch was standing at the edge staring at the pegs used to mark out the cabins. George disappeared then reappeared wearing her leotard, pink ruffled skirt, and ballet slippers.

Victor knelt and beckoned. 'Have you met my youngest? Quite the talent on the dance floor. I'll put on some music later and she can show you.'

Fin spent most of the evening fetching and carrying food, clearing used dishes, and washing up between courses to ensure they had enough plates. She longed to change into shorts and a loose tee but didn't dare.

Arch popped his head inside. 'Hey, why don't you come out? We could go for a walk along the creek bed.'

It was so tempting to head down and perhaps catch a breeze in the gully. Fin shook her head. Victor would be livid if she disappeared.

Arch persisted, his dimple dancing in his cheek. 'Don't worry about the dishes. I'll help you with those later. Are these the dessert platters? Let's take them out and use napkins instead of plates.'

Fin nearly laughed out loud. Napkins. She could hear Victor's voice. *We have standards, don't you forget that.* She managed a smile that barely moved her lips. 'It's all right, I'm nearly done.'

'Well, let me wipe up then.'

They worked side by side in silence. Fin scraped leftovers into newspaper, dunked each plate into the suds, then handed it to Arch to wipe. Her hands wrinkled in the lukewarm water, greasy with bits of debris. Light had shifted to a rich, red-gold sunset. She turned to hand him the final plate and her hand brushed against his. Her breath caught and somehow the wet plate slipped to the floor and shattered into pieces between them. They jumped apart just as Victor roared in. 'I can't believe how clumsy you are. Be a bit more careful with things.'

Without missing a beat, Arch stepped forward, 'Sorry, mate, that was me. I'll buy you a new one.'

Victor faltered for a heartbeat then waved his hand in dismissal. 'Don't worry about it, young chap. Bring out the clean plates and we might enjoy some dessert.'

Fin leaned against the sink and exhaled.

Arch raised an eyebrow at her before picking up the dessert platter and carrying it outside. Fin followed with the freshly washed plates.

Things were noisy on the deck. Joy was holding a wine glass aloft, hair half covering her face, feet bare, swaying and laughing while Mum watched. Victor was explaining his grand design for the house he planned to build to Cliff who listened politely, one eye regularly flicking over to his wife.

Victor picked up a melting hedgehog slice and frowned. 'Barb, what's this?'

Fin's pulse quickened. 'It's a selection from the Yowie Bakery.'

He took a bite and put the half-eaten piece back on the tray. 'Bloody rubbish. Not a patch on Barb's continental cakes. We'll get you over again when we can serve you something decent.'

Cliff helped himself to a couple of slices and held them in a napkin. 'Doug and Sheila have won awards for their stuff.'

Fin scanned the tray for some caramel slice and reached for it when Victor's voice boomed loud across the table. 'Barb, you really need to keep an eye on what Fin's eating. She is bursting out of her dress.'

Fin withdrew her hand like she had been slapped. She turned away and nearly walked into Joy, who looked unsteady. Her face was flushed, and the strap of her dress had fallen off one shoulder. 'Anuffer drink, please.'

Cliff shook his head and reached out to steady her. 'I think that's enough, love. How about a piece of that coconut slice you like?'

She stumbled over to the esky, tripped on a curled edge of carpet, and fell. Arch rushed over and knelt beside her. 'Mum, are you okay? Let me help you up.'

Two strides later, Cliff joined them. He rolled Joy over and picked her up. She hung from his arms like she was unconscious, blood oozing on her forehead, head tipped backwards, hair flowing loose, an empty glass miraculously intact, still clutched in her hand. 'Just one more.'

'Arch, mate, grab the esky. We might head off home. Your ma's hurt herself.'

Without a word, Arch picked it up, grabbed the car keys and walked to the Land Rover. Cliff gave a nod to Barb but ignored Victor. 'Thanks for the meal.'

They left with a squeal of tyres on gravel, streaming dust behind them.

George had chocolate on her face and streaked down her leotard. The pink skirt looked torn, one ballet slipper missing. Fin stood beside her, watching the dust settle.

Victor loosened his tie and shook his braces off his shoulders so they looped around his hips. The smell of his sweat was pungent. 'They are not our sort of people. Bloody chicken farmers, what do you expect?'

He turned to Fin. 'I forbid you to associate with that lout of theirs again.'

13

Three years earlier

FIN toyed with her gin and tonic at the Stones Corner Pub. She glanced at her watch, yet again wondering where George was, and shot her another text.

Where are you?

Forty-five minutes late. Fin shifted in her seat, and crossed and uncrossed her legs.

Fin stabbed at the slice of lime in her drink with her straw. She had an early shift in the morning. She had another look at the time and wished Anthony were here.

At eight, Fin shoved her empty glass aside and stood up to leave.

'Fin! Am I late?' George whirled inside wearing skinny black jeans, a leather jacket, and high-heeled boots, with a frayed satchel slung over one shoulder.

'One hour and five minutes. And yes, I am counting.'

'Jesus, I'm sorry, Fin. Sorry, sorry, sorry. There's so much to do and I just don't think I'll get it done.'

Fin dropped back into the chair with a sigh. 'Let's order.'

'You won't believe it, but I left my purse at Damon's place. It's complete chaos. I can't find anything.'

Fin bit her lip. 'I'll order a plate of fish and chips and we can share.'

'Could you get me a rum and coke? I'll pay you back, promise.'

The food came out. George drank her rum and coke quickly and asked if she could have another. Fin dunked chips into tartar sauce, no longer hungry.

George's fingernails were long and green, matching the streaks in her hair. Her make-up was thick and too dark. She talked non-stop, and her wild gesticulating nearly knocked over her second drink.

'I know you don't like Damon, but Fin, he's the one. He really is. It is all a bit weird, but Anthony and Damon never talk. He wasn't even there when Damon grew up, so it's kind of less weird don't you think?'

Fin stood up, leaving the now soggy chips and cold battered fish.

George teared up. She stood up too, walked around, and gave Fin a hug. 'I'm going to miss you. I really am.'

Fin didn't return the hug. 'Keep in touch. At least once a week or so.'

George wouldn't. She never did.

Fin reached for her bag draped over the back of the chair.

George dug frantically around in her satchel. 'I nearly forgot. I got you something.'

She shoved a crinkled brown paper bag into Fin's hand.

'Sorry, I didn't have time to wrap it properly.'

'Thanks.' Fin shoved it into her handbag. She gave George a peck on the cheek and walked out.

It was only the next day at work when Fin remembered the gift. She put her tuna salad aside and pulled out the crinkled brown paper bag. Fin reached inside and pulled out a small photo frame. Inside was a picture of herself as a kid standing on a podium in Speedos with a blue ribbon pinned to her chest, her eyes scanning the bleachers.

Fin gazed down at it, the day rushing back to her. The thrill of her success, the disappointment that none of her family had come to watch. She wondered who had taken the photo and how George had managed to get hold of it. Fin looked inside the bag again and found a scrap of paper torn from a spiral notebook.

Dear Fin,
You are the best big sis.
Always number one.
G

~

It was seven months since Fin and Anthony had driven George and Damon to the international airport and waved them off. George sent a message a week after they landed in America, letting Fin know they were settled in New York. A few months later she sent a grainy photograph of the Statue of Liberty with the words, *playing tourist*.

Then silence, despite multiple attempts by Fin to make contact.

Fin lay curled up on her side of the bed, facing away from Anthony. Sunlight fell in slats on the timber floor, shifting when the blind moved with a soft breeze. She felt his hand on her shoulder.

'Morning, beautiful.'

Six months of fertility treatment now and still no baby. Fin curled around her disappointment, her body's betrayal. She juggled her shifts around appointments, hopeful with each cycle that this would be the one.

Anthony traced a finger up to her neck, let it run slowly, feather-light down her spine and over her cotton nightie, awakening the glimmer of sensations she had forgotten existed. His hand snuck underneath fabric to rest on her hip. He tried to unfold her and pull her close into the familiar curve of him. Fin stayed stubbornly tight and refused to respond, any intimacy a reminder of her body's treachery.

Anthony sighed and rolled onto his back. She thought he might say something, mention the rising costs of fertility treatment or probe her sullen mood, but he didn't speak. He stayed close so she was aware of the warmth of his body and felt his breath against her skin.

It was starting to get uncomfortably hot when he rolled onto one elbow and spoke to the stubborn curve of her back. 'Have you thought about taking some time off? I'm happy to leave the bookshop in Freya's capable hands for a week or two.'

Fin's eyes were moist. She felt a tear slide along her nose and pause before sliding over the curve of her cheek, around the edge of her lips and onto the pillow. She caught it with her tongue and tasted the salt of despair. 'We have a series of appointments with City Fertility coming up.'

'That can wait. One or two weeks won't change anything. It's only been six months.'

'Plus six months of trying without any help.'

Anthony placed his hand on her shoulder. She took care not to wince. 'Maybe some time away, just the two of us relaxing somewhere beautiful will help us forget about it all for a while and give your body a break from the constant pressure of hormones, appointments, and deadlines. There can't be any harm in having a holiday.'

How to explain to him that every day of every week mattered? 'I'll think about it, check with work.'

She slipped out from under him, sat up and was about to head to the ensuite when her phone vibrated. It was George, her first contact in three months. Fin pressed the phone to her ear. 'George?'

Anthony sat up. His hair stuck up like a dishevelled kid, and his pyjama buttons were in the wrong holes, making him look lopsided. Fin turned away.

'Are you alright?' After all, the only time George called was when something was wrong.

Silence.

Fin's heart paused. Her breath caught in her throat. Maybe Damon had ended things and George was stranded alone in New York.

Fin felt Anthony's lips near her ear. He whispered something about getting pastries for breakfast. She nodded, keen to speak to George alone. She hoped George was still there.

'God, I miss you Fin. So much.'

'So, how is New York treating you?'

There was a sob at the end of the line. 'Well, the city is incredible. All buzz and lights, something happening all the time, but…' Another sob. 'Poor Damon is working so hard, he's so busy. I hardly see him. It gets lonely.'

'Why don't you respond to my emails? My messages? Do you even check WhatsApp? I'm worried about you.'

'I'm sorry, I really am. I plan to, and then get swept along by things and don't know what to say. I know that you won't approve and then I feel awful.'

Fin tried to work out what time it was in New York, gripping her phone so hard that her knuckles hurt. 'Just a *hello, I'm fine, let's chat later* would do and put my mind at rest.'

'You know how hopeless I am at that stuff. I promise I'll try harder to keep in touch.'

This was not the first time George had made such promises. She never followed through. Fin clenched her jaw.

'Are you there?' George sounded anxious.

'Yes. I was just thinking and remembering all the other times I thought you'd been abducted, murdered, or had disappeared without a trace.'

'But I never was, you always found me, looked after me.'

How many terminations was George up to? Fin pulled her knees up to her chest, her thighs pressing into her own barren womb.

'And I didn't forget your birthday. I sent you something. I bet it's late. You can't rely on the post.'

A present? 'I'll let you know the minute it arrives.'

'There's just one other thing.' George's voice was saccharine now. Fin hugged her knees with one arm and clutched the phone even harder with her other hand.

'I'm so sorry to ask you, but can you loan me some money? About ten thousand? We're in a bit of a tight spot. I'll pay you back the minute Damon does his first big gig. I just don't want to ask Mum and Dad and Damon refuses to ask Anthony. He told me his dad is a real tight-arse.'

Fin heard the front door open, then bang shut. She wanted to defend Anthony but instead clenched her teeth.

There was crinkling of paper out in the kitchen. Anthony loved lining up at the bakery and bringing them something wicked for breakfast. It was better he didn't know about George's request. Thinking about Damon always made him upset.

'George, I gotta go. Send me the details of your account and I'll sort it. A loan this time, mind you. I would like it back.'

A sigh of relief. 'You really are the best. I love you, sis. Muah, muah.'

'Love you, George.'

A click. Silence.

Anthony called out, 'How is George?' Fin hoped he wouldn't probe. He would be livid about the loan.

Fin slid off the bed. 'Just fine. Living the high life by the sound of things.'

The smell of freshly baked goodies wafted from the kitchen, and Anthony set out a couple of almond croissants, one of her favourites. 'She bought me a birthday pressie, just posted it a bit late. Typical.'

'I see.'

Anthony had just finished making tea and sat with the *Sydney Morning Herald* folded under his arm. He opened his mouth to say something, thought the better of it and pulled up a chair, scraping the timber floor.

Fin flinched at the jarring noise before pulling up the chair opposite. She reached for the colour magazine, opened it, and broke off a piece of croissant, careful not to catch his eye. 'How about a long weekend at Maleny?'

14

Teenagerhood

THE claustrophobic bedroom was nearly dark. Dusky evening light silhouetted the furniture crowded into the shared space. Fin held the creased bus timetable in her hand, torn about whether to see Arch again or not. It would have to be in secret. Once Dad made up his mind about someone, there was no shifting him.

She shuddered when she remembered snippets of the evening, a kaleidoscope of humiliation. The tight dress she loathed, George clamouring for attention.

'Dinner!'

The goulash, with big chunks of potato and chuck steak floating around in a thick sauce, was unsuitable on a stinking hot, humid day. Fin played with her food, the hard lump in her gullet making swallowing impossible.

'Would you like a piece of bread to mop up the sauce?' Mum pushed the basket with its thick slabs towards Fin, then continued fussing around George, cutting her bits of meat smaller. She even put out a saucer with a cube of sauce-drenched steak for Lucky, the mangy, stuffed dog. It was absurd the way Mum pampered George. At seven, George could cut up her own food and didn't need to pretend to feed her toy. Fin curled over her own plate and sweated into the food.

'I'm not feeling that great,' Fin said. 'I might just head off to bed.'

She lay in the dark, ran her hands down her curves, ashamed of her breasts and hips. The obscene fleshiness of it all.

Bursting out of her dress.

Despite spending so much of her life in Speedos, she never really looked at herself and had ignored comments about her breasts. She was so absorbed with improving her times and being selected for the squad that she never worried about being the first girl in her class to reach puberty. At ten, she sprouted buds on her chest, grew hair in awkward private spaces, and became impossibly tall and square. One year later, her period started: an inconvenient complication for a swimmer. She spent ages in the toilet attempting to insert a tampon with only the most rudimentary knowledge of her anatomy. There was no way she could ask Mum about that sort of thing. Her efforts at sex education were a few muttered words about not letting boys touch her 'down there', followed by a copy of the book *Where Did I Come From,* handed to her in a brown paper bag.

If only she had a full-length mirror to make a full appraisal of herself. Mum had a mirror above the dressing table, but you could only see your top half. Everything else was packed away in the shipping container, inaccessible. Who knew when Dad would build the new place?

Fin pretended to be asleep when George came to bed and heard Mum shushing her. If only Fin had her own room and a bit of privacy. How many fourteen-year-olds were forced to share a room with their seven-year-old sibling?

Fin's sleep was restless and by early morning she was wide awake. She stared out at the softening darkness, thready clouds blurring the moon.

Careful not to wake George, who was fast asleep on a mattress nearby, Fin pulled on shorts and a tee, laced up her sneakers and crept outside in time to see the horizon streaked with pink. She set off at a brisk pace up the hill and reached the crest. She let go and started to sprint down the other side. It felt good, pumping her lungs with air and making her pulse beat hard. She tried to run up the next hill but only managed short painful bursts. Panting, she reached the highest point, where Dad had brought them all on their very first day here. She could hear his words and remembered the gleam in his eyes and the way he spread his arms wide like a preacher.

'And this is where I will build our home.' He'd made a grand sweeping gesture. 'Whichever way you look, it is all mine. I've always dreamt of standing somewhere knowing that as far as my eye can see belongs to me. I will build a place where I can gather my family around me and stare out at my own land.'

He walked around the site then, still talking and gesticulating, the future mapped out in fine detail in his head. 'This will be the view from the living room. Large glass windows in three directions. Over here will be the kitchen, the work area looking over the cabins I plan to build for guests.'

He stepped back and waved one hand over windswept grasses bending in the breeze, before trampling them underfoot. 'And here are the bedrooms, set back and private, each with their own deck and private garden.'

It was the happiest Fin remembered ever seeing him.

Staring down, she could make out a tiny figure just outside the dot of the old hut. It would be Mum, starting the chores for the day. Fin took a deep breath then plunged down the slope, skidding on gravel, the sound of it crunching beneath her soles. There was a rush of satisfaction at sucking warm air into her lungs, a pleasure at the ache of muscles contracting as each foot landed, the sound of twigs and dry grass snapping with each step.

She arrived at the shack bent over, panting with sweat glistening on her skin. Mum came out with the pink tub, sloshed water onto the dry ground. The sun was well over the horizon now, the heat starting to bite. 'Where did you go?'

'Nowhere in particular.'

Mum looked wrung out. She suddenly seemed much older, fine lines etching her face, grey hairs streaked through brown. Fin thought of that photograph and how different her mother had looked.

'I found a photograph. You with another man.'

Barb stiffened.

'It's beautiful. Was he someone special?'

Barb clutched the pink tub, dirty suds clinging to the edge. She hesitated, and Fin glimpsed the shadow of a youthful vulnerability, then Barb turned away, tucking a stray hair behind her ear. 'There is only one special man in my life.' She squared her shoulders against the weariness of all that needed to be done. 'I've got to finish clearing up and get a load of washing on before your father gets up and needs me.'

Fin bit her lip. She was torn between doing the right thing and helping her mother when all she wanted to do was get away and leave the chaos behind her. 'I might just head into Ipswich. I need to get a few things for school.'

'Get yourself some breakfast. There's a bit of money in my purse if you need it. Do you want a lift?'

'Nah, all good. There's a bus.'

Fin rinsed off quickly under the makeshift shower her dad had set up, the cool water tightening her skin. She towelled off and wished once again for a mirror where she could look at herself properly. She grabbed a banana and her bag and took a shortcut through a paddock to the dirt road leading to the bus stop.

Once there, she found Ipswich at least five degrees hotter than home. The pavement shimmered, and the rising heat burnt through the soles of her shoes. It was like melting from the inside. Fin walked down the street, shaded her eyes with a cupped hand and admonished herself for not bringing a hat. When she stopped to sip warm water from her drink bottle, she caught sight of herself in a shop window and stared. Everyone always thought she was older than her years, and it surprised her how adult she looked. Tall and muscled, her breasts fuller than she realised. The woman in the reflection was unfamiliar to her, someone she met once and vaguely recalled but never bothered to get to know.

She walked into the store and made a show of wandering past racks of clothing. With money always in short supply, it was rare for Fin to get new clothes. Mum usually grabbed a few items from Target when they went on sale. Fin selected some clothes without looking at them too closely, wanting an excuse to go into the changing rooms. Stripped down to her panties, Fin examined herself from different angles and tried to see herself the way Victor saw her. Tall, a bit clumsy, and awkward.

Bum the size of a draught horse.

Looking at herself from behind, she squeezed her butt cheeks with her hands and frowned at them in the mirrored changing room. Standing under the harsh light of her own scrutiny, she sucked in her tummy, ran her hands down along her curves and longed to be svelte like Miranda, beautiful like George. Tears prickled her eyes. The thing about Dad was that he could be brutally honest, but he was always right.

A shrill voice called out. 'Can I help you with anything? Get you a different size?'

Fin realised she had been in the shop changing room for ages. 'No, thanks. I'll be out in a just a tick.'

Blushing, Fin dressed and handed back the items she had not even bothered to try on. She hurried out of the shop into the searing day and imagined her backside wobbling from behind. She clenched her buttock cheeks and walked more slowly, sucking her tummy in.

'Hey, are you heading back? Care for a lift?'

Arch was leaning out of his Land Rover, his cap on back to front, his elbow a sharp angle poking out the window.

I forbid you to associate with that lout of theirs again.

Crossing her arms over her breasts, aware of sweat trickling down her neck and between her cleavage, she prayed he would attribute her flushed face to the heat. 'Nah, I'll be right.'

'Hang on a tick,' Arch said. 'I'll be right back. Just let me park.'

Fin stood on the pavement in the meagre shade of a shop awning. A few minutes later he was there, hair plastered to his head, a dent where the rim of his hat rested.

He stayed a distance away from her and scuffed the toe of one boot on the pavement. 'Can I get you a drink? It's so hot.'

Fin bit her lip and looked away from his hopeful enthusiasm. 'No, thanks.'

He kicked a takeaway wrapper into the gutter with one foot. 'I just wanted to say sorry for the other night.'

Fragments of the catastrophic evening came back to Fin. Joy's long slim legs visible through the white sundress, the way Cliff carried Joy to the car, her head tilted back to reveal the translucent skin on her neck, one hand gripping the stem of an empty glass.

'Your mum, she was bleeding. Is she okay?' Fin looked over her shoulder as if she expected Victor to suddenly appear.

Arch stared down at his feet. 'Yeah, kind of. I reckon she'll have a scar.'

'I'm sorry to hear that.'

Arch reached a hand towards Fin then dropped it again. 'Come on, let's get that drink.'

She shrugged. 'I haven't got long.'

He led the way to the Central Milk Bar, the air conditioning a welcome blast of frigid air.

'What can I get you?'

Fin looked at the milkshakes with longing.

Bum the size of a draught horse.

'Just a soda water, thanks.'

'You sure? They make the best milkshakes in the world here.'

They sat down to the whirr of the blender in the background. Their drinks were brought to the table and Arch fiddled with his straw. 'I'm real sorry about the party.'

'Me too. Dad can be over the top.'

Fin had her hands around the glass and let the condensation wet them, avoiding Arch's eyes. He slurped and she imagined the creamy taste of his milkshake. He pushed it towards her. 'Have a taste.'

The thought of putting her mouth over the straw where his mouth had just been made her face hot. She dipped her head and took a small sip.

'See, I told you they're good.' His dimple danced in his cheek. He called out, 'Another strawberry milkshake, please.'

Fin licked her lips.

His brow creased. 'Are you angry about the party?'

I forbid you to associate with that lout of theirs again.

Fin reached over the table and touched his hand.

'I'm angry, but not with you.' She bit her lip and slowly withdrew her hand. 'I wish your mum hadn't fallen over and hurt herself.' There was so much more Fin wanted to say. A tear slid down her cheek.

'Here.' Arch handed her a paper napkin. 'None of it was your fault, Fin.'

The strawberry milkshake arrived.

His dimple disappeared when he looked serious, and she had an urge to make him laugh so she could see it dance again. He looked up, his eyes intense with something he wanted to tell her.

'It's Mum. I don't want you thinking she's always like that. She can be funny and generous too. I wish you could have met her sober.'

His words hung between them.

Fin kept her hands in her lap. 'Your dad is so kind. The way he picked her up…'

A pause that lasted a fraction too long.

'The thing is, Mum has a problem with drinking. We shouldn't have come.' He leaned forward, his voice trembling. 'I worry that something will happen to her one day. Dad does too, even though he never talks about it. We kinda tiptoe around her, and things go well for a while, a week or two, then it all goes wrong again.'

'Isn't there somewhere she can get help?'

'She says she can stop drinking whenever she wants to. And she does for a few days or sometimes a few weeks, then lapses again.'

Cold milkshake, strawberry sweet and thick with ice cream, slid down Fin's gullet and into her stomach. 'I'm really sorry, Arch.'

He rewarded her with the glimmer of a smile, a hint of his dimple. She glanced at the clock hanging above the counter and worried she might miss the bus. 'I really need to get home.'

He stood quickly, leaving the last mouthful of strawberry milkshake. 'Let me give you a lift. Please.'

Fin nodded and half hoped Victor might see them sitting in the truck together. 'I'd like that.'

They didn't speak driving back. Fin felt the vibration of the truck up her spine and inhaled the sweaty, musky scent of him, aware of how his tendons flexed when he shifted gears. They neared the bus stop. Home cast a shadow over her afternoon.

'Just drop me here. I'll walk the last bit.'

~

When term started the following week, the loneliness of no Miranda gaped inside Fin like a fresh wound. She sat and wrote several pages to her friend, pouring out her heart in a letter while George was at one of her dance classes. Nine pages later, Fin tore them up again and instead wrote a brief note.

Hi Miranda,

I hope you had a great holiday. I've decided I want to be a nurse and help people.

A lady cut her face at our place, and I really wanted to do something and felt so helpless. I think she needed stitches. Do you know what you want to do?

If I don't get my own room soon, there will be a murder committed. George is driving me mental. Just don't tell anyone. Ha ha.
Love always,
Your bestie, Fin

Fin didn't go out of her way to avoid Arch, but their paths no longer crossed after she started at the local high school. It made it easier to put thoughts of him aside and focus on her studies, determined to become a nurse. She worked hard and stayed back late, keen to make her parents proud. On weekends, she caught the bus to the library to escape Victor's requests for help building his empire. To her relief, Arch made no effort to come to their place, probably still too ashamed of Joy's antics.

Fin started tossing her school lunches away without even examining the contents. Instead, she grabbed an apple, taking care to choose the most perfect one. Smooth, unblemished, and just the right size. Without friends, she spent her lunch hour reading under a tree and sliced her apple into so many segments that each one was transparent. Hunger became an overwhelming and constant presence. She imagined buttered toast, perfectly crumbed schnitzels, hot porridge lathered in brown sugar. When Mum wasn't looking, Fin stole five dollars from her purse and used it to purchase soda water to fill herself up. Weeks later, when she ran her hands down her body in bed at night, she found sharper edges and angles, hip bones, the bumpy ridge of ribs rutted beneath her fingertips.

A few months later, during the Christmas holidays, her periods ceased. It was a relief. No more inconvenient cramps and discomfort or fiddling with sanitary wear. Careful not to draw attention to herself, she continued to accept the sanitary products her mother bought but discarded them, unused. Fin took more care with her appearance, but no one noticed her newly defined cheekbones or the way she moved food around her plate. Barb was in survival mode, teaching and keeping the household afloat, while Victor continued full throttle with his plans.

Six months after starting at her new high school, Victor looked Fin up and down. The bottom half of his face cracked into a grin. 'You're growing up, looking like quite the lady these days.' He wagged a finger at Barb. 'Look at Fin. I knew this move was the right thing for our family.'

He put his arm around Fin's shoulder. 'Let me take you into town and treat you to some pretty clothes.'

Standing in the mall, Fin felt light as air, swept up in the rush of sound, movement, and people streaming past. Victor dressed in a suit for the occasion and guided her into Myer. 'This is where people like us shop. A place where you get decent service and quality.'

Fin left behind her longing for stonewashed ripped jeans and Doc Martins and followed Victor, grateful for his undivided attention. She floated on gleaming floors and slid along the inviting spaces between racks of clothes. Victor chose armfuls of garments. He complimented the mature saleswoman's hairstyle and shoes and stood a little closer than was polite. 'We are so delighted to have someone of your calibre serving us today.'

He whisked Fin into the changing rooms. None of the items he chose were things she would have selected, but she stayed mute and enjoyed the thrill of his attentiveness. He flashed his credit card, then winked at the other sales assistant, who was only a few years older than Fin. 'That's my girl I'm buying clothes for. Doesn't she look great?'

My girl. Fin hugged his words to herself. At home, Victor insisted she perform a fashion parade in front of them. One outfit after another, she strutted her stuff and relished the cling of the fabrics along her new, lean body. Her collarbones angled sharp like coat hangers. She stood tall, shoulders back, aware of how Mum and George watched her.

That old life with Miranda and swim club seemed so distant, it was like a dream where she only remembered odd fragments after waking up. The correspondence between them had petered out to the occasional note or postcard. Fin put aside her disappointment and thought to herself that her old bestie might not even recognise her now that she was thin and beautiful.

That night, Fin's fingers slid over her new, pared-back body, paused at the rounded fullness of her belly. She had relaxed tonight, basked in the pleasure of the day, and indulged in a large serve of *käsespätzle*, the soft cheesy flavour still a warm memory in her mouth.

She ignored the old fleshy Fin who lurked in the shadows and threatened to emerge again. She slid her fingers between her thighs, careful not to make any noise.

George turned away from her these days. A privacy of sorts. Just when Fin inhaled in response to the ripple of sensations thrilling down her spine, George's voice sounded in the darkness.

'I can hear you.'

Ashamed, Fin curled around her body, willed its still throbbing desires into submission, and pulled the sheet over her head.

15

Three years earlier

ANTHONY chose a cottage just outside Maleny on a grassy hill with glimpses of the rugged volcanic peaks of the Glass House Mountains. Fin stood beside him, the haze a veil over the ancient landscape, the sun dissolving in red and gold across the horizon.

'When Captain Cook sailed past here,' said Anthony, one hand shielding his eyes, 'he thought they resembled the glassmaking foundries of York.' He dropped his hand and squinted. 'I re-read the Dreamtime story today of how these mountains really came to be.'

Fin sidled closer to him. He put his arm around her, the fiery orb slipping off the edge of the earth, its red-gold fingers streaked between blunt peaks.

'That's the father, Tibrogargan, and the mother, Beerwah,' Anthony said, pointing. 'And the other mountains are their children. One day, Tibrogargan noticed the seas rising and called out to his son, Coonowrin.' Anthony pointed again, but the sky was fading now, and it was more difficult to make out the shapes.

'He wanted his son to help his mother, Beerwah, who was pregnant with another mountain. Coonowrin ran away without assisting his mother, making Tibrogargan furious. Did you notice the funny shape of that mountain over there?' Anthony pointed into the dusk. 'Tibrogargan struck Coonowrin so hard, his neck became permanently crooked.'

Fin stared into the dusk. 'And did he ever forgive his son?'

'No, none of the family did. They cried so many tears, it created all the beautiful streams and creeks we enjoy today. Tibrogargan still stares out to sea, never even looking at his son, and poor Beerwah is still in the advanced stages of pregnancy.'

Fin nestled closer.

~

Early the next morning, Fin laced her walking shoes in the pink-streaked dawn light, regretting that they were only spending a long weekend here. Anthony suggested heading out before breakfast to tackle the seven-kilometre Maleny Trail before doing a longer walk on Sunday.

'Ready when you are,' she called, gazing at the soft mist rising from the valley.

There was silence.

'Are you coming?'

It was unlike Anthony not to be ready. He was such a morning person. He had coaxed her into doing this early walk and promised a visit to the Maleny dairy for some cheese tasting afterwards.

Fin wished she'd slept in another half an hour when Anthony emerged from the bathroom looking pale. 'Sorry, beautiful.'

She bit her lip and regretted her annoyance, still not accustomed to being called beautiful. 'Are you alright?'

His smile seemed watery. 'Fine, I might be coming down with something. I just feel very tired. Maybe I just needed this weekend away. Let's head off.'

'You sure?'

Fin noticed how grey and washed out he looked. 'You don't look yourself.' She placed a hand on his forehead. 'I wish I'd brought my home visit bag. All I've got is some ibuprofen and paracetamol.'

'I'll be fine. Just too many late nights.'

Fin frowned. 'Why don't we just stay here and enjoy the view? I'll make some breakfast and see how you feel after that.'

'No, I'm fine now. Really.'

Fin hesitated, but Anthony grabbed the backpack with their drink bottles and headed towards the door. She followed. Once they started, it would be fine. It was an easy seven kilometres with the promise of a platypus sighting.

Anthony parked his car near the showgrounds, and they set off along the curved path with trees and shrubs to one side and paddocks on the other. It was wide enough to walk side by side, the concrete path giving way to gravel crunching beneath their feet. To Fin's relief, Anthony sounded just like he always did. 'I saw a couple of platypuses here when I came a few years ago. You need to come early before it gets busy.'

At the viewing platform, they paused and waited in silence. Fin noticed Anthony was breathing heavily despite the easy walk. She wanted to ask again how he was but bit down her words. They stood for a long time, saw a ripple, and held their breath.

Nothing. It seemed the platypuses were in hiding today.

Fin reached for Anthony's hand and gave it a squeeze. 'How about we head back? I'm ready for some brekky. We can do the whole circuit another time.'

'Just give me a minute.'

'Are you alright? You really don't seem yourself today.'

He shrugged. 'I'm just run down.'

Anthony had stayed back late for three functions at the bookshop last week. When they got back to the cottage, Fin brewed a pot of tea, cut up some fruit, and toasted slices of raisin bread. 'Let's sit outside. I'll bring it all out.'

Anthony barely ate anything and left half his tea. 'Sorry to be such a wet blanket. I might just sleep this thing off.'

Fin reached over and put her hand on his forehead again. It was cool. 'I'm worried about you. I don't think you are getting a flu. I'll see if there's a doctor in town.'

'Leave it, I'm fine.'

It was the first time Fin had seen him unwell since they met. She pushed down her fluttering anxiety.

The day was filled with an uneasy quiet. Fin shook it off and tried to concentrate on reading her nursing journal. She made herself a simple lunch of bread, cheese, and olives and poured herself the remainder of the sauvignon blanc from last night. She stared out at the rolling green and saw a swing hanging from the sturdy limb of a tree. It made her eyes mist, and she imagined the happy shrieks of a little girl stretching her legs out and tucking them beneath the seat to make it fly past the leafy lower branches.

The dense heat of the day softened, and the trajectory of the sun left the living area in afternoon shadow when Anthony stirred. Fin unfurled her legs, the detritus from lunch still on the coffee table. Careful not to make any noise, she stood at the bedroom door and gazed through the crack before gently pushing it open. The room smelt stale. He opened his eyes and half sat, looking rumpled, his clothes from this morning draped over a chair. His smile was warm. 'So much for our holiday.'

'It doesn't matter. How about we give that dinner we booked in town a miss, just stay at the cottage and enjoy something simple. We've got some eggs, tomatoes, cheese. I'll make us an omelette.'

'Are you sure? I should be right after a shower.'

Fin crawled in next to him on the bed, curled up close, and placed one hand on his chest. 'If you're still really tired when we get home, I want you to make an appointment and have some blood tests done.'

His skin was clammy, and Fin wished again she had her home-visit bag with her so she could check his temperature and blood pressure.

'Don't worry, it's just some bug.'

Anthony pulled her closer and she inhaled the unfamiliar scent of stale sweat.

'I've just never seen you like this. I have a bad feeling about it.'

He didn't say anything, instead looked out at the dark shape of Tibrogargan.

Fin's phone rang. She leapt out of bed and hurried to the living area.

'Hello, Martha. What is it?'

'Rob died. I just thought you'd want to know.'

Fin sat down hard. 'He didn't seem too bad when I left.'

'I know. We all thought he only had weeks to live last year, then after his grandson moved here, Rob surprised us.'

'I'm in Maleny.'

'God, I'm so sorry, I forgot. I shouldn't have rung.'

'It's okay. I'm glad you did. I want to be there for Rob's family.'

The call ended. Fin realised Anthony was standing in the doorway, wearing only his pyjama bottoms, hair sticking up. His ribs seemed more prominent, and she wondered how she hadn't noticed that earlier.

'Work just rang me. One of my patients died.'

'They shouldn't ring you when you're on holidays.'

'Martha forgot. And I'm glad she rang. I've been looking after Rob for nearly a year now.' She stood up. 'I want to pack up and go home tomorrow.'

'But why? He's died. There's nothing you can do.'

'He has a family. I really want to support them.'

When Anthony stayed silent, she crossed her arms. 'Anyway, you're not well enough to go walking tomorrow.'

16

Adulthood

THE phone in the hallway vibrated and Fin rolled back over, still half asleep, annoyed that anyone would ring her so early. When it continued, Fin sat up, early light seeping into her room in the rental house she shared with two other nurses. They must both be asleep after a big night out. Annoyed, Fin stumbled into the hallway and grabbed the phone. 'Hello?'

'Fin, I need to talk to you.' George's voice was tearful, babbling.

Suddenly wide awake, Fin leant against the peeling timber wall, light falling in muted uneven stripes through the living room blinds, her mouth dry. George never rang. 'What is it?'

'I really don't know what to do. Mum and Dad will hate me.'

'They adore you. Nothing you do will change that.'

George started crying. 'I'm pregnant.'

Fin's heart thumped harder. Her fifteen-year-old baby sister was pregnant. George's confession landed hard. George was having sex or, even worse, some bloke had forced himself onto her. Fin pulled her thoughts away from unwelcome images, not sure if she wanted to know the truth. 'Who's the father?'

George's voice shuddered, the words coming out between sobs. 'It's Dylan, my boyfriend.'

The realisation that George had a boyfriend and was sexually active made Fin slide down the wall, her knees bent against her chest, the phone still pressed to her ear. 'George, I'll drive out to The Estate, and we can talk properly.'

'You won't tell Mum and Dad.'

'God, no.'

Fin let the phone drop into the cradle and returned to her crumpled bed. Surely fifteen was too young. After all, Fin, now twenty-two, was yet to have her first sexual experience. She lay in bed a little longer, the share house still quiet. Her two flatmates both had boyfriends and, from time to time, brought them home, the rhythmic *thump, thump* of Leisa's metal bed against the thin wall audible while Fin tried to sleep.

It had been months since she was last home and Fin did not relish seeing Victor again. She gritted her teeth, certain he would make some hurtful remark. She recalled that day, four years ago, when she was accepted into her nursing degree, the joy sucked out of it by his response. 'Why would anyone want a job washing bloody bed pans?'

Fin had graduated with not one member of the family present to celebrate her achievements.

After a shower, Fin stared at herself in the cracked mirror and fretted about what to wear to The Estate. After leaving home to study, she had filled out again, relaxed back into her natural curvaceous shape. She tried a long shirt over her black skirt and turned side on to see if it skimmed her curves. Finally, she opted for a maxi dress. It would have to do. She crossed her fingers Victor would not make a comment.

Driving towards Ipswich, she wondered how Mum and Dad hadn't noticed that George had a boyfriend and was having sex. Did Victor and Barb even care enough to see what was happening right beneath their noses?

Fin turned onto the stretch of dirt road before that bloody awful driveway and wondered if there had been any further progress to the house since her last visit months ago. She still resented Victor insisting they move into the bare skeleton of the main house a couple of months before she completed her final-year exams at school. His dream home was still only partially built and barely habitable. Fin refused to help and instead stayed in the library until it closed every night. She came home to a shambolic mess of boxes and an open suitcase where she kept her clothes. Her bedroom was a barren and unwelcome space lacking shelves or a built-in wardrobe. There was nowhere to put anything, not even a desk where she could study.

Teeth rattling on the final twenty-kilometre stretch of pot-holed road, Fin stared when she rounded that final bend and caught her first glimpse of the grim desolation that was The Estate. There was a sprawl of half-built house, two basic guest cabins, old stacks of unused timbers warping in the sun, and the incomplete stone wall, a legacy of Victor's attempts at stone masonry. She wondered if they still hosted guests in the cabins. George had confided once that very few guests booked in for the rustic experience of living on a building site, so Mum had increased her hours to full-time and taken on some tutoring to keep things afloat.

Victor must have heard the car and embraced Fin the minute she got out. 'We barely see you these days. I miss you.'

Fin softened and hugged him back, despite being embarrassed about her fleshy curves.

Barb stood back, her hands clasped together, her apron splotched with cooking stains.

'Mum, how are you?'

Fin went over and gave Barb a quick hug, followed by a peck on the cheek.

Near the front door, in the foyer, there was an enormous box ripped on the side, spilling macramé onto the floor. Next to it was a stack of bamboo bowls, painted coasters, and wooden trinket boxes. Some of the bowls and macramé blocked the entrance. Fin was careful not to step on anything. 'It looks like a craft market in here.'

Victor beamed. 'I travelled to Vietnam and Cambodia and bought a tonne of stuff. People are going to love it. I want to hire a warehouse downtown, sell it by the bucketload. The profits are huge. You've no idea.'

George emerged and stood in the shadows behind Dad. She held fingers like a gun to her head. Fin nearly laughed out loud and only just managed to make it sound like she was clearing her throat.

'What about the cabins? The resort?'

'People just don't appreciate escaping from their burnt-out lives in the city. The last lot complained non-stop and when I went to sort out issues with the pump, they suggested I needed to let them know what time I was coming. Would you believe it? I need permission to enter the cabin I built with my own bloody hands.'

Barb patted his shoulder. 'Let's go and enjoy some lunch. You can keep talking at the table while I bring out the food.'

Relieved to be spared further details, Fin traipsed behind them, keen to chat to George on her own.

Barb's voice was full of apology. 'Now, if I'd known you were coming, I would have made something special. You should have called and let us know.'

Fin raised an eyebrow to George, who shrugged.

'I just happened to have a day off and thought I'd pop out for lunch. I might bring George to my place for a few days and treat her to some city life.'

'George didn't mention it,' said Barb, glancing across to see if Victor knew about the arrangement.

Victor pulled up a chair and beckoned to George to do the same. 'Your sister has homework and was planning to spend a few hours at the library to finish an assignment with friends.'

Fin wished George had briefed her. Was this a ploy for getting away? Somehow it was hard to imagine George spending Saturday afternoon in the library. Fin hoped she sounded casual. 'Well, I can give you a lift if you like. Swing past and drop you off on the way home.'

Barb came out with a huge platter of cold cuts and cheeses. There was a loud knock at the front door. Barb was still in the kitchen slicing bread and Victor stood up, frowning. George slumped over her plate, toyed with her knife and ran a finger along its blade. She still looked willowy, slim, unchanged from the last time Fin visited. Of course, she was probably only early and not showing yet.

They heard Victor and another voice coming towards them. Barb appeared with a basket of bread. George looked up, her eyes wide and very blue.

'This is Dylan, one of the friends in George's study group.'

And the father of her child, thought Fin, her jaw tight. Dylan was tall, muscled, his hair short and dark, sleeves rolled up to his elbows, arms stippled with black hairs. He looked about twenty. His eyes cast around the room and paused at the insulation poking under the window. Fin imagined him naked and entwined with George and dropped her eyes.

Victor waved towards Fin. 'Our eldest, Fin, is here to escape the city smog for a day.'

'Do join us for lunch,' offered Barb, holding the breadbasket tightly with two hands.

Dylan slid in next to George and gave her a peck on the cheek.

The lunch droned on with Victor telling Dylan about his plans to start his business importing and selling crafts. Dylan sat with his arm draped over the back of George's chair, his plate piled high with salami, cheese, and buttered bread.

Fin stood and excused herself. 'I really need to go for a walk. I just want to visit some of my favourite spots and breathe some fresh country air.'

Victor barely looked up. George stared at her plate like a beaten dog. Barb offered to make coffee, her voice strained.

Fin started up the hill towards the main road and remembered how often she had walked that way to catch the bus while she was studying. The old path was overgrown, with no evidence of George catching the bus into town to study. Fin veered off and wondered whether the river still flowed and if you still could swim there. She was panting by the time she reached the water, furious with George for ringing her, with Dylan for making her sister pregnant, and with her parents for their self-absorbed ignorance.

Fin stripped off behind a rock, then slid into the water. She allowed its coolness to embrace her. It was a long time since she had gone for a swim. She stretched her arms out and powered through the water, disturbing the still surface. At the other side, she turned and swam back, without taking a breath, the cool wet numbing the ragged anger turbulent in her head. When she reached the shallows, her feet lowered and felt for the pebbled bottom, water dripping from her hair. And then she startled at a long shadow across the water. A low voice.

'It really is you, then.'

Fin crossed her arms over her breasts and stood waist deep in water, a pulse throbbing in her ears. There, standing on the bank wearing only board shorts, stood Arch.

17

Adulthood

FIN sat at the back of the church, the pew hard and uncomfortable. Rob had a large family and lots of friends, some of whom she had met during the months he was in and out of hospital. Tears pricked her eyes when she thought of Rob's kindness and quirky sense of humour. She thought about the faded black-and-white photograph of him in Borneo, taken during the Second World War. He gifted it to her, saying, 'I was a handsome bugger once. I wasn't always feeble and useless.'

They all filed out, and Fin was heading to her car when Rob's son cornered her.

'It is so lovely of you to come. My Dad talked about you all the time.'

'He was a good man. It was a privilege to look after him.'

'He was very fortunate to have a nurse like you.'

Fin fought back tears. 'I'm sorry for your loss.'

'Join us for some morning tea.'

'Thanks, I'd love to, but I need to head off. I've got an appointment.'

~

'You have one embryo left.'

Fin sat ramrod straight in the chair and stared past Dr Birmingham at the corkboard plastered with photographs of success stories: newborns bonneted, beribboned, and smiling at her. Martha from work had recommended Dr Birmingham after Fin confided they needed fertility treatment.

Anthony's hand reached over and gave Fin's a squeeze. 'We should give it a go.'

Fin nodded, unable to find her voice. It was their last chance. Her

89

miscarriages, the paucity of eggs retrieved, and the accumulated failures were a preparation for this moment. Somewhere nearby was a single cluster of cells suspended and waiting for her, ready to multiply and grow into her baby.

Dr Birmingham leaned across towards them with some paperwork.

'How about we get you to see Gina, our nurse coordinator, who will go through everything with you again. Don't hesitate to contact me if you have any questions at all.'

Dr Birmingham's words washed over Fin, who was confident she was one tiny step away from becoming a mother. She glanced at Anthony, who was listening intently, nodding in all the right places as if they hadn't done this several times already.

When they left with consent forms signed and a date set, Fin gripped Anthony's hand tightly. They were jostled by the lunch crowd in the Queen Street Mall. A clown stood near Rankin's newsagency twisting animals into balloons while a group of students poured out of the nearby McDonalds with bags of greasy food. For a moment, Fin allowed herself to imagine a flutter of movement, a tiny heartbeat dancing beneath her own.

Anthony's strained voice cut across her imaginings. 'Can we sit a minute?'

Fin was wrenched back into the noisy reality of the crowd hurrying past them.

'Do you want to have lunch somewhere?'

She guided him away from the main thoroughfare and led him to one of the shaded benches. 'I'm really worried about you. Have you made that appointment for a check-up?'

Anthony lowered himself onto the bench. The couple sharing a takeaway container of noodles shuffled along to make more room. Fin squeezed in next to him, took his wrist and felt his pulse. 'I'm going to call the doctor right now.'

He didn't protest when she scrolled through her phone and rang. A few minutes later, she reassured him. 'I'm driving you there today at five. There's been a cancellation.'

The last time Fin and Anthony sat side by side at the GP's office was when they needed a referral for fertility services. Dr Prasad had listened, filled in pathology forms, written a letter, and spent some time managing expectations. *Age is the most important factor impacting fertility. The success rate after one cycle of IVF for a woman under 35 is thirty percent and for a woman from 40-44 is only about ten percent.*

Fin glanced at the photographs of Dr Prasad's three children and tried not to resent their smiling faces beaming from frames cluttering one end of the desk.

This time, Dr Prasad's face was serious, her questions probing. 'How long have you been feeling this tired?'

Anthony, sitting forward in his chair, answered, 'Maybe two months. Work has been busy. I'm thinking of getting more staff.'

'Any change in your bowel habits?'

He nodded again, avoiding Fin's eye.

Dr Prasad waited for him to elaborate.

Anthony shrugged. 'More frequent and a bit loose I guess.'

A cold hand squeezed Fin's heart. She should have noticed something. After all, she looked after people every day who had neglected minor niggles and ignored symptoms.

Dr Prasad was speaking again. 'Let's just see what you weigh.'

Anthony slipped off his shoes, emptied his pockets of keys, wallet and phone. Fin longed to stand up and peer at the numbers, but sat tight, nails biting her palms. He was not a big man. In fact, he probably weighed less than her.

Dr Prasad typed something else into Anthony's file. 'Let's get you up and examine you.'

Anthony disappeared behind the curtain. Fin watched his shirt and trousers drop to the floor. Dr Prasad continued to ask questions. 'Any blood in your stools?'

Twenty minutes later, they walked back down the corridor with forms for blood screens and a referral for a colonoscopy early next week. Neither of them talked on the drive home. Fin's confident joy from this morning was squeezed out by the possibilities raised after Dr Prasad's interrogation.

It was only once they were home that Fin broke the silence between them. 'How about I make us something for dinner?'

'No, let me do it. There are a couple of salmon fillets in the fridge, and I planned to make something nice.'

'You sure? I can cook if you don't feel well.'

Anthony shooed her away. 'I want to do it. I was planning a nice meal to celebrate our baby project. I even chilled a bottle of Marlborough sauvignon blanc ready for tonight.'

Fin swallowed the hard stone lodged in her throat. She wondered if he looked thinner or if she was just imagining his trousers looking looser.

Anthony set the table with care, using his fine cutlery set. He lit a candle and set it between them. Fin wanted to help but instead watched him and tried to subdue the worst-case scenarios bottlenecking her thoughts.

He looked up and smiled, seemingly unconcerned about the investigations booked for next week. 'Dinner is served.'

Fin pulled out her chair, numb inside. She allowed the tantalising smells from the kitchen to distract her.

Anthony unscrewed the wine and poured it with a flourish. 'Call me old fashioned, but I can't help but think that the screw top bottles lack the romance and flourish of a cork.'

A few moments later, he brought out the meal: crispy herb-crusted salmon nestled on a bed of potato purée and asparagus. Fin realised her hand was trembling when she lifted her glass and tipped his.

If only it was any other day with the two of them blissful at the cusp of a lifetime of shared dinners.

He sounded like he always did. 'Cheers, beautiful.'

~

There was no easy way to break bad news. Fin knew that more than anyone.

The gastroenterologist, Dr Mills, came out to the waiting room.

'Mrs Fletcher?' Fin suppressed an urge to correct him. *It's Fin Steinbauer, actually.*

'Anthony Fletcher asked for you.'

Fin's legs felt wobbly. She had hoped Anthony was right, that he had just pushed himself too hard with the bookshop, but deep down she knew it was more than that.

Anthony looked vulnerable and old in his hospital gown with the anaesthetic not fully worn off.

Dr Mills was brisk but not unkind. After all, the only part of Anthony he was familiar with was his bowels. It seemed inside-out somehow that a person could explore your colon with a camera without knowing anything about you and then change your life with a few words.

'I'd like to arrange a CT scan. I've got your blood test results, and you are very iron deficient. We need to wait for the pathology results, but you have bowel cancer.' He paused, his arms folded over his surgical gown. 'I will send copies of all the results to your GP.'

The next few days passed in a blur. Fin asked for some time off. Saying the word cancer out loud made the whole scenario feel very real.

Back inside the GP's consulting room, Fin stared at the photographs of those three children, still laughing, carefree while resentment curdled inside her. What would Dr Prasad know about longing, grief, or loss? She would head home tonight to her children, no doubt conceived without a hitch, to a husband who was robust and well. Anthony's diagnosis was just another consultation at the end of a long day.

Dr Prasad pulled her chair a bit closer, her hands folded in her lap. 'I'm really sorry, it's not good news.'

Fin reached for Anthony's hand. It was clammy, but his voice sounded normal. 'What does the CT scan show?'

Dr Prasad turned back to her screen and angled it so they could see. She pointed to some spots on the scan. 'It confirms the diagnosis of bowel cancer. It is stage three…'

'Which means the lymph nodes are involved,' Fin interrupted. 'I'm sorry.'

Anthony squeezed Fin's hand this time.

The room went blurry, and she took some deep breaths to slow her heart rate down.

The room swam slowly into focus again, like coming up from underwater. Fin realised Dr Prasad was speaking to her. 'Can I get you a glass of water?'

'No, no, I'm fine.' She was determined to pull herself together and be strong for Anthony.

Dr Prasad continued. 'I have referred you to Dr de Silva who has booked you in for surgery. You will need adjuvant chemotherapy but let's do this one step at a time.'

She turned away from them and typed. The printer spat out a letter, which she folded and slid into an envelope before handing to Anthony. 'If you have any questions at all, please don't hesitate to contact me. I'm sorry to have to tell you such bad news.'

Fin did have questions, but they were questions about the embryo that she knew she wasn't allowed to ask.

Anthony spoke. 'I appreciate everything you've done.'

A moment later, he and Dr Prasad stood and were shaking hands.

Fin pushed herself out of her chair and felt Anthony's hand on the small of her back, his voice reassuring Dr Prasad. 'Thank you for being so frank with us.'

'Let me drive.' Fin held out her hands for the keys.

'Thank you, but I'd prefer to drive right now.'

Fin slid into the passenger side of the car. He backed out in one fluid movement, pulled out into the traffic, and turned right instead of left.

When they reached the highway, he accelerated, rolled down a window and let wind ripple through. It made speaking impossible. Fin wondered at the ordinary lives of the other people driving alongside them. She resented the cars with kids glued to devices and babies lolling in capsules. There was a whole bank of tears inside her somewhere, but her eyes were dry and her heart was heavy and cold like a boulder.

Anthony pulled off the main road and headed towards the sea at Victoria Point. He pulled into an empty carpark, turned off the engine and reached for her hand.

'Anthony, I should have noticed something.'

'It is not your fault or anyone else's. It just is.'

He leant over the middle console, and she felt the raw press of his ribs against her breasts. It was as if he'd shrunk and was already slipping away in barely perceptible increments. She pressed her face into his shirt and tasted the salted sea air on her tongue. A breeze caught her hair and blew it across her face while a squall of gulls wrestled over a cold chip. Survival of the fittest.

Anthony stroked her hair and rested his chin on her head. Her body was wrung out in the face of such perilous uncertainty. She had lost her last chance at motherhood. He reached behind her chair and handed her a toy rabbit with embroidered eyes, a pink nose, and soft floppy ears.

'I bought this for the nursery. Let's give that embryo of ours a chance.'

18

Adulthood

'DON'T stare,' Fin called out, frozen to the spot, her pubic hair drifting like a clump of weed in the water, her arms covering her breasts.

Arch turned away. 'It's just such a surprise. I didn't expect to ever see you again.'

With his face turned away from her, Fin took the opportunity to look at him. His shoulders were broad, a life of physical labour evident in the taut definition of his limbs. His hair was longer, still dishevelled, but with a natural wave that suited him. His legs were long, hairy, adult.

Looking away, Fin took a step back into the water and cleared her throat, loud enough for him to hear. 'Actually, I don't have a towel. I didn't expect to go for a swim.'

'Here, have mine.'

Arch reached in front of him and pulled up a towel with a faded pineapple on a background of blue. He moved towards the water and held it up at arm's length. There was nothing for it but to get out of the creek stark naked. Her fingers touched his when she reached for the towel, and warmth moved down her spine. She held her breath. They stood like that for a moment, the towel held between them like a promise. Arch spoke first. 'Why don't I join you for a swim first? I'm still happy to share my towel afterwards.'

Fin let go of the towel. She shivered when a breeze blew across her skin. 'That's hardly fair. Me starkers and you wearing boardies.'

He slipped them off in a single deft movement. 'Easily fixed.'

His face was still turned away from her, the towel and shorts now limp in the dry grass on the sloping embankment. Fin stole a glance at his nakedness before turning around and diving back into the water. She heard him noisy behind her, trying to grab her foot. Despite not swimming for years, she surged forward and kicked him loose. She heard the deep rumble of his laughter, muffled by the water.

In the middle, where it was deep, she stopped and started to tread water, and he joined her. It was difficult to reconcile the lanky young Arch with the grown man beside her. Shadows of his former self were still there but more chiselled and defined – he sported a one-day growth on his jaw and above his lip.

His foot touched hers underwater and it was intimate.

He stared at her now, his face earnest, his dimple just like she remembered it. 'Has anyone told you how gorgeous you are?'

Fin wanted to curl up and hide, ashamed of her shape. She shook her head. 'Don't, don't say that.'

Their feet cycled and she shifted back away from him. He looked away. 'I'm sorry, Fin. I understand. A woman like you would be with someone. I overstepped.'

She shook her head and bit her lip. 'No, there's no one.'

'Then I stand by what I said.' His face lit up. He paddled close to her again and found her hand underwater. 'Come on.'

He coaxed her to where they could stand. She let him. Her heart hammered so hard her chest ached. They stood waist-deep now, still holding hands. His hand felt large and safe, and his eyes sparkled like sun dancing on water.

'I thought about you all the time and wondered what you were up to.' His voice was deeper than she remembered.

Fin wondered why she had listened to Victor. It would have been so easy to keep in touch with Arch and stay friends. 'I'm sorry. I should have made contact.'

She remembered the party. Joy stumbling across the deck, slurred and unsteady. He shrugged. 'It's okay. It wasn't your fault.'

Fin found herself gazing at the hollow at the top of his neck, the way a dark hair curled there. She remembered sharing her caramel slice and his kindness in the kitchen. She leant forward and kissed him right in that spot and tasted the muddiness of river water on his skin.

He lifted her chin and stared into her eyes, searching for something.

'Let's dry off in the sun.'

There was a sheltered, cool area behind the rock, and he stretched his towel out while Fin stood behind him, her arms hanging loose. He beckoned, and they lay side by side, touching. They listened to the tinkle of water over rocks and the still air filled with birds calling to one other. Fin was aware of her side pressed against his, their legs stretched out, some leaves and debris stuck to her calf. A wallaby hopped near them, startled, then veered off, bounding away up the hill.

Fin sneezed.

Arch half sat up, rested on one elbow. 'What are you up to these days?'

'I'm a nurse, working in emergency.'

He plucked a long blade of grass and let it dangle from his mouth. 'That must be tough.'

She rolled to face him, resting on her elbow. 'I enjoy it.' She paused. 'How is Joy?'

He sat up, stared into the distance. 'She died a few years ago. Fell, hit her head, and haemorrhaged.'

Fin sat up too. 'God, I'm so sorry.'

'Yeah, it was awful. They treated her like flotsam at the hospital because she looked so terrible and was drunk.' Arch pulled his legs up to his chest and Fin wasn't sure if it was a tear or creek water that slid down his cheek.

'I'm sorry for that too. No one deserves that.'

Fin thought about her own dismissal of patients who stumbled into emergency reeking of alcohol at the end of a long shift. She vowed to be more compassionate.

'I wish she had seen someone like you when she arrived at hospital.' Arch looked at her now. She let her eyes drop.

He whispered. 'She might still be here with us.' Then he leant over and kissed Fin on the lips. When she didn't resist him, he lingered there, and she responded, allowing the kiss to continue open-mouthed, a fluttering in her groin.

'Are you sure?' he whispered, one hand behind her head now, his eyes crinkled with concern.

She kissed him again, her fingers tangled in his chest hair. He moaned, and they lay back on their sides, facing each other. Fin felt his hardness against her thigh, and she wanted him with an urgency, to know what it was to be with a man and learn the truth behind the muffled sounds and rhythmic *thump, thump* of the bedpost against her wall at night.

Arch paused, one hand light on her breast. 'I don't have anything with me.'

'It's okay. I do.' She reached for her purse and pulled out the condom her flatmate had dropped in there one night when they all went out together. *Just in case.*

She pressed her breasts against him, kissed his eyelids, his lips and his jaw, before she reached down and touched his hardness and quivered. The only time she had touched a man was gloved.

Arch was careful. He took his time and read her body with his fingers and tongue until he knew it better than she did. In the late afternoon sun, she allowed herself to become needy and to want him without shame. Would he know this was her first time? There was a breathless, sharp pain, and she cried out. He hesitated but she clung to him, willed him to continue. He reached down and touched her, shifted inside her. She succumbed to the sensations roaring across her skin and through her body and gave herself up to the pleasure.

When he brought her close, she gasped and arched her back. She wrapped her legs around his hips and pulled him close until he too moaned into her shoulder.

Afterwards, he held her in his arms for a long time while she drank in the unfamiliar scent of pleasure, aware of the pinpricks of a million nerve endings firing on her skin.

19

Two years earlier

JUST after four in the morning, the darkness softened, and a crescent moon hung poised on a wisp of cloud. Fin peed into a glass and dripped some urine onto the stick. When the second faint pink line emerged, she blinked a couple of times and half expected it to be a bleary figment of her imagination. She bit the inside of her mouth and felt a heartbeat in her throat. Anthony was fast asleep, his mouth slightly open, his hair and pyjamas rumpled with dreams. She wanted to be certain before she woke him to celebrate her news.

In the darkness, she filled the kettle and flicked the switch. There was another pregnancy test in her handbag. She forced herself to wait and delay the joy of seeing the second line emerge again. The kettle reached its piercing crescendo. A pink dawn gashed the horizon, first light on this most blessed of all days.

She jiggled a teabag up and down and smiled when she imagined Anthony's disapproving look that she hadn't brewed a pot. Just as she was about to discard the bag and get some milk, he was behind her, his breath stale from sleep. 'Up early today,' he whispered, his arms pulling her close.

She pressed against him, her back merging into his familiar curves. 'We did it.'

There was the indrawing of his breath. Fin had a brief vision of doing it all on her own and it made her legs weak. On the day they were booked in to have the embryo implanted, he'd leant over and placed his hand on her thigh. 'I might not be here to see our child grow up.'

His words were a chill that trickled through her veins. She shivered again recalling the cold, pragmatic way he faced his mortality. She had dismissed his concerns. 'Don't say that. You are booked in for surgery. Dr de Silva commented that you are fit and would cope well with the operation.'

When he attempted to say something else, she cut him off with a kiss. 'You are going to be a dad again. That is what you should focus on.'

An unease sat between them, neither willing to raise the topic of Anthony's diagnosis again.

Fin had nursed a couple of patients who died after the same diagnosis. She knew the statistics. With surgery alone, only fifty percent would be alive in five years. With adjuvant chemotherapy, the recurrence was reduced by up to fifty percent. Anthony was fit without other medical issues. He would be in the group that survived.

'I just wanted to be extra sure before I surprised you,' she told him. 'I planned to make myself another cuppa and pee on another stick before waking you.'

He brushed his lips against her hair and turned her around so they were facing each other. 'I insist I make us a proper pot of tea.'

He poured hers down the sink, then looked at her, eyes wide like a child. 'You don't think having a cuppa will dilute the result, do you?'

Fin laughed and placed one protective hand over her abdomen. 'I'm willing to risk it.'

Anthony filled the kettle again and went through his familiar tea-making ritual. Fin sat at the kitchen table and watched him pull another mug from the hook under the shelf and warm the teapot, swirling it around a few times before pouring it away again. He took care to measure the leaves then poured boiling water over the top. When he wrestled the tea cosy over the spout, she imagined him dressing their baby, its chubby arms resisting his efforts. It made her smile.

Anthony poured milk into the jug and pulled up a chair next to her. He used the handle to turn the teapot around several times, the way he always did, before placing the strainer over her mug. It seemed impossible that he would not be here while their baby grew into a toddler, then into a child sitting beside them, small fingers clutched around a cup of milk, fingers of Vegemite toast smeared around lips.

Fin reassured herself. He was having surgery tomorrow and

chemotherapy was already booked in. The whirlwind of appointments had been organised around the implanting of their child into her womb.

She smiled and raised her mug to his just as a tepid sun slipped through the window. 'To our baby.'

Another pink line emerged, this time with the two of them poised and watching. Anthony stared down at her belly, still unchanged, of course. He shook his head. 'It's awful, I know, but I don't even remember this moment with Damon. I must have been away for work. No wonder the boy resents me.'

Fin placed her fingers on his lips. 'Hush. That was a long time ago. This baby will know their daddy loved them even before they were conceived. The most wanted and cherished baby in the world.'

It should have been a positive sign that they learnt the good news on the day before Anthony was scheduled for surgery. And yet, Fin was aware of her hand trembling around her mug. She suddenly longed to know everything about him, anxious about all the things she had missed and taken for granted. Her thoughts escaped into the dark space of *what-ifs*. How was it that when life was running smoothly and the days seemed rosy and endless, she had taken life for granted and didn't linger and appreciate the perfection of him, of their life together?

~

Working at the palliative care unit was a blessing and a curse. Knowing too much and yet not knowing what she needed to know the most. How all the statistics became meaningless when it narrowed down to a single person you loved.

Dr Janssen was kind and insisted the roster was arranged around Anthony's surgery and chemotherapy. 'Make sure you let us know when you need time off. We'll manage.'

She sat opposite Anthony now and absorbed the details of his jaw, the small brown mole in the hollow of his neck, the way his fingers wrapped around his mug. His smile was tight.

'We will get through this,' she told him. She stood and moved next to him, pushed her belly against him. 'She can feel with us, you know. Research has shown that if I am sad or happy, the baby experiences the same intensity of emotion.'

Anthony placed one hand on her abdomen, his fingers cool on her skin. His hand remained on her belly, and she swore she was aware of tiny flutters, the sensation of the tiny clutch of cells dividing inside her.

He placed his mouth on her soft belly and whispered to the baby. 'You are very fortunate. I long to be as close to your mother as you, to hear her from the inside, feel what she feels inside her heart while nestled beneath it.'

The next day, Dr de Silva cut out twenty centimetres of Anthony's bowel along with six infected lymph nodes. It was four hours after seeing Anthony wheeled into the operating theatres before Fin was notified. Her legs felt weak when Dr de Silva finally spoke to her. 'It was a complicated surgery, but I remain optimistic.'

While Anthony was in the intensive care unit, Fin sat in one of the plastic chairs in the tiny visitor room, grateful there were no other family members waiting or making tea and coffee while visiting their loved ones. Fin rinsed a mug and filled it with water from the tap. She glugged it down and splashed water onto her face before leaving the visitor room and making her way to Anthony's bedside.

Intensive care was stark, white, and windowless. The clock on the wall said five but it was hard to tell if it was early morning or late afternoon. A nurse was fiddling with tubes and lines. Anthony looked unrecognisable, reduced to a collection of bodily functions to be regulated and balanced, the saw-toothed lines moving mechanically across the screen the only evidence he had a beating heart.

Fin felt so useless standing there and relying on others to care for Anthony. The nurse looking after him turned to her. 'Hi, I'm Ellie and I'll be looking after your husband. I just increased his pain relief as per orders.'

She pulled out a chair for Fin to sit in. 'I'm going to give him a proper wash.'

'Thank you,' whispered Fin, but Ellie had disappeared through the gap in the curtain.

She was back a moment later with a small tub of warm water and a washer. With great care, she washed away the dried bits of blood and iodine, keeping other parts of his body covered with a white sheet and pausing only to silence one of the alarms.

Seeing Anthony so vulnerable, Fin recognized how impossible it was to reach deep into another person's experience of helplessness, to understand how it hollowed you out and made your bones brittle as porcelain.

The body in the bed gave no hint of the man she knew and loved. It was a violation, having those intimate bodily functions exposed for all to see. For Fin, the antiseptic smell of hospitals was associated with palliation and death. Her legs felt weak, and she trembled when she stared at his unconscious form. His whiskery chin triggered memories of his skin warm against hers, the same bristles prickly on her cheek when his lips searched for hers, the taste of tea and mint on his tongue. The extraordinary beauty to be found in the ordinary details of a life shared.

With Anthony's body clean again, Ellie poured the water away. She smiled at Fin. 'You should head home and get some sleep.'

Fin stared at his frail, broken body, the absence of his warm voice a sharp blade between her ribs.

20

Adulthood

THE weather was dismal. Fin scanned for a park close to the clinic but ended up a few blocks away. George was crouched over in the passenger seat, her knees bent under her chin. Fin reached into the back for an umbrella. It did little to shield them from the steady, drenching rain. Her sneakers squelched when they stepped into the clinic, and she added their umbrella to the clutch at the entry.

They stood dripping water at the front desk. The receptionist barely looked up.

'Name?'

George stood mute, all sharp angles, not a skerrick of flesh on her. She stared at the floor.

Fin responded. 'Georgina Steinbauer.'

'Fill in the form and hand it back in when you're done.'

Fin grabbed the clipboard with the pen dangling on a piece of string. She gestured to George to follow, and they found a couple of empty plastic seats. Resigned, Fin started to tick boxes and scribble answers. It felt intrusive to be asked so many details. She glanced over at George, who hunched beside her, staring at the puddle on the floor. Why did they need to know these things? George would never see any of them again after today.

Fin pointed to the dotted lines at the bottom. 'Just sign here.'

Fin handed the damp form in at the desk and sat down again. She glanced at the other women dotted around the room. They avoided looking at each other. Only one was here with a partner who sat awkwardly beside her.

'Georgina Steinbauer.'

George stayed fixed to the seat.

Fin gave her a poke. 'That's us.'

They stood, and George shuffled over to the woman wearing scrubs who waited at the door. 'Is your mother going in with you?'

Fin resisted the urge to correct the woman and instead hissed at George, who looked about twelve in her skinny jeans, the oversized wet tee clinging to her tiny frame. 'Come on.'

Fin followed George and the nurse to a tiny cubicle.

'Strip off your clothes, including your underwear, and slip into a gown. The doctor will call you shortly.'

A gowned figure appeared and called George in. She hesitated. Fin squeezed George's shoulder and whispered in her ear, 'It will all be over very soon. I'll be waiting for you.'

Fin sat and waited on the hard bench. The rain softened and ceased, and a diamond of light landed at her feet. It felt like a promise, a reassurance that all would be well.

Aside from the puddled road and quivering raindrops dripping from eaves, it was difficult to imagine the earlier downpour. The sun had pushed through the thick bruise of clouds and smiled from a freshly laundered blue sky, indifferent to the events of the morning.

Fin drove George to the share house, grateful that they would have it to themselves today. 'When we get to my place, you should have a hot shower and I'll make us some toasties. I'll drive you back tomorrow.'

Fin reached to turn on the radio but opted for silence instead. After she pulled up into the carport and turned off the engine, she turned to George. 'How are you feeling?'

George's hands were pressed between her knees.

It was so hard to read George at times. She used silence as a tool, just like Victor. Fin immediately felt guilty and touched George on the shoulder. 'Come inside and sleep it off.'

While George showered, Fin threw their wet clothes into the wash and tidied the kitchen. Despite attempts at cleaning rosters and Fin's strategically placed notices to wash up and clear up, the sink was once again an array of dirty dishes. The remains of meals clung to plates and rings of tea and coffee stained the inside of mugs. The bench was a scatter of crumbs and half-empty packets of noodles, used takeaway containers, and drying crusts of bread.

Fin punched out some ibuprofen and placed them next to a glass of water for George before running a sink of steaming water, discarding rubbish, and wiping the surfaces. It soothed her, this ritual of bringing order to the world. When everything was cleared, she assembled a plate of cheese and tomato toasties and took them to her room, where George was curled up like a foetus on the bed. Fin stood poised with the food, then set it on her desk, slid out of her shoes, and curled up behind George, using one arm to pull her close the way she used to when they were children.

21

Two years earlier

THE private hospital room had expansive views over the city. Anthony sat on the made-up hospital bed, his veined hand resting on the spine of the book bent open across his knees. He was dressed in casual clothes, a polo neck shirt, and his dark cotton pants. He looked so normal out of the hospital gown that she could almost believe the last five days hadn't happened. Of course, there were the bruises of different ages along his arms from the cannulas, and he was thinner, but otherwise, he looked like a ghostly version of himself.

His face crinkled into a smile. 'Fin, it's so good to see you.' He gestured to the chair beside the bed. 'I should be discharged tomorrow. The surgeon dropped in early and is happy with my progress. The oncologist, Dr Payne, is coming this morning.'

A young man strode in, hair styled short, the front carefully tousled, a study in self-assurance. His sharp suit was cut to precision. Fin guessed Armani. He made firm eye contact with Anthony.

'Good morning, I'm Dr Payne. Anthony Fletcher?'

Fin hoped his expensive clothes reflected his success as a highly acclaimed oncologist. She felt shabby in her worn jeans and old shirt.

Dr Payne's gaze shifted to her, his smile practiced. He reached out his hand. 'Mrs Fletcher, I assume?'

She opened her mouth to correct him, then closed it again. His handshake was firm, and it gave her confidence.

Anthony swung his legs around so that he was sitting on the side of the bed. 'Thanks for stopping by this morning.'

Dr Payne stood tall at the end of the bed, arms folded across his

108

chest, and listened.

'We are soon to be parents,' Anthony continued, 'so I need to know my odds.'

Dr Payne's expression didn't change. Fin placed her hand protectively over her flat abdomen, annoyed Anthony had mentioned the pregnancy. She sat very straight.

'You are fortunate that your cancer was picked up when it was. If it had metastasised beyond the lymph nodes the odds would be against you.'

Anthony nodded.

'With the chemotherapy, we can improve the survival rates by thirty to fifty percent. It will take about six months to complete and there is a risk of side effects. Nausea, numbness and tingling in your hands and feet…'

Fin curled one hand into a fist while Dr Payne listed the potential risks and complications.

Afterwards, Anthony and Fin went down to the hospital café and sat at a corner table.

His face sagged. 'It's a lot to absorb. I've just thought of a million questions I want to ask that doctor.'

Fin opened and closed her fingers while Anthony fiddled with the paper napkins jammed into a metal box.

'I want to update my will and my enduring power of attorney.'

Fin grabbed his hand. 'It's going to be fine. Dr de Silva said the surgery went well. We just need to get through the chemotherapy.'

'Dr Payne said that thirty to fifty percent of people survive with the chemotherapy. I want to make sure you and the baby are properly looked after if I'm not one of the lucky ones.'

'You have to think positive.'

'It's important to be pragmatic.'

Fin clenched her jaw and realised she had tears sliding down her cheek.

Anthony handed her one of the paper napkins. 'I love you, Fin.'

When their coffees arrived, Fin let hers sit there.

Anthony reached for two sachets of sugar, tore the tops off, and poured them onto the foam. Fin watched a small crater form, the crystals dissolving. He picked up his spoon and stirred, then took a sip.

Fin kept her eyes resolutely down. He placed his cup back onto the saucer.

'You know, life has taught me never to take anything for granted.' Anthony took another sip of his coffee. 'I was so angry when Pip left me and started seeing Simon. I was outraged by the injustice of it. Another man sleeping with my wife and raising my son.' He jammed his cup down hard and some of Fin's coffee sloshed over the rim. 'I was so busy with unimportant things that I was never home with my family. Damon was usually bathed and in bed by the time I finished work. I was difficult to live with.'

Fin leapt to his defence. 'That's not true.'

'It was true back then. I worked relentless hours in a corporate job I hated. When I was home, I was short-tempered, and my son barely knew me.'

Anthony drummed his fingers on the table. Fin cradled her cup in her hands, still not looking at him.

'One year after I found myself single again, my mother died when an aneurysm ruptured in her brain. We were close, and I was devastated.'

Fin dropped her hands into her lap. 'I'm sorry.'

'It was a terrible time. But my mother was meticulous and had a will and her affairs sorted. She left me a small inheritance. I left my job and finally did what I always dreamt of doing and put a deposit on the bookshop and a house. A good friend of mine, Bruce, had run a bookshop for years before finally retiring, and he helped me in those first months. It was the happiest I'd been before meeting you.'

A mother tried to wrangle a screaming pram the size of a small car behind Fin, and she pulled her chair in, one hand over her own belly.

Anthony reached and took Fin's other hand into his own. 'Mum would have loved you. I wish you could have met her.'

Fin stared at his hand with its blue delta of veins and gave it a squeeze, overwhelmed by the uncertainty facing them, unable to conceive a future without Anthony in it.

22

Adulthood

EARLY the next morning, Fin woke up to George packing her small overnight bag.

'I need to get back.'

'What's the rush?'

'I've got something on.'

Fin sat up and watched George disappear and return with her floral wet pack. Fin realised with a pang that it was the same one she had taken on grade five school camp.

'Let me take you out for brekky and I'll drive you back after that. I want to spend some time with you. It's been a while since we hung out together.'

George zipped up her bag. She was wearing the same clothes she had worn to the clinic, unironed, straight from the washing basket. Her hair hung in messy strands around her face.

'Why don't you stay for a while?'

'Don't hassle me. I promised someone I'd see them.'

Fin hauled herself out of bed. 'I need to have a shower. Give me ten minutes and I'll drive you back.'

~

The traffic was heavy. George was mute, her eyes blank holes staring through the windscreen. Fin's belly growled, and she veered off to the local bakery. 'I'm going to grab something to eat and a coffee. Can I get you anything?'

George shook her head.

Fin bought a third-rate coffee and a large cinnamon scroll. She unwound the outside of the scroll and handed some to George, who took it and had a bite. Fin finished the rest and washed it down with a mouthful of milky coffee before pulling back out onto the highway.

'Are you still seeing Dylan?'

'No.'

'Did he even know?' Fin finished her coffee, one hand on the steering wheel.

'I didn't tell anyone.'

'Except me,' said Fin, softening. 'Are you using contraception?'

'I'm worried the pill will make me put on weight.'

'George! You are so thin I worry about you. Anyway, the pill doesn't cause weight gain, and there are other options.'

Fin realised that George was stuck out on The Estate and relied on Mum to drive her around. 'How about I arrange an appointment with a GP for you?'

George stared out the window. 'It's okay. I can manage. Ewan said he'd look after me.'

Fin nearly veered into the ute in front of them. 'Who the hell is Ewan?'

'He's my boyfriend. Anyway, they gave me a script for the pill at the clinic.'

'Jesus, George. You were with Dylan a week ago. Have you forgotten yesterday?'

'He loves me.'

Fin refused to look at her sister. 'Maybe it's none of my business, but you need to use protection and look after yourself. It's not just pregnancy you need to worry about.'

George ignored her. Fin recalled her own recent experience with Arch and her face went hot. She pulled back out onto the road and turned the radio up loud. U2's *Beautiful Day* blared out of the tinny speakers.

Fin pulled into a pharmacy. A few minutes later, she got back in the car, tossed a packet of condoms into George's lap and drove the final stretch to The Estate.

It was a relief to realise Victor and Barb weren't home. Fin carried George's bag to the door, then turned to leave. Fin had her hand on the car door when George ran up and gave her a fierce hug.

Fin clutched George close, her jumble of anger and frustration giving way to love. George disentangled herself and whispered. 'Thanks for everything.'

Fin drove away in a cloud of dust, knowing the events of the past twenty-four hours would never be spoken of again. Steinbauer history was rewritten even while it was happening until it became difficult to recall which bits were fabricated or embellished. The car juddered over a rutted stretch of road. It made Fin's teeth ache. She felt an irrational grief for George's baby. When she reached the turnoff to Liberty Chicks, she hesitated for a moment, then decided to drop in, the memory of Arch's fingers on her skin fresh and raw.

His house looked tired, one of the gutters hanging loose like a vagrant's arm while a faded curtain flapped at an open window. Her optimism dipped, but she pulled up and walked to the front door. The large brass ring landed loud and reverberated into the echoing silence.

Fin regretted coming and turned around. She thought about the second packet of condoms tossed into her handbag with shame. What happened with Arch had been a one-off. She had not bothered to contact him for years, and he would not be waiting for her now.

Just as she turned to leave, she noticed a cloud of dust in the distance. It rapidly drew closer. Fin used one hand to screen her eyes and squinted into the sun.

A motorbike.

It was Arch.

He pulled up alongside her and lifted the visor of his helmet. He was dusty and rugged, his brown leather jacket worn around the elbows.

'Fin, it's good to see you.'

His hazel eyes matched the sky.

Fin scuffed her shoe in the dirt. 'I just thought I'd drop by. I was heading back to Brisbane.'

'I saw a car heading our way and came down. It's not often we get visitors.'

There was an awkward pause, and Fin's pulse hummed.

'Hey, I was heading for a ride. I'll grab another helmet and you can join me.'

Before she could protest, Arch had disappeared into the large shed at the side of the house and emerged with a dusty helmet. He shook it clean and fitted it onto Fin's head. 'It was Mum's.'

It seemed irreverent to be wearing something belonging to Joy. Arch's fingers brushed Fin's skin when he pulled the strap tight. She shivered. A moment later, she was sitting behind him, her arms wrapped around his torso as they accelerated up the dirt road, gravel flying. She tasted dust in her mouth, felt it sting her eyes and was aware of the solid shape of him inside his leather jacket.

The bike revved up the hills, bounced off stones, veered around stumps and hollows. She leaned with him, and it was both exhilarating and terrifying. She wanted it to go on forever. He pulled up alongside the river. When she got off, she could still feel the vibration in her legs and felt wobbly. They took their helmets off and he came up behind her until she was aware of his heartbeat pressing into her back.

The light shifted and formed fresh shadows. Arch let go and took her hand. 'I want to show you something.'

Fin followed him, her hand sweaty inside his, her hair plastered to her scalp. Arch stopped in a sheltered area protected by a rocky outcrop. There was a small cross standing amongst a sprawling patch of purple daisies. Arch let go of Fin's hand and knelt. 'I scattered Mum's ashes here where she could see the sky, hear the water, and finally find peace.'

Fin knelt next to him and touched one of the blooms. She had a sudden urge to create something to acknowledge George's baby. Something more solid than a memory.

She collected stones and placed them in a small pile. Arch watched her. He didn't ask, and she was grateful. With great care she used the stones to make a spiral a small distance away from Joy. Fin stepped back to look at her handiwork and wiped her hands on her shirt. She spoke softly into the breeze. 'Rest in peace, baby George.'

'Rest in peace,' Arch echoed.

Fin clung to Arch as he navigated the tiny dirt track back to his property. Her bones rattled as his old trail bike revved its way across the paddock and up the final hill. He gunned past the main house, and just when Fin wondered where he was taking her, a rustic timber cabin appeared between the swaying gums. He killed the engine and they both pulled off their helmets. She gazed at the tiny settler's hut with its small veranda and corrugated roof.

'Well, what do you think?'

'I didn't even know this was here.'

'It's only a couple of years old. I needed my own space.'

'I like it.'

'It's Queensland blue gum and ironbark. It comes prefab and I just assembled it with a bit of help from Dad.'

A dog barked. Arch called out, 'Coming, Spike. He turned to Fin. 'Come have a look inside. I'll let Spike off the chain for a run.'

Fin went up the steps and ran a hand down one of the knobbed timber posts. There were two deck chairs at one end and Fin imagined the two of them sitting there and enjoying a drink. She remembered the condoms she had tossed into her handbag, now back at the car at least a kilometre away. It made her blush to think of her advice to George just a few hours ago. Standing on the threshold of Arch's place with the shape of his chest still fresh inside her arms, she felt reckless.

A black-and-tan kelpie-cross catapulted over and nearly knocked her down.

'Spike! Come here!'

Spike's tongue lolled pink and wet, slobbering over Fin's arms.

'Sorry, he's still a pup. I think he likes you.'

Fin knelt and tried to fondle Spike's ears, but he wriggled so much it was difficult.

'He's almost as hard to pin down as you.' Before she could defend herself, Arch ran a hand through his hair. 'Sorry, I should have invited you in. Would you like a hot shower? A drink?'

'Yeah, sure.'

Inside the hut was a small living area, sparsely furnished around a pot-belly stove with timber neatly stacked against one side. There was a basic kitchen with a few mugs hanging off hooks, plates stacked behind a timber ledge and an open pantry. There was a door at each end, partly open, leading to two bedrooms.

She felt his presence behind her, his breath warm, his skin like hers sticky with sweat. His arms pulled her close, and they stood like that while around them, late afternoon shadows gathered and held them. Fin softened in his arms and wondered if this was what love felt like.

She turned and dared to slide her hand under his clothes to touch his chest, her fingers absorbing the lightly muscled solidity of him. When he kissed her softly on the lips, it rippled through her and she kissed him back, the dusty warm taste of his saliva intoxicating. She pushed her fingers through his damp hair and pulled him closer.

He led her to the bedroom. They wrestled each other's clothes off, zippers catching, buttons uncooperative. He struggled to unfasten her bra and she helped him. With the sunset burnishing the sky, they found themselves bared and ready. This time, Arch was prepared and reached inside the bedside table for protection. Fin watched him open the packet and sheath himself before reaching with his fingers to touch her.

Afterwards, they lay in the half-darkness, cocooned inside the smells of sex and sweat, both encrusted with dirt.

'I love you, Fin. Stay with me.'

She stiffened, Victor's words a distant echo in her head. She shifted to get up. Arch reached for her hand and didn't let go.

'You could live here with me. We could make a go of things.'

'I've just finished my nursing degree. I'm working two jobs in the city.' Fin grabbed her clothes and held them against her nakedness. 'Maybe I could come and stay on weekends?'

It would be the perfect way to keep an eye on George, to keep her safe.

Arch reached over and trailed a finger down her cheek. 'I would like that, very much.'

23

Two years earlier

FIN lay wide awake, excited about the day ahead. She watched as darkness gave way to the soft glimmer of dawn. Eleven weeks and two days pregnant. In five hours, they were booked in to have the ultrasound where she would meet her baby properly for the first time, her dream of motherhood finally becoming real.

It was tempting to wake Anthony, but he looked exhausted after having his bi-weekly chemotherapy and heading back to the bookshop. She let him sleep in. She turned the shower on and stared at her nude body in the mirror. Her abdomen was slightly rounded now. When the mirror misted over, she stepped under the jet of water and enjoyed the way it sluiced down her skin and made it sing.

A couple of weeks ago, Anthony had wanted to discuss their finances in detail to prepare her should he not be one of the lucky ones, but it made her anxious. It was like tempting fate.

When he persisted, she promised him that after knowing the baby was fine, she would sit with him and work through his end-of-life planning.

Fin hummed to herself through the ritual of tea-making. She started by swirling hot water in the teapot to heat it up, then measured a couple of scoops of Anthony's favourite leaves and poured boiling water over them. Finally, she pulled the woollen tea cosy over the snout and reached for the special china and matching jug he preferred. Today felt celebratory, so she set up the small table for two on the back deck and laid out warmed croissants and homemade jam from the markets before covering them with a tea towel. The local birds were cheeky enough to swoop in and snatch food left uncovered and unattended.

'Good morning.'

He stood at the double glass doors and watched her, dressed in his casual pants and deep green shirt. She felt a rush of relief that he looked his normal self today. It was almost like the last weeks had been a bad dream.

'Anthony.'

She came over and hugged him. 'Breakfast on the deck today. A celebration.'

They sat in comfortable quiet, just like before, sipping tea and listening to birds squabbling while gazing out onto Anthony's flowerbeds.

He insisted on taking his two-seater Fiat 124. Fin laughed. 'We won't be able to fit the baby capsule in here. We might have to sell it and get a sensible family car.'

He looked horrified. 'Never.'

The ultra-sonographer was young. Late twenties. She was also pregnant and looked like she was due very soon.

'Hello. I'm Anita. I'll be doing your ultrasound today. Hop up on the bed and pull your shirt up for me.'

She smiled at Anthony. 'How about you sit just there. Can you see the screen?'

Fin realised she was shaking. She nearly slipped on the footstool when she eased herself up onto the examination table.

'Careful. I don't want you falling off.'

Fin glanced over at Anthony. His eyes were glued to the screen, even though there was nothing to see yet.

Anita squirted cold goop over Fin's belly and pushed the probe down. It was all a grey blur and then there was the baby's head, eye sockets, lips, hands, feet, and a heartbeat.

'Anthony, look.'

His eyes were still fixed on the screen. He leaned closer and seemed to absorb the details with his gaze when the baby moved. Anita shifted the probe. 'Look, bub is waving to mum and dad.'

Fin's hands went up to her mouth, hardly daring to breathe as one tiny hand moved up and down, then stayed poised with fingers splayed.

Anita paused with the probe. 'Do you want to know the sex?'

They nodded in unison.

'A girl.'

She was perfect.

'All looking great.'

Anita kept up a steady stream of speech and took a series of measurements. Fin just kept staring at the screen, wanting to imprint every single bit of the scan in her mind.

'Let me get some great stills that you can share with your family. I might get you to wait outside.'

When they drove home, Fin was very quiet, one hand on her rounded belly. She lingered inside each moment of the scan and kept replaying the baby floating inside and waving.

Anthony interrupted her thoughts, both hands at the top of the steering wheel. 'We should tell everyone now.'

Fin had reprimanded him after he had told Dr Payne, explaining it was bad luck to make the news public before they were sure. There was no reason to keep the baby a secret now, but Fin wanted to relish the warm bubble of just the two of them knowing for longer. The thought of Victor making some unwelcome comment would suck the joy out of it. Much safer to hold onto their happiness and relish it alone.

'I'm just worried if my father finds out, he'll spoil it somehow. Can we leave it a bit longer?'

Anthony's shoulders dropped a little. He reached one hand over to her thigh. 'Sure, whatever you prefer.'

24

Adulthood

FIN pulled her case off the top of her wardrobe, excited to be spending two whole weeks with Arch. She smiled when she thought about the last time she stayed for a long weekend. Cliff came to the hut wearing a clean, checked shirt and new jeans. When Fin went to open the door, he'd taken his hat off, an esky at his feet. 'I just thought I'd drop you young folk some lunch.'

He declined to stay, putting his Akubra firmly back on his head and driving back to his own place. He'd made them egg and lettuce sandwiches, put in a couple of beers, and added two caramel slices – still Arch's favourite.

This would be the first time in two years she had taken more than a couple of days off. After finishing her degree, she continued to work punishing hours. It gave her a legitimate excuse to avoid going home. *Sorry, I'm too busy.* Last year, she even volunteered to work over Christmas.

The phone rang as she zipped up her bag.

It kept ringing, so she picked up. 'Hello?'

'Is that you, Fin?'

She nearly dropped the phone. George only rang when something was wrong.

'George, what's up?'

Her voice sounded muffled, like she had her hand over the mouthpiece. She whispered. 'I need your help.'

A rising unease overcame Fin's frustration that George hardly ever made contact.

'Has something happened?'

There was a pause. It went for so long that Fin thought she had hung up. Then George's shaky voice whispered again. 'I'm pregnant.'

Fin was furious. Once was a mistake, an understandable mistake. This was sheer carelessness. It was time George took some responsibility. Fin took a deep breath, determined to keep her voice calm.

'George…'

'Sorry, Fin. I can't talk. I gotta go.'

~

Fin's car bounced along the dirt road. At the last minute, she turned off at Arch's place. She drove past the old homestead, expecting to see Cliff out the front in his battered chair smoking a cigarette. The place looked shuttered, the weary cane chair empty.

Fin pulled up outside the settler's hut, but it was all locked up. Dread crept around Fin's heart. Arch rarely locked the place, and he knew she was coming today. Usually, he made a point of finishing early and waited, all showered and wearing jeans and a clean shirt, his hair still damp. It always made her ache to see how pleased he was to see her.

The trail bike waited dusty beside the shed and Arch's dual-cab truck was gone. Worried now, Fin headed back to her own car. He was probably at Yowie with Spike, buying some of that caramel slice they both loved. Fin turned her car around and drove on towards The Estate.

A dusty, black Jeep Wrangler sat in the driveway. Fin wondered who it belonged to. It was unlike Victor to have visitors. She pushed open the door and peered into the hallway, lined with boxes spilling an assortment of artifacts. She pulled a macramé pot hanger out of a box and let it dangle off one finger. With the exclusive resort still only half built, Barb was working more than full time now, tutoring on weekends just to make ends meet.

'Hello, stranger.'

Victor appeared. Fin dropped the pot hanger back.

'You should take it, no, take a few of them. They would brighten up your place. All handmade by a collective in Bangladesh.'

'Hi, Dad.'

He embraced her hard. 'I really missed you. You never visit us.'

'I'm working shifts. I don't have much time.'

'Well, you came on a good day. That sister of yours has brought her boyfriend, Ricky, along. He is quite something.'

Fin wondered what had happened to Ewan and why George had not mentioned Ricky. Was this man the father of George's child? Fin clenched her teeth and questioned why she bothered to come at all. She followed Victor down the hallway.

'Here's our eldest who has forgotten about her family.'

Fin forced a wan smile. Barb carried a tray of cups and the coffee pot over to the table. George was seated beside a solid bloke who looked about ten years older than her.

Victor flourished an arm their way. 'Meet Ricky who has completed his degree in finance and was clever enough to fall in love with our George.'

Fin pulled up a chair as far away as she could from Ricky and mumbled. 'Nice to meet you.'

Barb beamed. 'How wonderful to have you here.'

Fin doubted the comment was meant for her. Barb bent down again and busied herself with pouring coffees. She sliced wedges of the *gugelhupf* sitting on the white plate in the centre of the table. 'Fin, hand me your plate and let me cut you a piece.'

With Victor sitting there, Barb focused on keeping everything smooth, a responsibility that required her full attention.

Fin handed Barb her plate, then added milk to her coffee and gave it a vigorous stir. Some of it sloshed into her saucer and onto the tablecloth.

Victor frowned. 'Barb, get a cloth to clean it up. I don't want to stain the tablecloth. It's Austrian linen, a rare piece.'

Fin stood up first, her chair grating along the floor. 'I'll get it.'

Barb was already up, eyes wide. 'Let me soak it right away.'

She started clearing the table and shifted everything to the sideboard. Fin helped. 'It's only a small drip of coffee; just let me wipe it up.'

George was holding the remains of the cake aloft. Barb whipped the soiled cloth away and billowed a clean one over the table. Everyone pulled their chairs up again while Barb and Fin put the coffee cups back. Victor watched, arms crossed. 'I'm afraid the coffees are cold. You'll have to make a fresh lot.'

Barb scuttled out with the coffee pot, then returned a moment later and gathered the cups filled with cooling coffee. Ricky swirled a teaspoon round and round his thumb using his index finger, while George's hands were folded in her lap. Her question lobbed a landmine into the tense silence. 'Are you staying at Arch's place again?'

It sounded like an accusation. Fin pushed her cake away, the betrayal landing hard in her gut. How did George know about Arch?

Victor's eyes narrowed. 'Is that the bloody chicken farmer? I thought I told you they were not our sort of people.'

Fin's anger bubbled to the surface. 'That was years ago. He happens to be a kind, hard-working fellow. His business is very successful.'

Victor stared at her. 'His mother died a bloody alcoholic. Poor stock, if you ask me.'

Fin flung her napkin across the table. 'I might just head home.'

She stood up, grabbed her handbag, and headed towards the hallway. Barb followed her, hands clutched as if in prayer. 'Don't be silly, Fin. Dad just thinks you could do better, that you are too good for that family. Don't leave.'

Fin paused and glanced back at George. Their eyes locked. It would be easy to drop a casual remark, thought Fin. To land a fatal blow and comment on the pregnancy.

Barb reached over and touched her arm. 'You mustn't be so sensitive. We all want what's best. Come on, I'll set out some bread and cheese for lunch, and we can all sit down and enjoy an afternoon together.'

It was late afternoon before Fin, her hurt still raw, managed to corner George on her own out in the yard near the car.

'What the hell, George?'

Fin watched George's big eyes grow wide. She glanced over her shoulder, her voice hushed. 'It was a mistake. Ricky wouldn't cope with a baby right now. He's setting up his financial planning business.'

Fin had nearly forgotten the pregnancy after George's deliberate provocation.

'How did you even know about Arch?'

George dropped her eyes. 'Sheila at the bakery said something. *Isn't it lovely Arch and Fin are seeing each other?* Anyway, what's the problem? Are you embarrassed about him?'

'Of course not.' Fin felt her face heat up and looked away.

'Well, what's the matter, then?'

Fin pressed her lips together. 'You know Dad hates Arch.'

'You shouldn't lie to him.'

'I didn't. I just prefer to stay with Arch than…' Fin nodded towards the house.

George scuffed her toe in the gravel. 'Are you going to help me?'

'Are you using contraception?'

'I can't take the pill. I started getting these awful migraines. Ricky is not that keen on condoms, so sometimes he just pulls out.'

'I'll book you in early next week, but I am not prepared to keep doing this.'

'I know, I know.'

George dropped her face into her hands and started sobbing. 'I really like him. Dad likes him.'

It was on the tip of Fin's tongue to suggest that Dad was not the one dealing with the consequences of Ricky's sex life.

'I'll see you Tuesday morning.'

Fin backed the car out and turned around. She saw a cloud of dust settle around George, who looked like a child standing on the gravel driveway beside the black Jeep Wrangler. It reminded Fin of when George was an innocent kid, and of the nights when they curled up together and sought refuge in each other's warmth.

The car roared in Fin's ears. Its low-slung belly navigated the ruts and holes in the bloody long, dirt road with difficulty. When she came to the turnoff, she barely noticed the truck coming the other way and was forced to stop when it pulled up in front of her. Arch jumped out and left the door open with the engine running. Spike barked, leashed in the tray.

'God, Fin, I'm so sorry. I should have left a note and explained.'

His eyes pleaded with her, his hair dishevelled. Fin averted her gaze.

'It was Dad. He was up on a ladder fixing the guttering and fell off. He had a stroke.' The whites in Arch's eyes were visible.

Fin couldn't imagine Cliff lying in a hospital. 'I'm sorry.'

She followed the truck back to his place. There was a reassurance to the spartan simplicity of it. He shut the door and held her close. The scent of his shampoo and the earthy smell of honest work were the realest things she had experienced all day. Maybe she did love him after all.

She felt her mouth open under his, and when his tongue touched hers, her worries became weightless. They stumbled to the bedroom, shedding clothes. The sensation of her body pressed along the contours of his was excruciating. She gave herself up to the thousand pinpricks rippling across her skin and arched her back in a contented gesture of release.

Afterwards, she wept, fragile as a raw egg, the thin shell of her loneliness cracked. He soothed her even while she knew that she should be soothing him. It was in that moment she recognised her desire with Arch was not for that pure moment of physical fulfillment but a desperate need to be touched, loved, and known.

'Arch, I might try to get a job at Ipswich Hospital. I'll be able to help with Cliff after he's discharged.'

Arch pulled Fin so close there was no space between them.

Over the next weeks, Fin packed up her life in Brisbane, started a new job, and moved in with Arch.

25

Two years earlier

IT was still dark when Fin got up and repacked Anthony's bag for another of his chemo sessions. A port had been inserted in his upper chest now, and every second Wednesday, Fin dropped him at the hospital where he had his bloods checked and his infusions. In her mind, she ticked off each session and tried not to worry about the follow-up scan scheduled to see if the chemo was working.

She folded a clean set of clothes into his small bag and packed two of the books he was reading, and his ear pods. She added his toiletry bag with his toothbrush before zipping it up. He experienced dreadful nausea, and cleaning his teeth helped. There was solace in getting all the details right and bringing an order to the process. It was a way of avoiding the big question to which only time would provide an answer.

Anthony cleared his throat. 'We should tell everyone about the baby now we know everything is all right. We even have pictures to show them.'

Fin felt dizzy and steadied herself, one hand on the bedpost. 'I worry about telling my family.'

Anthony put his hand on her shoulder. 'We are nearly halfway now. You don't think he'll be excited about his first grandchild?'

Her knuckles were white around the bedpost. 'Let's tell everyone else.'

He looked ready to disagree, then sat down on the bed next to the bag, resigned to her decision. 'I might just keep a picture in my wallet to show people.'

She whispered, 'Thank you for understanding.' The pregnancy was the thing that kept her moving forwards through the nightmare of Anthony's treatment. 'How about I make us a pot of tea?'

Fin clung to the reassurance that simple routines like meals and cups of tea provided. It was a comforting way to divide the day into manageable segments.

Anthony looked grey and wrung out. 'I can't face anything.'

The nausea always started the morning they drove to the hospital, even before the infusion started. Fin turned away and wished she hadn't asked.

'You go ahead and make yourself one. We can head off afterwards.'

'No, I think we should just go.'

The traffic was still light, and it was not long before they arrived at the hospital. Fin reached for his bag on the back seat. Anthony tried to take it off her. 'It's all right. I'm not an invalid just yet.'

'Let me carry your bag. It makes me feel like I am being useful.'

It was irrational, but Fin wanted to scrutinise Anthony's infusion and ensure everything was properly checked. One tiny error might be enough for a metastatic cell to escape and proliferate beyond the lymph nodes. Fin forced herself to take a slow breath to interrupt the scattergun of her thoughts.

Anthony took the bag. 'I'll ring when I'm ready. Go and buy some nice things for the baby. I'll be back home before you know it.'

Fin kissed his cheek, his familiar scent already masked by the pervasive cling of hospital antiseptic and sickness. 'Ring me the minute you're finished.'

'Promise.'

When Fin's phone vibrated three hours later, she knew immediately something was wrong.

'Mrs Fletcher?'

She had not found the right moment to correct Dr Payne, and it seemed too late now.

'Speaking.'

Surely, it was too early to pick Anthony up.

'Your husband has developed a fever. We plan to admit him overnight and start some antibiotics.'

Fin's hands were clammy. 'Is he going to be all right?'

'We plan to run some tests and do a chest x-ray. He is immunosuppressed, making the risk of infection high.'

Had he answered her question?

'I'll come in right away and bring some of his things.'

The house closed around her. The roof popped and a branch scraped the window and made her jump. Outside was grey, boulders of dark clouds hiding the light. Fin turned on the kitchen radio, longing for sound to drown the anxiety jackhammering the inside of her skull.

Her phone rang again.

She responded breathlessly. It was Barb.

'Is that you, Fin?'

'I'm in a bit of a hurry right now.'

'We wondered if you would like to come for lunch on the weekend. We have some great news.'

'I'll have to get back to you.'

'Is everything all right?'

Fin's back slid down the wall until she sat on the floor, knees bent, and phone pressed to her ear. 'It's Anthony. He's in hospital with an infection.'

Saying it out aloud was a relief like a valve had opened, the pressure released.

'I'm so sorry to hear that. You said he was having surgery.'

Fin had mentioned the surgery but avoided the word cancer. Barb sent a bunch of flowers and a card. *Get well soon, Regards, Victor and Barb.* George and Damon had not even sent a text message. The surgery seemed like a lifetime ago now.

'Give him my best wishes. He is welcome too.'

Fin hung up.

It was only once she was backing out of the drive, the threatened storm whipping branches into a frenzy, that Fin realised she had not asked what Barb's news was.

~

Anthony looked ashen, the same colour as the sky draped over the city. Fin pushed aside the dinner tray and kissed him on lips that were dry as dust. She fished around in her bag and pulled out a plastic container of tea leaves and a mini strainer, followed by his favourite mug. 'Just wait there a minute. I'm heading to the tearoom to make you a proper cuppa.'

Fin swirled the small strainer around the mug and watched the water darken to a deep amber. Just as she shook the leaves into the bin, a familiar voice sounded in the corridor. Her body went rigid, an animal hypervigilant to danger.

'Tony, you look bloody terrible. We'll have to get you out of this hospital and get some meat on your bones.'

Fin's hand shook. She suppressed the urge to flee. It was unfair to leave poor Anthony alone with Victor. She rearranged her loose top to hide her protruding belly.

'Dad. Imagine seeing you here.'

'Can't have the man languishing here alone. Barb called while I was driving home, so I came past. I'll get her to freeze some decent meals so you can feed Tony properly.'

Fin slammed the mug down so hard tea sloshed over the side.

Anthony reached for it and cast her a grateful glance then nodded at Victor. 'Thanks for dropping by.'

'I can't stay long. When you run an international business, there's little time for sitting back. I picked up another shipment of goods after seeing my accountant. Do you have a good accountant?'

Victor pulled his wallet out of his back pocket. 'Here, let me give you his card. I suspect you won't need someone of his calibre running a small bookstore, but you never know.'

Fin opened her mouth to defend the bookshop when a pink-uniformed lady popped her head in the door. 'Finished with dinner?'

Victor shook his head. 'I can't believe the crap you feed people in hospital.'

She swiped the full tray from the table, forcing Victor to step aside.

Anthony sipped his tea. 'This is just what I needed, Fin.'

Victor placed the accountant's card on the bedside table and tapped it with his finger. 'You won't regret making an appointment with this fellow. I'll put in a word for you. And before I forget, Barb has invited the two of you over for lunch on the weekend. You should stay on in one of our exclusive cabins, get some fresh air into you. It will do you both good to get out of the city air for a while.'

Anthony shifted. 'Thanks for the offer, we'll let you know.'

To Fin's relief, Victor frowned at his watch. 'I can't stay. Must rush.'

He headed to the door, one hand raised. 'See you on the weekend. Ready to celebrate some exciting news.'

Fin lowered herself onto the bed. 'I'm sorry.'

Anthony's fingers teased her hair. 'Don't let him get under your skin. I'll be discharged tomorrow, so we can humour him by having lunch there. It might be time to tell them about our baby.'

Fin didn't respond. She knew Victor would spoil it somehow.

When Fin left the hospital, it was dark. She switched her phone back on. A message from work, another from one of her nursing team asking how she was and one from George.

A flutter rippled through Fin just seeing George's name there. Maybe she was asking about Anthony after all and wishing them both well. Fin wanted to ask George to be the baby's godmother.

She scrolled to George's message. *Hope all is going well with you. We have exciting news. I'm pregnant.*

26

Adulthood

IT was three years since Fin moved into the main house with Arch so she could support Cliff. Arch wriggled closer to her on the worn lounge and placed his hand on her thigh. 'How was work?'

Fin sat unresponsive. 'Awful. I was looking after a toddler with a fever when they brought in half a nursing home with food poisoning. It was so frantic, a young woman with pain and bleeding nearly died when her ectopic pregnancy ruptured.'

'Let me cook tonight.'

'Are you listening? She nearly died because I didn't triage her appropriately. She didn't even know she was pregnant.'

'Fin, you're a great nurse. Don't blame yourself.'

'She's still in intensive care with only one fallopian tube because of me.'

'But she's alive.'

'Just forget about it.'

Arch shifted, leaving a small gap between them. They sat side by side, not speaking, the news a muted series of flickering images. She stood up. 'Back in a minute.'

She came back with a glass of wine and sank back into the lounge. Arch frowned at her. She ignored him.

'I'm grateful you're helping with Dad, but I don't think you should give him alcohol.'

Another veiled criticism of her own drinking, a well-trodden path Fin chose to ignore.

'Why can't he enjoy a beer?'

'It's bad for him, that's why. Have you forgotten Mum?'

'Joy had an addiction. It's an entirely different thing. Cliff gets pleasure from his evening beer. You're being unreasonable.'

Fin moved further away and ensured no part of her touched him.

'I forbid you to give him alcohol.' Arch hesitated. 'You seem to be drinking quite a bit yourself.'

Fin drained her glass, stood up, went to the kitchen, and poured herself another.

He folded his arms across his chest.

Fin sat down, as far away from him as possible. Even after he showered, the faint scent of chicken shit clung to his skin. She wondered if all relationships were like this. A series of small compromises, an accumulation of debts and misunderstandings brushed over until one half caved under the weight of it all. If it were not for Cliff, she would have left long ago, back to city lights and pavements.

Arch continued, 'He's fragile and on medication, I've seen the damage alcohol can do.'

She stood up. 'I have an early start. I might just head off to bed so that I can sort Cliff before my shift.'

Arch thrust the remote towards the TV. He changed from the news to some quiz show and turned the sound up loud.

Fin changed into her pyjamas, cleaned her teeth, and tiptoed to Cliff's room, the smell of sickness staining the walls. There was enough light to show him asleep, mouth open, sparse hairs sprinkled on his chin, his cheeks sunken.

She shivered when she went over her conversation with him early this morning. He had waited till Arch was out with the chooks then grabbed her hands, desperation bulging his eyes.

'Please help me. I don't want to live like this anymore. Dependent and useless, a burden to you and Arch. I beg you, do something.'

Fin understood that Arch was never to know. Unable to meet Cliff's eyes, she imagined mixing him a cocktail of drugs, staying with him while he fell asleep. A sweet release from his life of dependence and pain. Cliff's life was outside on the farm, fixing things, doing things, not transferring from a sickbed to a wheelchair, his wasted buttocks pocked with bedsores. She turned him using the foam underlay, wasted sheets of muscles hanging off bones.

Fin's eyes brimmed with regret. 'I'm sorry, Cliff, I just can't.'

Now, looking at him, she wondered if she was doing the right thing.

Fin turned away, feeling nauseated.

'Fin, is that you?' Cliff called out, his voice soft.

She knelt beside his bed. 'I'm here. Can I get you anything?'

He coughed. It sounded moist. Fin put her hand on his forehead, relieved to find it cool.

'A box of tissues, please.' He hesitated. 'And a plastic bag for the used ones.'

Fin came back with a fresh box and put them beside his bed then opened the plastic bag and hung it from one of the bedside table drawers. She stroked his forehead. 'I might get to bed. I've another early start.'

Despite her fatigue, she lay awake for a long time, eyes closed. It must have been some hours later when she felt the mattress dent and Arch slip in beside her, his breath warm on her neck. Eventually, his breathing settled to the steady cadence of sleep. Fin was careful to leave a space between them. She thought about their earlier conversation, how he just didn't get it.

Only last week, she told him about the three-year-old who came in unwell with bruises and sores around her mouth. Investigations confirmed a diagnosis of leukaemia. Fin stayed back after the shift to talk to the mother while they waited to be transferred to Brisbane.

Arch listened, brow creased. 'Jeez, Fin. Why don't you just give it up, work with me on the farm? We could have a couple of kids and spend more time together.'

She'd clenched her teeth, opened the fridge, and got a beer for Cliff, then poured a wine for herself. With Arch's disapproval burning a hole in her back, she helped Cliff into the wheelchair and wheeled him onto the deck, where they watched the sunset together.

After they finished their drinks, he looked out into the dusk. 'I really appreciate everything you do, Fin. You're a damn fine nurse.'

Fin rolled away from Arch, pulled her knees up and savoured that moment again, embarrassed by how much she appreciated Cliff's praise.

~

On the way home the next afternoon, Fin swung past the bottle shop to get some more beers for Cliff and a bottle of wine for herself. He really enjoyed that evening drink looking out over his farm the way he had always done. She didn't want to upset Arch and checked if he was in before taking her haul inside.

'Arch?'

The house was still. Arch was outside working. She heard the distant sound of the tractor. Arch had constructed four large mobile chook caravans and each week moved them to a new spot.

His free-range organic eggs were selling so well there was a waiting list of customers hoping to tap into the demand for ethically produced food, all happy to pay a premium.

Humming to herself, Fin placed the alcohol in the fridge, then headed to Cliff's room. He was in bed, his half-eaten plate of food attracting flies, the stench making her nose crinkle. He had soiled himself again. 'G'day, Cliff, how about we get you cleaned up?'

'Jesus, love. Help me, please.'

Fin paused in her tidying up. Cliff's blue eyes were wet, tears trickling down his cheek. Her heart clutched and she knelt beside him, holding his good hand between hers. 'I'll get you sorted right away.'

She filled a basin with warm water, grabbed a washer and his razor. With a sheet tucked under him, she rolled him over, slid the soiled clothes and bedding out, and bundled them together before beginning the laborious process of washing him. His skin was tissue-paper thin, crusted with sweat, urine, and dried faeces.

'You're a good woman, Fin. I hate to be a useless burden like this.'

'Hush, it's good for your soul.'

Lying on his side, he spoke muffled into the pillow. 'When Joy was still alive, we promised each other no heroics, no loss of dignity. I failed her. When we took her to the hospital, she was treated like she was nothing. They assumed it was just the drink and treated her like dirt and delayed investigations. She was a beautiful person, talented and smart.'

Fin wiped him dry, replaced the dressings on his pressure sores and remade the bed around him.

His eyes were glazed, and he stared so intensely at her she had to look away.

'I love you, Fin. Like a daughter.'

Fin was overwhelmed by the rush of tears to her eyes. Her own father had never once uttered those words. She took Cliff's coarse and workworn hand into her own.

Soon, the washing machine hummed in the background while Fin cooked up a batch of bolognese. Freshly showered, Arch came up behind her and nuzzled her neck. 'We should celebrate tonight. Liberty Chicks has been nominated for a Food Industry Award.'

Fin turned the heat off and reached for a serving spoon. She dished up three bowls and busied herself cutting Cliff's spaghetti into easy mouthfuls. 'Well done.'

'I even got us a bottle of champagne.'

Fin paused and turned around. It was Arch's olive branch after making remarks about her drinking. She softened. 'Congratulations, you should be proud.'

He placed his finger on her lips then took her hand and led her to a small table he'd set up outside with two glasses and a bottle of Chandon Brut. She left their dinner cooling on the bench and wondered if she should wheel Cliff out to join them.

Arch stood and eased the cork off with a loud pop and Fin watched it explode into the evening. When he handed her a glass, she lifted it against his. She wanted to feel happiness for him, but her mood stayed flat. The air around them cooled and Fin shivered. Arch reached for the folded blankets on one of the chairs and handed it to her.

'I might go and help Cliff with his dinner.'

Inside was dark, and only the ticking of the old clock in the living room could be heard.

She went into the dim kitchen where three bowls of food sat congealing. Fin flicked on the light, placed Cliff's bowl in the microwave and called out. 'Dinner's not long.'

The microwave pinged and she used a finger to test the temperature as if he were a baby.

She walked into Cliff's dimly lit room, screamed, and dropped the bowl, spraying mince, tomato, and parmesan around the room. A moment later, Arch was at her side, still reaching for one arm of his tattered brown cardigan.

Fin stood in shock.

Arch made a strangled sound, nearly slipped on shards of ceramic, splats of spaghetti and sauce, and threw himself on the bed, one arm of his cardigan hanging vacant.

Cliff lay blue-mouthed, eyes staring lifeless, his head locked inside the plastic bag Fin had left for him the day before, empty foil sachets of drugs scattered across the floor. Arch ripped the bag off, tore at his father's striped pyjama top, and started compressions. The mattress sank with each push of his hands.

Fin froze at the realisation of what she had done.

Numb with shock, she walked through the mess.

Arch pumped with a fury. She pulled at his shoulder.

Then she looked down and her heart froze. Cliff's spidery writing on a paper napkin beside the bed, with the words, *Thank you.*

Arch collapsed onto his father's cooling body and wept.

27

Two years earlier

FIN got up early, ready to head to the hospital to bring Anthony home. Her phone pinged. She glanced at the screen. It was Victor. *George is making us grandparents. Come for lunch so we can celebrate.*

Fin's jealousy was unreasonable. After all, no one knew that she was pregnant. She regretted not listening to Anthony when he suggested telling everyone, but there was no going back. If only she had been the first to announce her pregnancy.

She caught sight of herself in the mirror in the hallway, focused on her thick thighs, aware that her hip and collar bones were now sheathed in fleshy softness, her belly round and enlarging, her baby taking up residence and asserting herself. George and Damon had not even bothered to make contact to wish Anthony well after Fin had messaged George about the cancer diagnosis. Anthony must have let his son know, and yet, not so much as a card or a text from either of them. Everything was always about George.

The roads were still quiet. Fin arrived, found a park, and headed to the elevators. When a woman with a young fellow in a wheelchair pushed ahead of Fin, she bit down her irrational anger and punched the fifth level several times.

Anthony was disconnected from his fluids and antibiotics and sitting up reading when she strode in and slammed her bag onto the chair.

He raised an eyebrow. 'Everything all right?'

She shrugged, arms crossed. 'Fine.'

'Have you heard Damon and George's news?'

'Bloody George. Stealing the limelight is a speciality of hers.'

137

Anthony reached for her hand. 'Hey, that's a bit unfair. You were the one who wanted to keep our news a secret.'

Fin perched on the edge of the bed, arms limp by her sides. She hated it when he was so reasonable.

'Damon really loves George. This baby means so much. Having his own child will change him, I'm sure of it.'

Fin wanted to tell Anthony about the other babies, how careless George was with important things, and how she could barely look after herself, let alone a baby.

'George didn't even send a card when you were having surgery.'

'Don't be too harsh. Damon has occasionally been keeping in touch with me. I am really hoping to mend bridges.'

Fin picked at a loose thread in the blanket and didn't say anything. Anthony's hand was warm over hers. 'Are you ashamed I am becoming a grandfather at the same time as becoming a father again?'

'No, of course not. I just wanted this to be about us.'

'This is about us. George and Damon having a baby doesn't change that.'

~

Fin glanced at Anthony as she drove them to The Estate. Just having him home the last two days, wearing his own clothes, drinking cups of tea with the spine of a fresh book broken across the arm of the lounge, made the future seem solid again. He smiled. 'We'll have a bite to eat, join in the congratulations, then I'll beg fatigue, and we can head home.'

Fin's hands gripped the steering wheel and guided the car over the rutted dirt road, wishing the day over.

Anthony stared straight ahead. 'Are we going to tell them our news today?'

'Not today.'

The engine stuttered over potholes. Anthony's hand clutched the grab handle.

'Have you thought about names for our daughter?'

She shook her head.

'I rather like Scarlett.'

Scarlett. She liked it, liked that Anthony had been thinking about names. 'Sure.'

'I'm delighted. I sort of expected you to disagree.'

Fin pulled up in the gravelled drive, relieved Victor and Barb were not waiting outside for them. When Anthony stepped out of the car, his movements were careful like an old man.

Barb appeared at the door and greeted them with a measured smile. 'It is lovely to see you both.'

Anthony reached and pecked her cheek.

Fin's arms hung loose. 'Good to see you, Mum. I'm sorry it's been a while.'

Fin realised she meant it.

'I'm afraid lunch will be a simple affair. Victor isn't home yet, he's been busy at the markets trying to offload some stuff.'

They stood in the hallway, lined with boxes spilling macramé, decorated bowls, wooden figurines, and tribal masks. Fin and Anthony glanced at each other, then followed Barb past the expanding detritus to the living area.

Barb waved one hand at the gaping rooms with pipes exposed, incomplete walls, and canvas nailed over window frames. 'Victor is working very hard with this business venture and has not had a minute to do the finishing touches on the place. Now, with George having a baby, he will do up one of the cabins and turn it into a cosy home.'

Fin clamped her mouth shut before she reminded Barb the place had been half-finished for twenty years.

'Once Victor sells his imports, he plans to have a big working bee and just do the whole place over a month or so. Unfortunately, people don't appreciate the value of Victor's products. They are unwilling to pay decent money to have a beautiful piece in their homes.'

Anthony put his arm around Fin. A sharp stab in her pelvis made her tense.

Barb flapped a tea towel in the air. 'I made soup, a good old-fashioned goulash. Victor mentioned you were a bit run down and this dish is full of good things. Meat and vegetables, and a few homemade gnocchi to fill you out a little...'

There was a loud bang at the front door. Victor appeared, the bottom half of his round face cracked open by a smile. 'Well, well, well. What a great surprise to see you both here. Have a seat, make yourselves at home. Barb, how can you let our guests stand around like this? Go and get them a coffee.'

'Darling, I was going to serve the goulash. It's lunchtime.'

He frowned at his watch. 'Time flies past when you have a schedule like mine.'

He thumped Anthony on the back. 'I suppose you know the news. We are going to be grandparents, you and I.'

'Dad, you told us, remember? You invited us for lunch to celebrate.'

'Come here, my girl. You don't visit your old dad enough. I miss you. Just imagine how wonderful it will be to have a young child growing up here. We are so excited, aren't we Barb?'

Fin avoided looking at anyone, aware of her own enlarging belly.

Soon, they were all seated around the table with baskets containing rounds of an Italian loaf and pats of yellow butter on white saucers. Barb brought out a tray with four steaming bowls and placed one in front of each of them. Anthony shifted closer to Fin and asked her to pass the bread.

As Fin handed the bread to Anthony, she said, 'I didn't know George and Damon were moving back.'

Victor layered butter onto his bread, dropped a chunk into his soup, and stirred it until it was coated. 'Well, not immediately, but I can't imagine them raising our grandchild in a big, dirty city like New York. They'll long for fresh air and the freedom of home.'

Fin's belly cramped harder this time. She dropped her spoon back into her soup and pushed away from the table, sucking air in through half-closed lips. 'Excuse me, I'll be back in a minute.'

She nearly didn't make it to the toilet, the blade of cramping doubling her over. She punched a fist into her pelvis and cried out.

When Fin stared into the bowl, it was stained with blood.

Fin crumpled, face in her hands, grief tearing her asunder from throat to pubis while blood continued to drip against cold enamel.

She used a face washer folded over twice to line her underpants and stumbled back to the table. 'I'm not feeling well.'

Anthony looked at her. 'What's up? You look pale.'

Victor talked, his voice rising and falling like wind wheezing through trees.

She stood up, one hand on her belly. 'I just need a walk.'

She left Anthony in the fray and walked out without any dissent from Victor.

Fin ignored the intense cramping that came in waves from some place deep inside her. Fists curled, she ran through the pain and felt warmth slipping away between her legs. She kept going through the bush, not allowing herself to stop. Heaving, she reached the place where Joy's ashes nourished daisies.

Further pain doubled Fin over and she groaned and curled over in the dirt, sharp stones pressing into her side. Fin panted through the tightening spasms, relieved when they died away. She inhaled and her lungs filled with air, sharp and clean.

Two glossy crows perched nearby, their beaks curved and eyes shiny. One throaty caw later, their gleaming wings lifted them into the air, leaving her surprised at the muscular size of them up close.

'Fin?' Anthony's voice, far away.

Sound began to filter through the retreating membrane of pain.

'Fin, where are you?'

An echo reverberated across the valley like a dream.

A chorus of cicadas; the still flow of the brown river below. And then another rising wave obliterated thought and everything receded into the slippery, dark vault of sweating agony while she hovered at the edge of consciousness.

Time disappeared into the rise and fall of pain, a tide that swept her along helplessly until it squeezed her so hard, she cried out. It cracked her open, two parts of a whole, and she was overcome by an overwhelming urge to push.

'Fin?' High-pitched, closer.

Thighs bloodstained, her body spent with exhaustion, Fin stared in shocked disbelief at the dark blood oozing from between her legs onto the dirt.

The still baby was tiny, her skin translucent, one hand unclenched. Fin screamed her loss into the indifferent world, past the long grasses bent and broken where she lay, across the hard shape of the rocks near the river below.

'Scarlett,' she sobbed. 'Scarlett.'

At nineteen weeks and five days, she was not even stillborn: a non-entity, unworthy of acknowledgment. Fin kept whispering the name, and a soft wind carried it across the water, a faint echo of her loss. After the placenta landed with a swoosh beside them, a red-backed fairywren tipped its head and paused a moment, curiosity a bright sparkle beading its eye. Then, just as quickly, it was gone.

Grief and guilt curved Fin's spine around her tiny daughter, longing to stitch her warmth to this child and breathe life into her purple lips. Scarlett. It was the perfect name. Fin's daughter, light as ashes or a blown kiss, soon to join the ghosts woven into this very same earth.

Shadows lengthened and Fin used a sharp rock to dig a shallow grave. She gathered rocks, worn smooth by water, and arranged them into a small cairn. Sweating, she stood back and viewed her efforts, the stones white and pure like ghosts. Fin crouched down and placed a finger inside herself then smeared clotted, dark blood on the rocks, staining them with her sorrow.

With her pulse rushing in her ears, her knees cracked with dirt, she went to the river, slid out of her clothes, and let the coolness of the water rinse her clean. The adrenaline and oxytocin that had fuelled her efforts receded to a dull throb radiating from the hollow spaces inside her.

'Where are you?' Anthony's voice reverberated off rocks.

Fin stayed until she glimpsed the pinprick of a single star between the clouds winking at her. She imagined the tiny, fresh spirit released into the sparkling blackness of eternity.

Scarlett was reduced to stardust, alive only in the shimmering night sky, a distant hope for a future that was now out of reach.

28

Adulthood

THE funeral was held in the small hall in Yowie. Above them, a bank of clouds threatened rain. Fin sat up the front next to Arch, his grief solid beside her. Without speaking about it, she knew they would never divulge Cliff's hand in his own demise. Fin found herself unable to look Arch in the eyes, certain he would see her complicity. If only she had thought to remove the evidence, laid Cliff under the sheets, his lips blue, and spared Arch the awfulness of finding his father's body.

Fin pulled herself back into the moment. The words uttered by the celebrant sounded insincere and failed to give substance to the man who had loved her in a way her own father never had.

When Arch stood to read his eulogy, Fin gave his hand a quick squeeze, her own grief a painful stone in her gullet. She would miss Cliff's wheelchair on the wide veranda, the two of them enjoying a cuppa while she read the newspaper out loud or watching the sunset with a drink before dinner.

Arch stood at the front and looked out over the small group gathered to honour his father's passing. The sheet in his hand trembled, but when he spoke, his voice was clear and confident. Fin sat with her knees pressed together and let the words she wrote to honour Cliff knit themselves into her memory.

Cliff's final words were engraved in her heart. *I love you, Fin. Like a daughter.* By the time Arch nudged himself next to her again, silent tears slipped down her cheeks and landed one by one in her lap. He leant close and whispered. 'Dad really loved you, Fin.'

By the time the final song, Lynyrd Skynyrd's *Free Bird*, sounded from the speakers, the sun had muscled through and softened the atmosphere. A single cone of light found its way through one of the slatted windows and held the coffin in its beam, dust motes spinning like tiny planets orbiting in perfect symmetry.

Everyone started to sway to the ballad sounds of the first part of the song and Fin joined in, her arm tucked under Arch's. When the guitar exploded into a strumming rockfest at the end, people raised their arms in the air and started dancing as if they were at a live music event. Fin's hips moved of their own accord, and she shimmied with Arch's arms around her, careful to keep her eyes averted from his.

It was a couple of weeks after the funeral when Arch suggested that they visit Victor and Barb. 'Your father must have moved on by now.'

Fin's shoulders tightened. 'He never lets go of things.'

Arch grabbed his keys and let them jangle from one finger. 'If he says anything, I'll pull him up. Don't worry, I'll stick up for you.'

Fin sat rigid in the passenger seat and stared out of the windscreen while Arch drove the few kilometres to The Estate.

'Soften up. It'll be fine. Your mum made a cake, and we'll just stay for a short while. They're family, after all.' His voice went soft. 'And I don't have any other family left.'

Fin stared out the window. Arch had not lived with Victor's subtle criticisms, thinly veiled as advice. He had never experienced Victor's long, sullen silences, those days when the three of them would tiptoe around, his presence a thick cloud filling the house while Barb made pleading efforts to appease him. *Victor, dear, let me make you a coffee. I made some of the kiflel you love.* Fin still hated the way these controlling silences were never mentioned after he started to speak again. It was like nothing had happened.

Arch pulled up behind George's old Datsun. 'Maybe I'll offer to help him with those cabins he planned to build.'

Fin wanted to warn Arch. She wished they had driven her car instead of Cliff's old truck. Despite having plenty of money to get a new one, Cliff had been too attached to his old faithful. *I don't want one of those newfangled things with fancy engines I can't fix on my own.*

Arch grinned when they pulled up on the gravel driveway. 'Hey, Fin.

Don't worry. I'll tell him about our award, show him how well we're doing.'

Fin put her hand on his sun-browned forearm, muscled from hard work. It reminded her of Cliff, and she pulled away and stepped out of the old truck.

Fin pushed the door open and heard Barb listening to songs on the radio. When they followed the sound to the kitchen, they found her dusting a Linzer Torte with icing sugar. The table was set with white plates and polished silver, a small bowl of whipped cream like a cloud in the centre. Barb startled. 'I'm sorry, I didn't hear you come.'

Arch leant against the doorframe. 'Great to see you, Barb.'

She dusted her hands off, her cheeks pink. 'Victor won't be long. He's settling some guests into one of the cabins. They have a discount because things aren't quite finished yet.'

Conjured by her words, Victor appeared, oddly dressed in a suit with a bow tie. Arch, as ever in his faded jeans and checked shirt, didn't shift from his position in the doorway. 'Great to hear your innkeeping is taking off.'

Victor pulled himself to full height. 'I'll have you know, I am not innkeeping. I am running exclusive rural retreats.'

Arch shrugged. 'If you need a hand finishing those cabins off one day, I'm happy to come over one weekend.'

Fin's mouth dried up.

Barb interjected, 'Let's have morning tea. I've just brewed the coffee. Fin, grab the milk and sugar, would you?'

Fin snatched up the jug and sugar bowl and headed for the table. Barb fussed around the coffee percolator while Arch and Victor followed Fin out. She placed the jug and sugar bowl on the table. 'Where's George?'

Victor pulled out a chair just as Barb came out with the large coffee pot and started to pour. He winked at Barb before looking at Fin. 'It was great timing you dropped in today. We have big news.'

Fin stole a glance at Arch, who added milk and three sugars to his coffee.

'George is moving out. She has met a very impressive fellow, Miles. He has a senior role at Sterling Real Estate. You know them? They are very successful. They plan to marry next year, and it will be quite an event. We might hire a marquee, set it up, and allow people to stay on in the cabins.'

Barb cut wedges of cake, then used the silver slide to transfer them to plates. 'George mentioned having the wedding at Mount Tambourine.'

'Don't be ridiculous. Why would she want it somewhere else when we have this magnificent spot here?'

Fin forked some cake into her mouth, hurt George hadn't mentioned Miles to her first.

Barb broke off a tiny piece of cake with her fork. 'You are right, dear. She might have thought it was too much work for us.'

Victor rolled his eyes. 'This woman has no idea; she talks without thinking.'

Arch dropped his fork onto the plate. 'We have some big news ourselves.'

Fin choked on her cake and held a napkin to her mouth. Arch waited for everyone's attention.

He leant back, one arm casual over the back of his chair, one leg stretched under the table. 'Liberty Chicks has been nominated for a Food Industry award. I already signed a large contract with the organic food company, Earth, and will need to employ more staff.'

There was a silence that extended long enough to be uncomfortable. Fin watched as Victor picked up his coffee, took a sip, then jammed it hard back into the saucer so everyone jumped. 'Barb, this bloody coffee is lukewarm. How can you expect our guests to drink this?'

Barb stood up, the scrape of her chair loud. She gathered all the cups and coffee pot on the tray and fled to the kitchen.

Arch stood. 'I might give Barb a hand.'

Fin sat numb, cake crumbs dry in her mouth, Victor a dark presence near her. He stood up and muttered. 'I can't believe that my eldest daughter is stuck with a bloody chicken farmer.'

Fin's heart sank like a brick in a well. She stared hard at her plate, relieved when he walked out and left her alone.

~

That evening, Fin didn't feel like cooking. She made them each an omelette, her shoulders tight.

Arch shrugged. 'He's just a grumpy old bastard. I think he was so excited by George getting married, he didn't absorb our news. Once he sees how successful Liberty Chicks is, he'll come around.'

Fin hurled the finished omelette across the room, infuriated by his relentless and misplaced optimism. Arch put his hand out, cautious. She batted him away. 'George didn't tell me. She always tells me everything.'

Fin thought about the terminations, how she had kept George's secrets, and never breathed a word. She stormed to the bedroom, slammed the door, and crawled into bed. It might have been ten minutes or an hour when the door opened and Arch came in. He undressed and curled himself around her. His hand slid over her belly, rested there and pulled her close. Despite her anger, her body responded to him. She resented her body's betrayal, its base need for physical reassurance. Arch reached over and nibbled her ear. She softened against him.

Arch's fingers moved under her tee, paused, and awaited her consent before touching her breasts. His consideration undid her. She shifted from under his arm, and still lying on the bed, wriggled out of her jeans and pulled her tee over her head. She rolled back towards him and took the lead with a fresh urgency that was less about desire than control. Her fingers dug into his back, her nails marking his skin, and she felt his surprise. He tried to kiss her, to slow her down but she wrapped her legs around him, unwilling to delay, needing to release this hatred growing inside her. The sex was a brawl of intimacy, all tongues and fingers, sweaty entanglement, and deep thrusting.

Afterwards, Fin rolled away, raw and released, her anger spent. Arch fell asleep, snoring gently, the weight of his arm across her chest. She must have fallen asleep because she woke up sweaty, with the image of Cliff's watery eyes staring at her, the plastic bag tight around his neck. She lay wide awake for what seemed like hours, those final images of Cliff imprinted in her imagination like a sordid nightmare.

Just as first light entered the world, she slipped out of bed and ran a hot shower, scrubbing her body hard until her skin felt red and raw. At the end she stood under icy cold water, willing the memories to disappear in a swirl together with the night's sweat, dirt, and intimacy.

Fin stood in the half-light of the kitchen, wearing only undies and an old tee belonging to Arch. She became aware of Arch behind her.

'Is everything all right?'

She shook her head. Pink dawn filtered into the kitchen, and its familiar shapes emerged from the shadows around them. 'Cliff…' she stuttered, then stopped, knowing she could never share her guilt with Arch and break his heart. 'I'm sorry, I just can't do this anymore.'

Arch dropped his face in his hands. 'It's my fault, isn't it?'

'No.' She swallowed the words filling her mouth.

She left him standing in the kitchen, went and pulled on jeans and an old shirt, then laced her boots. 'I'm heading to the river.'

'I want to come too.'

Fin wanted to go alone but waited for him. Ten minutes later, she was tucked behind him on the dirt bike. He let it roll down the hill until it gained momentum, then let the clutch out with some throttle until it burst into life. The noisy revving synced with the dull, throbbing headache pulsing inside Joy's helmet.

When they stood together in the fresh quiet near the water, Fin collected some stones while Arch watched. She gathered them in her shirt, and he followed her to the place where Joy and Cliff's ashes mingled in the dirt. Fin wavered when she looked at the small shrines honouring George's babies.

She knelt and arranged the new stones into a heart, then stood back, wiping her hands on her shirt. She spoke in a hushed voice. 'Cliff asked me for something, and I let him down.'

Saying it out loud was when Fin knew for certain. She needed to get back to the city, away from The Estate, from Arch. 'I want to honour his memory and study palliative care.' She reached for his hand and gave it a squeeze. 'I'm sorry, Arch. I'm moving back to Brisbane.'

His hand stayed limp inside hers. 'Give it some time, we can sort things out. You can live here while you study.'

Fin shook her head.

'Take some time off, so much has happened. Your work is always stressful. Dad died. Think things over. Don't decide now.'

'I need to go back.'

Fin clung to the familiar shape of Arch, the vibration of the bike making her teeth rattle.

After Cliff's death, she was certain about what she wanted to do. She longed to lose herself in the wisdom of stories told by people with only the final page of their lives left to live.

At home, Arch moved around the kitchen. He cracked eggs into a bowl and tossed some bread into the toaster. 'Please, give it a few weeks.'

She sat, resolute, at the table, her hands around a mug of tea. The comforting smell of toast wafted through the room. 'I've been thinking about it for a while. No matter how tired I was, I always loved coming home to Cliff and looking after him. He was the father I never had.'

Fin choked up. 'Those last months of life are so precious, and every person deserves to have love, kindness, and care when every moment counts. It is what I am meant to be doing.'

Arch turned the heat off, clattered plates onto the bench, and piled scrambled eggs onto warm toast. He turned to her, his arms limp by his sides. 'But I love you, Fin.'

She turned her face away from him. 'I know, Arch. I'm sorry.'

29

Two years earlier

THE river curved past the ghosts scattered along its banks and the couple curled in the grass. Anthony lay beside Fin and held her. They stayed like that for a long time. There was the hint of rain in the air, the indistinct shape of clouds thick in a deepening sky. Anthony started to shiver and gently coaxed her to come with him.

It was dark when they drove home. Fin wet and dishevelled, Anthony still shivering despite putting on a jacket. The inside of the car was taut with emotion, and Fin found it difficult to breathe. Anthony's fingers were white around the steering wheel.

'I was frantic when you didn't come back. I went looking for you and called and called. I eventually followed that rough path near your parent's place, the track you once told me about.'

Fin didn't respond, lost in imagining her daughter. Brown haired, freckled, and curious. Faceless and always just out of reach. She made a strangled noise and spun slowly into the black vortex of her grief.

Anthony drove, his face contorted with pain. 'She was my daughter too. I am always here for you.'

Fin sat with her knees pulled up to her chest, head bowed. There was dirt under her fingernails and smeared across her tear-stained face. Every bump jarred her raw insides.

Anthony didn't speak again until the bitumen was smooth beneath them. 'I love you, Fin. When you walked out pale and unwell, I knew there was something very wrong.'

Fin stared out the window. It was dark now. The moon was obscured by cloud. There were no stars to be seen. Scarlett's light was invisible. A sky in mourning. 'I needed to get away from them.'

Anthony's knuckles were prominent white knobs. The silence between them was clogged, the two of them inhabiting their private worlds of pain. Fin clenched against the unrelenting ache deep inside.

At the hospital, Fin was whisked away. Anthony had called ahead. Their roles were reversed now. Fin lay helpless and hooked up to bags of fluid while blood was taken and drugs injected. The hours passed in a blur of anaesthetic, procedures, and questions she stumbled to answer. Weren't the doctors the ones who should be providing answers?

The next morning, Fin found herself trapped beneath stiff white sheets. When she first woke, she believed she had experienced a nightmare. Then she caught sight of Anthony, sitting on a chair beside her. He looked wretched, wearing his crumpled clothes from yesterday, his hair mussed, and eyes bruised by fatigue. He brightened when she opened her eyes. 'You're awake.'

The truth seemed even harsher under the cold light of another day. The sudden realisation that she would have to live through this day and then another and another for years and years was overwhelming. Fin slid her legs from under the sheets and let her feet touch the linoleum. It felt cold, just like she did inside. 'I just want to go home.'

Anthony stood and placed one hand on her shoulder. 'The gynaecologist is coming by any minute.'

Fin slumped at the edge of the bed. He sat beside her and used one arm to pull her closer. 'I am so sorry. Sorry I wasn't there. Sorry you went through it on your own.'

So many *sorry*s.

They sat side by side, Fin silent, her capacity for tears drained.

'Josefine Steinbauer?'

She nearly didn't respond, accustomed to being called Mrs Fletcher at the hospital.

'I am sorry for your loss. It looks like you had an infection, cytomegalovirus, or CMV. It is a mild infection in adults but can be fatal to unborn babies.'

Fin looked up, stricken. 'How did it happen? Where did I get it?'

The doctor in his scrubs looked at her and shook his head. 'It's just bad luck. Nothing you did or didn't do.'

~

Fin sat on the floor in the nursery and stared at the mobile hanging still over the cot. Anthony stood in the doorway. 'Join me on the back deck. I'll make us tea and we can sit together.'

'I just want to be on my own.'

'You shouldn't be on your own right now.'

Fin started to cry again. 'I just want to go backwards. Not go to my folks. Go back to the day before.'

Anthony came and crouched beside her. 'Me too.' He paused, then spoke very softly.

'Would you like the freedom to find someone who can give you a baby? Someone younger and not nudging at death's door?'

Fin imagined a fling with a faceless stranger or having a donor's seed planted inside her and felt a tiny flutter of hope.

'Of course not.' Her voice was sharp. She refused to look at him.

Sleep, when it came, was the only anaesthetic that provided relief, however temporary, from the gaping emptiness that filled her womb. Over the next weeks, Fin stumbled through life and its endless routines. She held her losses inside, nourished and nurtured them alone. She refused to take any more time off work or to seek counselling. Anthony tried to reach her, but she remained uncommunicative, drowning in her own loneliness and grief.

It was two months after the miscarriage before Fin agreed to join Anthony for a shared pot of tea on his deck, just like they used to do. Late afternoon sun dappled across the yard but did little to bridge the fresh wound of loss gaping between them.

Fin's phone vibrated and her tea quivered. It was George. Anthony raised an eyebrow before pouring himself a second cup. A rush of emotions washed over Fin. She imagined curling up beside her sister again and feeling pale skin soft against her own.

'Hello?'

'Fin, is that really you? It is so good to hear your voice. I feel so far away.'

'Well, New York is far away.'

There was quiet sobbing down the phone. Fin pressed it closer to her ear and imagined worst case scenarios. A sudden fear chilled her to the marrow. 'Is it the baby?'

'I'm thirty-four weeks now. I'm huge. I look like an elephant.'

Fin exhaled. It was hard to put a name to the emotions clawing under her skin. Part of her longed to touch George's taut belly. It was not fair. It should have been Fin who was breathless and fecund with little feet and hands rippling her insides. A stab of jealousy skewered her. A strangled sound escaped her lips.

Anthony put his paper down and mouthed. 'Are you okay?'

Fin turned her attention back to George. 'Thank goodness the baby is fine.'

George was crying softly into the phone. Fin wondered if there was some way George knew about Scarlett, but it was impossible. No one knew except Anthony. Fin glanced over at him. Had he mentioned something to Damon?

'I hate to ask, Fin, but I wonder if I could borrow some money again.'

Something exploded inside Fin.

'You haven't even paid back the last loan. What the hell is going on?'

Anthony leant towards Fin. She turned away.

Hiccupping sobs on the phone now.

'I'm sorry, Fin. I just can't ask Dad. He would expect me to come home, and I can't. I must support Damon and be here for him. I love him.'

Fin was relieved that Victor's dream to raise his grandchild on The Estate was quashed but was determined not to budge on the money.

'I just can't keep sending money over. Come back home, get a job.'

The tears dried up. There was an uneasy quiet that went so long Fin thought George had hung up.

'Forget about it. I'll sort things.'

Fin readied to end the call when George added, 'Say *hi* to Anthony and tell him his grandchild is fine.'

Anthony sat still while two cups of tea cooled between them.

'What's with George?'

'She needs more money.'

'We should send her some. Enough to tide her over. She might need it for the baby and her medical appointments.'

'I thought Damon was working. If they can't afford to live there, they should come home.'

Fin read Anthony's silence as assent. He stood up, gathered the tea things, and went inside. A shadow fell across the table, the sun blocked by a cloud. Fin's hand went down to her own flaccid belly.

A breeze whispered through the trees and a red-backed fairywren landed on the railing, its tail cocked, head to one side, curious, the daubed paint saddle startling. Fin reached out a hand, certain it was the same wren that flitted past when Scarlett was born, even though that was surely impossible. It gave a series of high-pitched calls that rose and fell before lifting away, diaphanous, its wings, rapid as heartbeats. It was gone in a wink. Hope and beauty, both brief and transient.

Back inside the house, the toy white rabbit with its cross-stitched eyes stared at her from the bookshelf. Fin turned away. Heart banging hard against her sternum, she snatched the rabbit up and returned to the nursery. The walls echoed with the ghost of her longings. Fin placed the rabbit inside the cot. Its staring eyes pierced the membrane of her grief. Weeping, Fin crawled into the cot with its pristine sheets and shrank herself to fit, curled up in a ball, pain slipping through the guard rail of her denial.

A sliver of light pierced the gloom. 'Are you in there?'

She stiffened, her sobs settling to sniffs. Anthony stepped inside, uncertain. 'Fin, get some professional help. Talk to someone.'

She stayed still and didn't respond.

He whispered into the greyness. 'I've made some soup. Please join me.'

His footsteps moved away from the door. Fin unfurled, crawled out of the cot, and walked to the kitchen where the scent of garlic and herbs filled the kitchen. He stirred hard, the timber of the spoon scouring the bottom of the pot.

'I know you won't agree, but I transferred some money over for George.'

Fin balled her fists. 'How dare you. You don't know anything about George and my family.'

He pulled the pot off the heat and turned the gas off. 'I am not doing it for George, or for Damon. It's for the child. I do not want my grandchild at risk because I didn't help. This baby belongs to all of us and is related to you and to me. It is an opportunity for us to be a family; to forgive past wrongs and grievances. Children give us hope, an opportunity to do things differently.'

'It's not fair. I have spent my life picking up the pieces while George goes from one disaster to the next. She will never learn if there is always someone there propping her up.'

Fin walked out of the kitchen and snatched up her handbag.

At the front door, she turned around and screamed, 'I hate you!'

She slammed the door so hard the house shuddered.

30

Adulthood

THE wedding date dominated everyone's life. Fin was grateful that her work at St Vincent's Hospital palliative care unit kept her so busy. Victor was so excited that he worked long hours to complete the cabins and even took Arch up on the offer to help. Fin wanted to warn Arch, to remind him what Victor was capable of, but it was hard to put into words. His slights and jibes were disguised, the only evidence they had occurred was the aftermath that reverberated inside her head years later.

Barb was hopeful the wedding would finally force Victor's grandiose project to a conclusion. She wrote comprehensive lists of what needed to be done, lists that Victor ignored.

It was after a hideous twelve-hour shift when Fin stumbled through the door of her unit that her phone started to ring. She dumped her bag and grabbed the cordless handset, her eyes adjusting to the dark.

'Fin, I've been trying to call for ages.'

George sounded upset. No doubt another wedding crisis.

Fin sank into the sofa and half-wished she had let the phone go to messages.

'I've had a long day.'

'Can I come and stay with you?'

'Now?'

George's voice dropped to a whisper. 'Please, Fin. I need to talk to you.'

Fin flicked on the lamp and watched yellow light pool over the coffee table, scattered with nursing journals, old newspapers, and her used plate and mug from breakfast. She wondered what she had in the

156

pantry to eat. It had been over a week since she'd shopped for food.

'Is it about the wedding? Can't it wait?'

Fin pressed the receiver between her ear and shoulder and walked over to the fridge.

George's voice sounded strained. 'Please.'

There was a tray of Liberty Chick eggs sitting lonely on the shelf. Barb had foisted them onto Fin last week when she drove home to help. She really thought she couldn't face an egg again after living with Arch, but they were surprisingly comforting to come home to when she was too tired to cook.

'Well, don't expect too much. I might make us an omelette. Where are you anyway?'

'In the phone booth at the end of the street.'

Fin nearly dropped the phone then looked over her shoulder.

'Jeez, George. Why didn't you say so right away? Come on over.'

Fin replaced the receiver and almost immediately there was a timid knock. She opened the door, and her hand flew to her mouth.

She pulled George inside and slid the safety chain into place. There was a bruise blooming on her face, a laceration bleeding on her lip, and she cradled her arm.

'What on earth happened to you?'

George pressed into Fin's shoulder and started sobbing. Huge heaving shudders left a trail of blood and tears on Fin's uniform.

'Come and sit down while I clean you up.'

Fin moved George gently to the old sofa, filled a bowl with warm water, and grabbed a cloth and an ice pack. She dabbed at George's lip, pressed ice against it, then wiped gravel from George's cheek and forearm. George winced every time Fin touched her. Fin punched out a couple of ibuprofen and handed George a glass of milk. 'Here, take these. It will help with the pain.'

'Now I'm going to make us each a cheesy omelette, and you are going to tell me what happened.'

George curled up and made herself very small. 'It was Miles.'

Fin dropped what she was doing, shock making her rigid. 'Miles? How long has this been happening?'

George stayed tight and closed. 'He said he was sorry, that he really loved me. He didn't mean it.'

'Jesus, George. You have to call the wedding off. The man assaulted you.'

'I can't call it off. It's next week. Dad has spent a fortune. There are guests flying in from overseas. It will be all right. I'll sort it out.'

'You cannot marry this man. Forget the guests, the wedding. Dad needed to renovate the place and finish it off. You did him a favour. Mum is delighted to finally have a functional bathroom and kitchen. Let me ring them and call it off.'

George looked up wide-eyed. 'No! You can't. It's too late.'

'It's never too late. This is insane. I'll sort it out, talk to Mum and Dad. They will kill him.'

'Dad loves him. Says Miles is the son he didn't have. Miles has offered to sort out the finances and help with setting things up for Dad's businesses. Sometimes it feels like he is marrying Dad and not me.'

Fin clenched her jaw. She sat next to George and took her hand. It was trembling. 'Once Dad learns Miles has done this to you, he will insist you call it off. I promise.'

'Please don't tell anyone tonight. Let me sleep on it.'

Fin punched a pillow. 'Have you reported him to the police?'

George shook her head. 'It was an accident. Miles pushed me and I fell. I think he was shocked too.'

The next morning, George's eye was dark and swollen, her shoulders rounded, her eyes downcast. 'Can I stay here till my eye clears up?'

Fin slammed bowls on the bench, poured cereal, and waited for the kettle to boil. 'I am driving you to Mum and Dad's after breakfast so they can see you like this. We are calling off the wedding. After that, you are welcome to stay.'

George started sobbing, her head in her hands. 'I realised Miles was cheating. I was suspicious when I saw him with one of the estate agents and when he was in the shower, I checked the messages on his phone.'

'What a bastard.'

The kettle's piercing noise died away, and Fin jiggled two teabags in two mugs. She pushed one towards George. 'Get some breakfast into you.'

George kept sniffing, poked around at the cereal floating around in her bowl, and barely ate a thing.

'You will feel better once you eat something. At least drink your tea.'

The phone rang.

'Hello?'

Fin clutched the receiver, looked at George's hunched body and felt a renewed fury at Miles.

'Is George with you?'

Fin covered the mouthpiece and mouthed at George. *It's Mum.*

'As a matter of fact, she is right here. We're having breakfast.'

'That is such a relief. Miles is here, worried sick about her. She had a fall and just took off.'

Fin bit back her response.

'Will the two of you come around later? There is a list of wedding things we need to discuss.'

'There is something *very* important we need to discuss. And yes, it does involve the wedding.'

George looked up now, eyes wide. She drew a finger across her throat and shook her head at Fin.

'See you in an hour or so.'

Fin hung up.

~

Victor stood with arms crossed, Barb next to him, wringing her hands in the corner of her apron. Miles looked poised for flight, his eyes moist. 'I love you, George. You know that. We are good together. I'm sorry. It was an accident.'

George stood tightly coiled, her eyes trained on the ground.

Fin narrowed her eyes at Miles. Anger coursed through her body, and she balled her hands to stop herself from punching him in the face. 'Is that so?'

Miles turned to George, her face swollen black around one eye, lip fat, her body bent and broken. 'Tell them, George. Tell them it was an accident. I didn't mean it. I'm sorry.'

George stared at the floor, her voice barely audible. 'What about Fleur, the real estate agent you kissed?'

Victor's arms had fallen to his sides and his eyes moved from George to Miles and back. Barb's fingers stilled. She whispered, 'The wedding is next week.'

Miles stared at George. 'Please…' His eyes darted around, his face white. 'It was nothing.'

Victor waved one hand in dismissal. 'Your mother is right, the wedding is next week.' He put one hand on Miles' shoulder. 'This man loves you and is a decent person. He is nervous about the wedding and made a silly but understandable mistake. Marriage is about give-and-take and forgiveness.'

Miles took a step towards George, and Fin held one hand up. He faltered. 'I'll make it up to you, I promise.'

George shuddered. A long silence followed.

Fin went over to George and put an arm around her shoulder. She looked Miles in the eye, her voice low. 'There will be no wedding next week. Take your things and go.'

George's shoulders softened under Fin's arm. Miles stayed fixed where he stood. The quiet elongated.

Then George spoke. 'It's over, Miles.'

An inhalation from Barb.

Fin held George upright. 'You heard her. Go.'

The tension in the room eased when Miles picked up his things and walked out. Barb shook her head, her voice a whisper. 'The wedding is next week.'

Fin snapped. 'There will be no wedding. George is coming home with me. You can let everyone know.'

Victor put his arm around Barb, pulled her close. 'He promised to help me with the resort. He said I could use my artifacts to decorate the cabins, that I should set up a gift shop here and sell them.' He shook his head at the unfolding of events. 'I loved him like a son.'

Fin turned her back on her parents and ushered George out the door and into the car.

They drove in silence for most of the way. When they were nearly back at Fin's place, George looked up at Fin, her distorted face shiny with tears again. 'There's just one more thing.'

Fin's hand tightened on the steering wheel.

'I'm pregnant.'

31

Two years earlier

IT was late when Fin reached the bookshop. She hadn't intended to go there, but the thought of being alone amongst the shelves of stories waiting to be read was comforting. She dug through her bag for the key, stepped inside, and left the light off. She ran her fingers along the fresh spines and wished she could slip between the covers of a book and disappear into its pages. The thought amused her. *Forty-year-old woman missing. Found as a surprise new character inside a Sally Hepworth novel.*

The world felt insubstantial, something she could step away from and easily leave behind. The reality of surviving day after endless day was intolerable. She had refused the medication prescribed. There were pills for sleep and still others to subdue her grief. Fin refused the oblivion they offered. Night after night, she watched the shifting of darkness to light while her mind churned restlessly with grief for Scarlett.

George's life was so effortless. Once again, she had fallen pregnant the minute she met someone new and, at this very moment, was blooming with a baby. When George encountered difficulties, the solution was a phone call away. *I hate to ask, Fin, but I wonder if I could borrow some money again.* Someone was always lured in by George's learned helplessness and her inability to take care of herself.

Fin had always believed that if you strived for things and worked hard you would be rewarded. Now she recognised how arbitrary life really was. The good things, the bad things, we didn't deserve any of them. They just happened. In the time it took to inhale and exhale, a lifetime of yearning could be snatched away. The earth continued to spin, unmoved by the grief and suffering played out daily on its surface. There was no fair or unfair; there simply just was.

In this fog of despair, Fin realised that inside her bag she had all the medications she had not taken, as well as the narcotics Anthony no longer needed after his surgery. She had planned to take them to the hospital pharmacy at work to be discarded. Her heart accelerated, dizzy with the possibility of escape, grateful Anthony insisted she get her scripts filled despite her determination not to take anything.

She pulled out the paper bag of medications and made calculations in her head. Sleepers, antidepressants, and a couple of sheets of Anthony's narcotics. It was essential to get this right and do things properly. She imagined falling asleep, dissolving into permanent oblivion, relieved of the nightmare of living through her losses for another day.

Trembling, she walked to the back of the shop to the small tearoom and turned on the light. At the sink, she filled a glass with water, set it down with trembling fingers. She readied herself to punch out tablets when her phone rang. Fin's instinct was to ignore it, but she had a sudden urge to hear another voice, one final time.

'Fin?'

Bloody George.

'Fin. Are you there?'

'Yes, I'm here.'

Not for long, she thought to herself. She stared into the bottomless void and longed to fall inside, for it to swallow her pain forever.

Fin exhaled through clenched teeth. Bloody George. Ever unreliable, ungrateful. Still pregnant.

'Fin, you're scaring me.'

Fin sank into Anthony's old sofa, the springs long-dead, and pushed the phone hard against her ear. She imagined speaking her mind for the first time. What would George say if Fin told George how much she resented the way Barb and Victor favoured her, and how jealous Fin was of all those pregnancies? She had a sudden urge to tell George about Scarlett, who should right now be growing and developing, ready to push her way into the world. She started to weep, her tears big and endless and out of control. All that love she had to give and no baby to give it to.

'God, Fin. I'm so sorry. I really am. I should have called more and asked how Anthony was after the diagnosis. I'm just so terrible. I'm sorry.

You are so lucky. He is such a good man, the best.'

Fin lay down now, the phone still pressed against her ear. How had she not thought about Anthony? He must surely be grieving the loss of Scarlett. His daughter. Why had she not wept with him, shared the depth of her loss, and clung to him? She knew once she started to weep, she would fall apart and dissolve in a salty torrent of grief.

George again. Tearful now, her voice a notch higher. 'Fin, I miss you so much. I love you, I really do.'

Fin remembered those days, long ago, when the two of them had shared a bed. The way George followed her around, her trusting eyes big and needy. An unspoken, solemn bond that not even Victor could destroy. George's voice dropped lower again, her words spoken through hiccups.

'You know Anthony helped us out. Did he tell you?'

Fin sank deeper into the couch and disappeared into its sagging cushions.

'Fin, I need to tell you something.'

Now George was crying properly, her words muffled.

Fin hung on, her fingers tight around her phone, the muted light suddenly too harsh.

'Oh, Fin. I should have told you, but I'm so ashamed.'

Fin's heart squeezed, adrenaline driving it so hard she felt pulses throbbing in her ears.

'Damon has a problem with alcohol. He's in detox.' George broke down again.

Fin sat up again. 'Jesus, George. Why are you even there? What the hell?'

'I can't leave Damon here alone. The baby is due soon and I don't know what to do. He doesn't want Anthony to know. He'd never talk to me again if he knew I was telling you.'

Fin stared over at the foil packets of pills scattered across the bench. It was as if she had been underwater holding her breath and had suddenly come up for air. The consequences of her plan stood in stark relief before her. George struggling alone with a baby, Anthony learning the truth about his son while Fin lived on in others' nightmares forever, a truth reverberating into the life of George's unborn child who would soon push her way into the world.

Fin heard someone fumbling at the door and froze.

An intruder. She dropped the phone.

There was no window large enough to escape through. Fin did a rapid inventory of the drawer. Cutlery, a bread knife, and some scissors.

The front door opened. Had she left it unlocked? Fin swore under her breath. She would not fit under the sofa. She should ring the police.

She reached for the phone on the floor, George's scared and pleading voice silenced.

Footsteps approached. Fin punched triple zero into the phone.

Just as emergency services responded, a shadow shifted near the tearoom door.

Fingers shaking, Fin dropped the phone again. It went silent. It was too late to extinguish the light. She stood and pressed her back against the bench, groped for the scissors, and held them like a weapon in front of her.

'Fin?'

She dropped the scissors and they clattered to the floor, the blades open near the phone.

'Anthony.'

She ran to him and buried her face in his shoulder. He held her close, and she wept once again, inhaling the warm familiarity of him.

'How did you know where to find me?'

'Let's just call it a hunch.'

He helped her to the old sofa and pulled out a teapot from one of the overhead cupboards, together with an old tin of tea leaves. 'This calls for a cuppa.'

He glanced at the foil packets strewn across the bench, pushed them aside, and went through the motions of brewing a pot of tea. Fin watched the way he heated the pot, swirled the water around then tipped it down the sink. His hands shook while he measured the leaves and poured boiling water over the top, before heating two mugs. His voice cracked when he picked up one of the foil sachets, the tablets still sitting unused in their blisters. 'Is it me?'

'No!'

The muscles in his face relaxed when he handed her a mug of tea.

She wrapped her fingers around it, grateful for something to hold on to. When he sat next to her, his thigh touched hers. Fin sank into the comfort of physical closeness and was filled with shame. 'I'm really sorry.'

'I should have spoken to you before transferring the funds to George.'

Fin wanted to confide in him and tell him about Damon. She wanted to ask for his help to get George and the baby back to Australia but didn't want to betray George's confidence. She had already caused enough trouble. Perhaps George was using Anthony's money to fly home.

'You did the right thing. I was frustrated and angry with George and jealous of the baby.'

Anthony put his tea down and pulled her close again. 'It will be our baby too, you know. She is made up of bits of all of us. We all love her.'

~

In the weeks that followed, Fin took some time off work while Anthony continued with his chemotherapy and did some shifts at the bookshop. She started taking an antidepressant. The medication helped more than Fin thought it would. She even used the sleepers a few times and started to see a psychologist about Scarlett. There were still terrible days when getting out of bed proved an effort, but she learned to honour her vulnerabilities and respond to herself with compassion. Every day she had fresh insights into the minute details that stitched a life together, and she learned to cultivate hope.

In December, during the week without chemotherapy, Anthony suggested they go out for brunch. 'I'll leave the bookshop with Freya for a couple of hours and meet you at Stones Throw.'

Fin wore a pretty dress, left her hair loose around her shoulders, and applied a slash of lipstick. She arrived exactly on time. He was already there, waiting for her in the courtyard, a pot of tea in front of him. He stood up and gave her a hug.

'It feels like a first date,' she said into his shoulder, breathing in his presence like a tonic.

Fin sat down and gazed at him. She absorbed all those delightful and familiar details. The shape of his fingernails when he poured tea, the single freckle under the left side of his chin, the pulse beating in the hollow above his collar bone. 'It's like I've been living behind frosted glass.'

She wrapped her hands around her mug and had a sip, felt the delicious warmth of tea slip down her gullet, the flavour of Earl Grey lingering in her mouth. 'You were right. The medication really helped. I mean, I should know that more than anyone, but I thought I should be able to cope. I mean, look at you…' Her voice trailed away.

'I turn up for my cocktail of drugs every two weeks.' He reached over and placed his hand over hers then lowered his voice. 'It's good to have you back.'

'I'm sorry. I just fell into this black hole and disappeared. I miss her so much.' Fin's voice cracked.

'I know. I miss her every day too.'

Fin's phone pinged.

She stared down. *Ebony Josefine Fletcher arrived safely. 2823g*

Fin held the screen up to Anthony. 'You are a grandfather.'

Another ping. A picture appeared on the small screen. A squished pink face, skin crinkled, rosebud mouth, one tiny hand poking through a shawl. They both stared at it then looked up at the same time.

Fin looked away first, her eyes moist.

Anthony placed a hand over hers.

He sent a message to Damon congratulating them. Fin knew that he continued to reach out to Damon regularly, despite not receiving messages in return. She ached to tell him the truth but did not want to break her promise to George.

'Does he make you angry?'

'Furious at times. But I know I am partly to blame. When he frustrates me the most, I remind myself that I want Damon to know how much he was always loved despite my failings and my inability to convey that to him when he was younger.'

Fin refused to meet his eyes. Instead, she pored over the photograph of Ebony in minute detail. Fin used her fingers to enlarge the photograph until it blurred, and the little pursed mouth disintegrated into pixels.

32

Adulthood

FIN was driving George back to The Estate two days after the wedding that didn't happen. 'Are you sure you want to go back home?'

Fin sounded sharp. George flinched. Her face was nearly healed now and another pregnancy had been terminated.

'Dad borrowed so much money for the wedding. I owe him.'

'It was his decision, from what I recall. He wanted this grandiose function at The Estate. Didn't you want a small dinner at Mt Tambourine?'

George shrugged. 'He loved Miles. The two of them got on so well. I ruined things.'

'The man assaulted you. Thank God you got out while you could.'

'I hope Dad isn't disappointed in me.'

'You did the right thing, whatever Dad says. Anyway, you can always come and stay with me.'

They drove along in silence for a while, Fin reluctant to turn on the radio. Before they turned off onto the long driveway, George whispered, 'Sorry.'

'You have nothing to be sorry for.'

'I'm sorry about the baby.'

Fin's throat closed. She pulled over and stared out the window at the long stretch of parched lands subdivided by posts and wires. The loss hit her hard this time. Fin had driven George to the clinic but waited in the car instead of going in with her.

'I tried all sorts of things. I can't take the pill because it makes my migraines worse. I let them put that thingy in my arm, and I just didn't

167

stop bleeding. It was awful. I was fitted for a diaphragm, but we went away for a weekend, and I forgot to pack it. I feel so stupid.'

Fin stared into her lap. 'I'm sorry. I didn't know.'

'I was going to tell Miles I was pregnant, when I realised he was cheating.'

'What a bastard.'

George just shrugged. 'When Miles came home, I confronted him. I picked up my phone to ring Mum and Dad. He was furious and told me marriage was about trust. He said if I was not happy with something I should speak to him and not air our dirty laundry elsewhere. That's when he hit me across the face and pushed me. After I fell, I had a bit of a bleed and thought I'd lost the baby.'

Fin put the car into gear and roared back onto the road. George's head banged against the door and a cloud of dust lengthened behind them. At The Estate, Fin jumped out of the car and slammed the door so hard the sound reverberated across the property and brought Barb to the door.

'My darling girls, thank goodness you're here.' Fin opened her mouth to speak but Barb continued without inhaling. 'Your father is furious with that no-hoper our darling George nearly married. Come in, come in. We have arranged an apprehended violence order on Miles to ensure he never comes near us again.'

Fin raised an eyebrow at George before hurrying after Barb.

Victor was red-faced on the phone. He jammed the receiver back into the wall when they arrived. 'Girls, thank God you are both here. I was just discussing things with the bank manager who kindly lent us some money for this wedding of yours.'

Victor shook his head, embraced George, and nodded at Fin. 'Come, girls. Let's sit down. Darling, go and make us some coffee and bring us some of those *kipfel* you made.'

He put one hand over George's. 'My poor girl. I always knew that man was a bad egg. It is such a relief he is gone. I tell you, if he ever sets foot near you or this property again, he will regret it.'

Fin threw up her arms. 'A week ago, you said he was like a son to you!'

'Complete and utter rubbish. I never liked that man. He thought he was better than us because he worked as a salesman flogging prestige property. He even tried to tell me how to suck eggs with my own business.' Victor dismissed Fin with a wave of his hand. 'If you can't contribute anything useful, just don't say anything.'

Fin pushed her chair out and stood up. She gave George a pointed look and snatched up her keys. 'I might just leave you all to it.'

Fin thought Victor would come after her and beg her to stay longer. She lingered near the car. Victor was rewriting the past to create his own convenient new truth until all of them became uncertain about what had really happened, even while Miles was being shamed for his treatment of George. Fin let go of her fierce, protective fury. What did it matter if Victor reconfigured the narrative and twisted it a little to downplay his complicity if George was safe?

Fin started the car, backed out, and drove slowly away from The Estate. She could just make out the newly finished cabins in the side mirror. No doubt Arch's work. He had always been meticulous. She thought about him with a pang, then pulled herself away. Her life was not here. It was in Brisbane. When she passed their special spot, she pulled over and got out of the car.

She listened to the sound of water gliding over rocks and carving its way through the landscape. She felt the gravel knobbly under her soles and smelt the oily eucalyptus that perfumed the air. She parted the shrubs that protected the spot holding the ashes and memories of those who were gone. The area looked dishevelled and unkempt, the stones she had placed now overgrown with weeds and barely discernible. Nature reasserting herself over these lives spent, absorbing their substance and breaking them down while erasing evidence of Fin's endeavours to commemorate their living and their passing.

Fin bent and set to work clawing back this sacred space in defiance of nature. She pulled weeds and cleared dead branches, gathered fresh stones, and reassembled each shrine with painstaking care. The earth was dry and unforgiving, the vegetation tough and unyielding.

Fin had not realised how much anxiety was knotted through her bones these past months. Now Miles was exiled, Fin's muscles eased. She realised how fearful she had been that she would lose George to this loathsome man who did not love or understand her.

She sweated and smelt exertion on her skin. Her body loosened as she worked, and she felt lighter as her anxiety and anger dissolved in the sun and dirt. She gathered fresh stones and washed them in the river before assembling them into a perfect circle for George's recent baby. Fin stood up and looked at the grove of love she had re-created. A returning of loved ones to the earth. Dust to dust.

33

Two years earlier

IT was Christmas Eve, and Anthony had a special book event at the shop. Several local authors were coming in to give a brief presentation, followed by book signings. He had arranged canapes, champagne, and fruitcake, and the evening was booked out, with all proceeds going towards support for victims of the fires raging around the country. He invited Fin, but the twenty-fourth of December was sacred in the Steinbauer household.

Fin stood in the driveway next to Anthony. 'I wish I could come.'

'I'll bring home a bottle of bubbles for us to share.'

Victor and Barb celebrated in the traditional European way and spent the day preparing a special meal and decorating the tree. They opened their gifts after dinner before cutting the *baumtorte*, a rich, multilayered cake filled with marzipan and topped with chocolate. Barb also made batches of Christmas biscuits. Fin promised to bring Anthony a selection to enjoy with the champagne.

The Estate stood stony-faced in the heat, staring down the brown paddocks. Fin pulled up and turned the car around so that she could make a quick exit if needed. She reached for the bag of gifts she had brought and went inside, the heat of the late afternoon intense. 'Hello?' she called down the empty corridor.

She continued to the living area, where Victor was taking meticulous care setting the table. Barb was in the kitchen preparing the food.

'Are you expecting someone else?' Fin looked at the four settings.

'I'm setting up for Tony.'

'I told you he has a function on at the bookshop.'

Victor wiped his damp face with a spare napkin tucked into his

171

trousers. 'Some people have no sense of family or tradition.'

Fin chose not to rise to the bait. 'I'll put the presents around the tree. Anthony has wrapped a couple of things too.'

Barb came out looking red-faced and flustered. 'Merry Christmas, Fin. I'm running a bit behind. Can I get you something?'

Victor's eyebrows met in the middle. 'For God's sake, darling. Go and get dressed in something decent. It's Christmas, after all.'

Barb threw Fin a desperate glance. 'Just watch the carp, will you? I won't be long.'

Fin disappeared into the kitchen, grateful to have something to do. It felt like a sauna and there were dirty dishes piled up on every surface. Victor didn't believe in dishwashers. Fin pulled out one of Barb's aprons and began the laborious job of clearing up, wishing she was relaxing at the bookshop with a glass of bubbles and a canapé. She gave the carp a poke and basted it in more butter and lemon. The heat from the wood-fired Aga was unbearable. Fin moistened a tea towel and draped it around her neck, letting the water drip under her dress.

She had nearly worked her way through the dishes when she became aware of Victor shouting at Barb. She poked her head around the corner. Victor wore his braces and paced up and down, agitated, his thumbs hooked under the elastic. 'That useless creep. I always knew he was no good for our girl.'

Fin flinched. 'What did she say?'

Victor stopped pacing when he saw Fin. 'I rang George for Christmas, and the poor girl is alone with our granddaughter. Did you know?'

'Know what,' asked Fin, hoping it was not about Damon.

'Poor George, she just started crying and when I asked about that lout, she told me he has a problem with alcohol. He is not even there with her.'

Fin's heart sank. Why had George told Victor? Damon would never be welcome here again. Victor paused for a moment, then pointed a finger at Fin. 'You should go to America and bring George and her baby home.'

Barb nodded, the way she always did when Victor spoke. She looked pale, her *dirndl* limp with perspiration. He jabbed the air with his finger.

'It's hard to believe Tony hasn't gone already. What sort of man is he? He must know his son had a drinking problem. He is not welcome here.'

Fin ground her teeth. '*Anthony* loves Damon and has supported George financially more than once.'

A burning smell came from the kitchen.

'My carp.' Barb ran into the kitchen, where curls of smoke escaped from the Aga door.

The carp was blackened, the potatoes crisped. Victor was flapping the sweat-drenched napkin to clear the smoke. 'Useless bloody woman. Can't even manage to prepare a nice Christmas dinner. I've had that carp swimming in a trough for the past two days and you've ruined it.'

Fin grabbed the oven mitt, reached inside the belly of the Aga, and pulled the remains of dinner out, the smoke thick now. She went to open a window, then remembered that they didn't open. She coughed, her eyes stinging.

Victor waved the napkin at Barb as he stumbled out of the smoke-filled space. 'Darling, don't just stand there with your mouth gaping; make us all a coffee and bring out some of those vanilla *kipferl* and *linzer* biscuits. Did you manage to make those without incinerating them?'

Fin knew she would have to break Anthony's heart and tell him about Damon. Better he found out about his son's drinking issues from her than from Victor.

Barb came over with the coffee pot and poured Victor's first. She added milk and four sugars and stirred it before placing it in front of him.

He waved his arms in the air. 'We will clear out the cabins, they are full of my imports. George and the baby can stay there while I renovate the guest wing of the house.'

He reached over and grabbed a couple of biscuits, then looked at Fin. 'You can organise the flight to bring them home. Leave the hard yards to me. We need our baby girl and granddaughter home.'

Fin pushed her coffee away. 'George won't want to stay out here. She can stay with me.'

'Don't be foolish. Of course she will stay out here. We can assist with childcare and support her. You'll be working.'

Fin knew there was no point arguing. She stood up, wondering how many savings she had left after all the IVF and the funds she had sent to support George. The chances were that Victor and Barb had even less. All of Barb's income went to service their debts.

'Are you leaving already? You haven't even finished your coffee. Stay for dinner.'

At the mention of dinner, Barb hung her head.

Fin didn't bother answering. She slung her handbag over her shoulder. Victor stood and grabbed her by the shoulder. 'We will all be together again, a proper family at last. I always thought it was a shame Tony is so much older than you, and now we know what sort of person he really is. You should have found yourself a young fellow, someone your own age. You might even have had a baby of your own.'

Fin wrenched herself free. 'His name is *Anthony.*'

34

Adulthood

FIN was having lunch in the tearoom at work before heading out for an assessment of a new patient. She flicked through a magazine while waiting for her sandwich to toast and paused to read an article about a woman who opted to use a sperm donor to have a baby. Fin's heart beat harder. She glanced over her shoulder, rolled the magazine up, and shoved it into her bag. When her sandwich was toasted, she folded it into a piece of paper towel and hurried out before one of her colleagues arrived wanting to chat.

Fin drove to a carpark near the river, her toastie growing cold. She opened the magazine and scanned the article about the woman, Jacinta, who was pictured sitting on the back deck of her home, holding a plump-cheeked baby with wisps of curly hair. Fin touched her finger to the photograph and devoured each word of the story.

'I always wanted to have children, but my husband kept delaying, wanted to wait until we were financially secure. By the time we divorced, I was thirty-eight years old and didn't have the time to wait any longer. I discussed my situation with my GP, and she referred me to a fertility clinic where they suggested a sperm donor.'

There were more pictures of Jacinta holding her son, Damien, up in the air, his arms and legs outstretched like he was flying, his eyes sparkling with laughter.

'It was the best decision I ever made. I adore my son. Motherhood is everything I imagined and more.'

After work, Fin drove to the bookshop at Stones Corner and scanned the shelves for books about single motherhood. The fellow at the counter came up behind her and she startled.

'Can I help you find something?'

Fin felt her face heat up when she looked down at the collection of books in her arms. 'I'm fine, really. I'm a midwife. Just doing a bit of research.'

Fin wondered why she told a fib and felt the need to justify her selection of books. After all, if she was planning on becoming a mother on her own, she needed to own the decision, both for herself and the child.

'I'll take these, thanks.'

'If you need any others, I'm always happy to order them in for you.'

He slipped a bookmark with contact details inside the cover of the book on top of the pile and placed them into a paper carry bag for her.

'Thanks for that.'

Fin fumbled through her bag and realised she had left her purse at home. 'I'm sorry,' she faltered, her face hot, 'I'll have to leave them.'

He pushed the books over to her. 'Just take them and come back and pay.'

Her hand brushed his. A warm feeling spread to her toes. She grabbed the bag of books and looked at him. His eyes were soft and kind, and he had a freckle under his chin. She absorbed the details then fled, heart pounding.

Her purse sat on the kitchen bench, mocking her. She drove back and waited at the counter. The owner was deep in conversation with a tall, broad-shouldered man with silvered hair. When the bookshop owner saw her, his smile lit up his eyes. 'Excuse me.' He shook hands with the tall man. 'I have a special customer.'

The fellow turned, caught sight of Fin, gazed at her a moment too long, then left.

'That was quick.'

Fin fumbled in her purse, then swiped twice before her card worked, apologising each time. At last, the green tick appeared with the word *approved*. It seemed forever before the receipt printed out. He handed it to her, and she stared at the delta of veins on the back of his hand. She took care not to touch him this time.

That evening, it started to rain, the raindrops a steady rhythm on the roof. Outside, the wind buffeted tree branches and whistled along the guttering. Fin settled down to read, her imagination filling the unit with a baby and all its accompanying paraphernalia. She calculated how much time off she would need and how she might juggle work and single parenting. Eyes closed, she lost herself in a future where her baby was in her arms. Soft, perfect skin, dark wisps of hair, a greedy mouth latched onto her nipple. Fin furnished her unit with a change table, cot and pram, scattered rattles and cuddly toys across the floor. She imagined inviting a guest inside and having to say, *Sorry about the mess, I've been up to my eyeballs with the baby.*

Unbidden, Victor came to mind. She could only imagine what he would say about a donor baby. He must never know. This would be her secret, something to be shared with the baby, who would soon be part of her life.

When the doorbell rang, Fin wondered who it might be. She left the book, page bookmarked, on the sofa.

'Hello?'

'Fin, it's me, George.'

Fin fumbled with the deadlock. George stood, her hair in wet strings around her face, a long tee plastered to her skin, nipples visible under the thin, wet fabric.

'George, you are soaking wet. What on earth are you doing wandering around looking like that on a night like this?'

It was hard to tell if George was crying or if it was the rain sliding down her cheeks.

'Come in. Just wait and I'll grab a towel, dry you off.'

Fin hurried to the linen cupboard and returned with two large towels. George stood shivering, her arms limp by her sides.

'Let's get this wet gear off and I'll run you a bath and make something hot to drink.'

Fin led her into the living room. She peeled George's wet clothes off and let them drop to the floor. When George was stark naked, Fin rubbed her dry and wrapped her in a towel. She led her to the bathroom, where she ran a hot bath and added a few drops of scented oil. George had still not spoken. She stood, shoulder blades sharp, her nobbled spine rounded, long hair dripping water onto the tiles. Fin tested the water as if she was preparing it for a child, then coaxed George to get in.

'Now I'm going to make us some hot chocolate and I'll be right back, and you can tell me what's going on.'

Fin collected the pile of sodden clothes, pulled George's phone from the pocket of her shorts, and put it aside. She heated milk and dissolved cocoa and sugar in two mugs, then carried them to the bathroom and sat on a stool next to the bath. Without saying anything, she handed George a mug and waited.

'Why can't I find a decent man?'

George sank lower into the water, her knees bent and poking out, the mug held aloft. It occurred to Fin that, just like her, George was clumsy and unversed in her relationships with men. Sex and seduction were never discussed at home. They both groped their way through relationships with ineptitude and shame.

'Titus was so much fun. I thought he really liked me. Then, after I moved in, he changed. Nothing I did was right.'

Fin waited, and waited some more. Was George so unlike Barb? Her desperate need for affection was a beacon inviting compliance and servitude. Had Barb ever been happy? Fin recalled the photograph of her mother, young and smiling with another man. Perhaps Fin was the fortunate one, her desires muffled deep in a silent space inside, not beholden to any man.

'I wore that pink shirt I like with my shorts, and he lost it. He said I was a fucking slut and no girlfriend of his was going out looking like that.' George was trembling. 'I reminded him that I was wearing it when he asked me out and he went into the bedroom and started pulling all my stuff out of drawers, throwing it around the room. He ripped my dresses and skirts off hangers, and I was on my knees gathering it all up and trying to calm him down. It was bucketing rain and he was shouting at me. He ripped the shirt off my back and I got scared. I grabbed the nearest thing and pulled it on. It was one of his tees. I really thought he was going to hurt me, so I ran and then kept walking until I ended up here.'

'Geez, George. Why didn't you just ring? I would have picked you up.'

'I didn't know if you'd be angry with me. If I just turned up, I thought there was a greater chance you might let me stay a few nights.'

'You're always welcome. You know that.'

'He's got all my stuff, my clothes, my makeup. It's all at his place. I've only got my phone.'

'Forget about it. We can get a few things tomorrow. We should report him. Does he know where I live?'

George shook her head.

'Let me get you something to wear. Maybe one of my leggings and a shirt. Nothing else will fit. If he tries to contact you, just don't reply.'

On cue, George's phone pinged. Fin reached for it. George's eyes widened.

'It's him, isn't it? What does he say?'

'We are blocking him. I'm getting you a new sim card tomorrow. Leave it with me.'

'Tell me, what did he say?'

Fin held the phone out of reach. George reached up and tried to snatch it from Fin. It fell into the bath.

'I hate you. You've destroyed my phone.'

George fumbled through the froth and pulled it out. It was completely dead.

'Good riddance. At least he can't track where you are.'

Fin ordered pizza, something Victor forbade at home. Barb brought one home once and set up the table with white plates, knives, and forks. She slid two pizzas onto a couple of large platters. By that time, they were cold.

'Why are we eating this shit?' Victor had raved. 'Why not take the time to prepare good, wholesome food for the family?' Fin and George gobbled up the cold slices until they were so full they could barely move.

Even now, years later, it tasted of rebellion.

Outside, the rain continued, and they sat at either end of the sofa, feet touching in the middle while scoffing pizza, drinking shiraz, and watching *Bridget Jones' Diary*.

George snuggled into the blanket.

'Do you think either of us will ever fall in love and get married?'

Fin shrugged. 'Maybe, maybe not.'

She went to the bookshelf, pulled out one of her old nursing textbooks, and found where she had hidden the photograph.

'Look, this is Mum. Do you know who that man is?'

George stared at it, brow furrowed. 'No idea. Maybe it was one of her dancing partners.'

'Maybe. She looks so happy in that picture. I don't know if I have ever seen her like that.'

George giggled. 'An affair? God, Dad would kill her.'

'I asked her about the photo once and she seemed hesitant, said it was an old friend. I think she is in love with him. Look at the way they are gazing at each other.'

'Dad is her first ever boyfriend, remember? It is one of his favourite stories. That he had dinner with her family, and they were engaged the next week.'

'Do you think they were ever in love?'

'Of course they were. I think people just get tired of each other when they have been together for too long.'

'I wonder. Maybe Barb did have a fling once and that's why he's so awful to her.'

'I can't imagine it. Mum having sex with another man?'

George rolled about laughing. Fin didn't join in.

George picked up the book Fin had sitting on the arm of the lounge. She scanned the blurb. 'Are you really thinking of having a baby with some man you've never met?'

Fin reached over to snatch the book away. 'Of course not. I'm just doing some research.'

George grinned. 'Why would you want to have a baby without doing the best bit? Maybe we should try and set you up with someone who will bonk your brains out until you fall pregnant and then you can give him the flick. Beats having a syringe put the tadpole up there.'

Fin pulled her feet away from George's on the lounge and reached for her wine glass. 'Sex is overrated.'

35

One year earlier

FIN grabbed her keys from their dish on the kitchen bench to drive Anthony to one of his chemotherapy sessions when her phone pinged. It was a new photo of Ebony. Fin lost herself, gazing at her wispy hair, tiny hands, and startling blue eyes, and imagined her baby smell, how soft and squishy and perfect she would feel. Just the way George used to be before she grew up and whittled down to sharp, bony edges.

Anthony glanced at the image. 'You are besotted.'

Fin took care to sound nonchalant. 'How is Damon enjoying fatherhood?'

He shrugged. 'I don't probe.'

Fin worried about Damon's drinking and longed to ask George for details, to swoop in and fix things up. However, she worried that if she started to ask questions, she would not get her weekly photo fix. George never mentioned Damon in her brief texts; just added short captions.

First smile.

A new dress.

Hello Aunty Fin. Can't wait to meet you.

'We better go.' Anthony was at the door, waiting.

Fin hurried out, pulled the door shut behind her, and locked up. The last weeks were a blur and at times it seemed she only got to spend time with Anthony on the drive to the hospital.

He glanced over at her. 'You don't have to take me, you know.'

'I want to drive you. It's not something you can do alone.'

'I just don't want to wear you out. You are hardly home.'

'I've been rostered on to do extra shifts to help prepare, should this pandemic come to Brisbane.'

'Are you worried?'

'A bit.'

He put his hand on her thigh. 'It will all work out.'

He sighed next to her in the car. 'I worry you gave up your dream of having a baby staying with me.'

Fin thought back to that night at the bookshop, where it felt like the only option was to escape. A chill ran down her spine. 'It was our dream, our loss.'

An image of Scarlett, lifeless and lying stained with blood and mucus in the dirt flashed through her mind, and the car behind her honked. The lights had turned green. She accelerated.

'Are you alright?'

Fin forced a smile. 'Just thinking about things.'

'You seem distracted.'

'I just wish George and Damon would bring Ebony home.'

She turned into the car park and manoeuvred the car into an empty spot.

'What if they choose to stay there?'

It had never occurred to Fin. 'Of course they won't do that. Their families are here.'

She bit her lip, guilty that she knew all about Damon's drinking, the reason George was trapped on the other side of the world.

Anthony cleared his throat. 'The minute I get the all-clear, I think we should go over and visit.'

'To New York?'

'Why not? We could help them with Ebony and have a holiday.'

~

That evening, Anthony was exhausted and went to bed early. Fin poured the remnants of a bottle of wine into a glass. Deep down, she knew George would want to come back with the baby but was staying because of Damon. Even if she had not promised George, it seemed unfair to burden Anthony with more stress now.

Fin held the phone up to snap a selfie. She was texting it to George with a row of hugs and kisses when the television screen captured her attention.

'The prime minister Scott Morrison announced today that Australia would close its borders to all non-residents of Australia, effective from 9pm on the twentieth of March 2020. These enhanced border measures are in response to the coronavirus outbreak. Treasurer Josh Frydenberg suggested in an interview that this travel restriction could remain in place for up to six months, subject to medical advice. Australian permanent residents and their immediate family members, and New Zealand citizens who can show they are normally residents in Australia, will be allowed entry to Australia but will need to self-quarantine at home or in a hotel for fourteen days from date of arrival.'

Fin's gut dipped. What did that mean for George and the baby? They would be fine, surely. After all, they were Australian citizens. At a meeting at work today, further precautions were being put in place to protect their very vulnerable patients. A shiver ran down Fin's spine.

She sent George a WhatsApp message. *You should head home. They are starting to close the borders.* She bit her lip and paused. *How is Damon?*

There was ongoing discussion about the virus by health professionals and epidemiologists. Fin sighed, pointed the remote to blank the screen, and pushed away her wine glass.

It occurred to her that Victor and Barb might not being keeping abreast of things with his militant view about television. Barb had the radio on all day but preferred stations that played music she could hum and dance to. She dialled their number.

'Mum. Have you heard the announcement on the news?'

'What announcement?'

They really did live under a rock at times. 'The government is closing international borders to non-residents of Australia.'

'Let me get your father.'

No, Fin wanted to protest. *I would rather talk to you. I want you to make a decision without running it past Victor first.*

Barb was already calling him. 'Darling! It's Fin. Something about things closing. It sounds serious.'

Jesus, thought Fin. They really had no idea, living such an isolated life on The Estate.

'Fin, my dear. What is going on? You have upset your mother.'

'Do you even listen to the news? Scott Morrison is closing

international borders to non-residents. I just think we need to get George and the family home sooner rather than later.'

'What's the problem? She is an Australian. One with a baby. She should be fine.'

'For now. Things are changing rapidly. I think we should be cautious.'

'Well, I told you. I'm busting the arse renovating here to make it comfortable for George and the baby. If there's a problem, you sort it out. I can't do everything.'

Fin clenched her fist. 'Keep abreast of the news. This is fast becoming an emergency and you should stay informed.'

'Darling, one of the reasons we live out here is to get away from all the bastards and their idiocy. I don't give a shit about the news. If they want to close borders, let them. We have everything we need out here. Bring your sister and our granddaughter home. You should come out here too and get away from this rubbish you are listening to.'

Fin hung up.

She sent a WhatsApp message to George. *You should pack up and come home, with or without Damon. Australia is closing its borders.*

When there was no response, an uneasy feeling knotted Fin's stomach. She tried to ring without success. A deafening silence. Fin tried to pull her mind back from worst case scenarios. Death, illness, injury, eviction. Why didn't George respond? It was so typical of her. She only ever made contact when she needed something or was in trouble.

Fin shook off her unease. She remembered what Anthony had said when George didn't respond to her message thanking her for the latest photo. *George is a young mother and probably trying to get a bit of sleep. Leave it till tomorrow and she'll message.*

Fin knew she wouldn't be able to sleep and didn't want to disturb Anthony. She checked her phone several times overnight and tried to distract herself with a book. In the early morning, she turned on the radio. There were more reports of this virus from Wuhan being identified in Australia. The situation around the world was dire. People were dying, hospitals were overfull, there were mass graves in Italy.

Fin switched over to music and lay on the sofa imagining George in New York trying to manage with a baby and no money. Perhaps George had lost her phone. She was always forgetting things and leaving stuff behind.

Fin checked her phone again. Still, there was nothing.

She hauled herself off the sofa, her limbs heavy with sleep deprivation, her heart weighed down by all the things she couldn't control.

36

One year earlier

FIN woke up late, relieved to have a day off after so many extra shifts in these strange lockdown days. It was early April and things had been eerily quiet at work, like a held breath waiting for disaster. Fin realised Anthony was already up. She pulled on her jeans and a tee to join him. There was so much she needed to talk to him about: his own vulnerability should the virus take hold here in Brisbane, Damon, and the urgent need to get all of them back home to Australia.

He was dressed as if he were going to work, standing next to the toaster, waiting for it to pop. She was relieved he was home and wanted to warn him not to go out, even for essentials. Just in case.

'Anthony, thank goodness you're here.'

'What's up?'

'I need to talk to you.'

'Now?'

'Why don't you relax, let me make breakfast and then we can talk,' Fin said.

The toast popped and he lathered it with butter and raspberry jam, made it into a sandwich and took a bite. 'I can't right now. Maybe tomorrow.'

'What's the hurry? It's not like you need to be anywhere.'

'I'm heading to the bookshop, sorting a few things.'

'What are you doing there? I thought it was closed.'

'I'm trying to keep things afloat. Packing up online book orders for customers. Who knows how long all this will go on for?'

He walked towards the door. She heard the clatter as he grabbed his keys, and the throaty gurgle of a moist cough.

'Don't go,' Fin pleaded. 'I'm worried about you. You are so vulnerable.'

'I won't be long. I need to ensure I have customers when all this ends.'

'Aren't you worried about George, Damon, and Ebony?'

'There is nothing I can do from here. I might as well do something useful at the shop, so I have one when things get back to normal.'

He opened the front door and stepped out.

Fin was tempted to shout *Damon is an alcoholic.* There was a crunch as his back fender hit the gutter, then she heard him drive off. She took some deep breaths and pushed her anxieties aside for a few more hours.

Holding a mug of instant, she switched on the morning news, anxious about the new border closures and quarantine requirements. She changed channel, determined to step away from the vertiginous pull of uncertainty. But a few minutes later, she found herself again scrolling through newsfeeds, stoking her anxiety.

Still no word from George.

Fin calculated the time in New York and sent several more messages, careful to keep them light-hearted. *How are things? Would love a pic of Eb. Hello??*

An hour later and still nothing. Fin decided to pull out her trump card. *I'm telling Anthony about Damon. He needs to know.*

A deafening silence.

It was early evening in New York. Why was George not responding? Surely if you had a baby, you would be at home with your phone nearby. Fin had to come clean and tell Anthony everything. George would be furious, but there was no other option. Ebony's wellbeing was at stake. She sent him a text. *I need to talk to you. How about a nice lunch on the back deck?*

No response.

It was two in the afternoon. Fin banged plates around, made a pot of his favourite pumpkin soup, warmed some bread rolls, and had lunch on her own. On impulse, Fin checked out some American news sites. It sounded apocalyptic. On the same day that Queensland closed its borders, 17,800 cases had been confirmed in New York with 199 deaths.

It turned out that one-third of the cases in America were in New York. She scrolled through the daily case numbers and the death toll. The numbers were eye watering – one day with 23,000 cases and 365 deaths. Surely George and Ebony would be fine. It mostly affected the elderly, didn't it?

When Fin's phone rang, she grabbed it, breathless. It was Barb, in tears. 'Victor fell off the scaffolding. He was trying to spruce things up for George and the baby. I have to drive him to hospital in that truck of his.'

'How bad is Dad?'

'He is shouting instructions to me. His leg is bent. I might have trouble getting him into the truck.'

'You have to call an ambulance.'

'He is insisting I take him.'

'Just say no and call an ambulance. I'll meet you at Ipswich Hospital.' Her voice casual, Fin added, 'Have you had any news from George?'

'You know how she is. Her life must be so busy with Damon's career taking off and a new baby. You must tell her about Victor.'

When Fin arrived at the hospital an hour later, she was refused entry. The staff were wearing plastic gowns, masks, and shields.

'Look, he's my father and I'm a nurse. My mum really needs the support.'

'Sorry, new protocols. Leave your number, and we'll let you know the minute there is some news.'

Fin waited for news in her car. She tried to contact Anthony, but he didn't reply. Her earlier frustration was replaced by unease. It was not like him not to respond. Fin took a punt and rang Freya.

'Hello?'

Freya sounded hesitant.

'I'm worried about Anthony. Do you know if he's at the bookshop?'

'He might be. I left a couple of hours ago. He called me in to help pack up the online orders and then…'

Her voice faded.

'Freya, please tell me. Then what?'

'I just thought he would have told you. That you knew.'

'Knew what?'

'He no longer needs me and let me go.'

'I'm so sorry. I didn't know. This whole lockdown business won't be forever. I'll talk to him.'

'Leave it. I understand. I'll find something else.'

Two hours later, a kind doctor rang. 'Your father, Victor, is stable. He has several fractured ribs, a fractured collar bone, and fractured left tibia and fibula. He is currently having surgery.'

Fin rang Barb. 'Why don't you come home with me? Dad's stable and there is nothing you can do now.'

'No, I've decided to stay here. He'll want me here when they finish operating on his leg.'

~

Anthony wasn't there when Fin finally arrived home. He didn't respond to her messages until late evening. Fin was so relieved that her anger at his hours of silence, just when she needed his support, evaporated. 'Is everything okay?'

'Fine, thanks.'

'You didn't respond to my texts. I tried to call. Victor had an accident. I've been at Ipswich Hospital.'

Anthony was silent on the other end of the phone.

'Talk to me. Where have you been all day?'

'I told you, I was at the bookshop.'

'Why are you ignoring me?'

She hated the accusation in her voice.

'I left my phone in the car.'

He sounded defensive and not himself.

'What's going on?'

'Freya left. She's not working with me anymore, so I had to do everything myself.'

Fin stood in her kitchen, her mind all over the place. He had never lied to her before. Was Freya lying? Fin wondered whether to mention her phone call to Freya. She shook away the unease in her head. There would be some simple explanation. 'I'm worried about you. Are you sure you are all right?'

'Just exhausted.' He cleared his throat. 'I'm sorry about Victor and that I wasn't here for you. How is he?'

Her legs went weak with relief to have her familiar Anthony back.
'He fell off scaffolding, but he's stable. Where are you now?'
'Heading home. You can tell me all about Victor soon.'

37

Adulthood

FIN wandered out to the kitchen and watched the sun dance along the windowsill. She flicked on the kettle for her morning cup of tea. It was nearly six months since George had moved in and she was still as messy as ever. Her things were scattered around the lounge. A faux leather jacket, one strappy shoe lying on its side, its companion mysteriously missing, a couple of glossy magazines, and a bulging cosmetic bag split open to reveal lipsticks and mascara. It made Fin smile. George was working now, doing the accounts for a family-run jewellery business, and doing an art class a couple of evenings a week. With Fin's shift work, sometimes they barely saw each other, but seeing her stuff everywhere made Fin feel less alone.

Just as Fin was about to make herself some breakfast, she noticed a huge pair of scruffy Converse at the front door. They clearly belonged to a bloke. It seemed presumptuous of George to flaunt her sex life like that in Fin's home. The two of them must have come home late after she was asleep. Fin hadn't heard anything.

'Morning.'

Fin startled. George was standing there in a tee that only just covered her butt, her nipples visible.

'I see you have a friend here.'

'Yeah, Jules is doing the art class with me. We went to The Valley last night and got home about two. I might just get in and make us a coffee.'

Fin wanted to say something, to ask for a warning before George just brought a man home, but instead forced a weak smile. 'I'm heading

191

out. I might have brekky at a café.'

Fin wanted to remind George to clean up afterwards but bit her lip. When Fin grabbed her handbag, she jangled her keys and made a point of stepping over the shoes near the front door. George didn't notice. She was busy fiddling with the coffee plunger.

~

Fin found a carpark near Stones Throw Café and glanced across the road at Books at Stones. There was an author out the front signing books and patrons queued along the footpath waiting. She would just pop in to get a newspaper and check if there were any good events coming up. Perhaps the nice owner, Anthony, would be there. Fin dismissed the thought even as it made her smile. She had been back several times and he always smiled at her, offered to help her find what she was looking for. The truth was she didn't really know what she was looking for, but she felt drawn to the bookshop and made excuses to drop in.

The bookshop was busy with people milling between shelves and children already occupying the small table and beanbags in the corner. There was the happy buzz of satisfied customers browsing, the crisp smell of unread pages taunting her. She kept promising herself to not purchase another book until she at least read the top two on her growing to-be-read pile, but with a little persuasion from Anthony, she usually relented and invariably bought just one more.

She leant to pick up a newspaper when she was aware of a presence behind her and looked around to see Anthony.

His smile was cautious. 'Hello, it's lovely to see you. I put aside a couple of titles you might enjoy.'

Fin felt a warm prickle up her neck. He was always so helpful. Her resolve to not buy any more titles faltered. The truth was, she always read everything he suggested. He had an uncanny knack for choosing the perfect titles.

'I actually just came to get the weekend newspapers to read.'

He beckoned and reached up along the shelf full of books on hold for regulars. 'This is a gorgeous book, you'll love it.' He handed her Kate Grenville's, *The Secret River*, then grabbed a second book. 'I seem to remember you enjoy Sally Hepworth. Have you read her latest?'

His smile was warm, and she found herself agreeing to buy both books as well as a *Sydney Morning Herald*. His hand brushed hers when he handed her the brown paper bag, and that warm feeling fluttered through her again. Fin swiped her card, hoping her face was not as red as it felt. They stood awkwardly while they waited for her receipt to print out.

Anthony cleared his throat. 'I wonder if it would be presumptuous to invite you for a coffee.'

The sounds in the shop faded into the background. Fin's mouth went dry.

He licked his lips. 'I am sorry. I expect you're busy.'

Fin's tongue moved again. 'Now?' She was so aware of him behind the counter, his blue shirt, a freckle on the left side of his chin, his long fingers tearing off her receipt. 'Aren't there rules about taking customers out for a coffee?' Fin felt her mouth twitch at the corners.

'I've not needed any rules before now.'

She half looked away, her smile broad now. 'Sounds great.'

His face softened into a relieved smile. 'Just a minute.'

He beckoned to the grey-haired woman putting some books away on shelves. 'Freya, I'm heading out for an hour or so.'

Then his hand was on the small of Fin's back as he guided her across the road, past the customers waiting to have their books signed. They found a table for two at Stones Throw.

After Arch, Fin had only had a couple of brief relationships; neither of them making it to one year. It felt unfamiliar to realise her skin was alive, sitting opposite this quiet, grey-eyed man whom she knew well, yet didn't know at all.

A smiling waiter brought out a coffee for Fin and a pot of tea for Anthony.

'I'm so delighted you agreed to join me. I've been working up the courage to ask.'

The wonder of it made Fin feel breathless. She laughed, and then he laughed too. He poured tea, added milk. She sipped her coffee. The quiet between them felt comfortable, like a space that should be there. After he placed his cup back on his saucer, Anthony's eyes locked onto hers. 'I was worried you might stop coming in for books, I sold you so many.'

The way he gazed at Fin made her sit up taller and feel confident, like a woman who regularly accepted spur-of-the-moment dates for coffee on a Saturday morning.

'My to-be-read tower is teetering. I might need to take a week off work, head to a beach somewhere so that I can get through them all.'

He paused, his teacup aloft. 'Are you suggesting we go away for a week?'

Fin gulped some of her coffee before lowering it back onto the saucer. 'Maybe we could try a weekend?'

Her heart felt wild against her sternum, the colours in the café vivid. It seemed her life had been an incomplete jigsaw and she had suddenly found the missing piece.

'How about Peregian Beach next weekend?'

Fin searched her head for her roster, unable to recall if she was working. She smiled at him. 'Sounds perfect.'

~

Time brushed past Fin over the next few days. Being in love with Anthony made her feel beautiful, and she took care with what she wore and made an extra effort to look her best. She smiled at herself when she glimpsed her reflection in the glass sliding door. George crinkled her brow. 'You seem very happy. Are you in love with someone?'

Fin felt that familiar warm prickle in her neck and tried, unsuccessfully, to stop herself from grinning. 'Maybe.'

George tipped her head, curious.

'I'm actually heading away for the weekend, so you'll have the place to yourself.'

Fin disappeared into her bedroom and pulled down a suitcase. It seemed too big for a weekend away, but she was not leaving anything to chance. She wanted to pack a range of clothes to be prepared for every eventuality. Her bathing suit had seen better days. It had been a long time since she'd been swimming. Fin pulled out her phone and made a list of things she would buy before the weekend. It started to ring.

'Fin, I thought we could leave on Thursday night. I booked a lovely place overlooking the water. Does that suit?'

She tried not to sound too eager. 'Just let me check my roster. I'll get back to you.'

She left it exactly an hour then rang him back.

He sounded relieved. 'Let me pick you up, say, four, and we can enjoy a nice dinner when we get there.'

She panicked and wondered what she would wear. She decided to head out for a new dress and bathers.

George was lounging on the sofa, flicking through a glossy magazine. 'Who is this mysterious man?'

'George, you have to promise not to say anything to Mum and Dad.'

The thought of Victor meeting Anthony and criticising him was unbearable.

George looked at her wide-eyed. 'So, who is he?'

'You know the bookshop at Stones Corner? It's the fellow who owns it, Anthony.'

38

One year earlier

THE morning after Victor's hospital admission, Fin stood in her kitchen, exhausted after tossing and turning for most of the night. She had just boiled the kettle to make a pot of tea when the phone rang again.

It was Barb, her voice tense.

'Fin, darling, I wonder if you could come to the hospital.'

'Now? It's so early. I'm not allowed in, remember? No visitors.'

'He is determined to discharge himself against medical advice. The doctors have been patient, but they are so busy. Victor has his heart set on finishing those renovations for when George and Ebony arrive.'

'With a fractured leg and fractured ribs?'

'You know how determined he can be.'

More like stubborn and stupid, thought Fin, switching the phone to speaker and putting it on the bench while she unscrewed the lid of the orange juice and poured herself a glass.

'What am I supposed to do about it?'

'Reason with him, tell him it's more important to recover and let the doctors do their job.' Barb paused. 'Please.'

Fin hesitated. The thought of confronting Victor made her heart sink.

'Mum, have you even heard from George in the last few days?'

'Not in the last few days. She has sent a few photos of Ebony who is such a darling. You know our George. She gets busy and distracted and forgets or loses her phone.'

Fin gritted her teeth. Did Barb not worry her daughter and granddaughter were living in the epicentre of this pandemic catastrophe

196

in a city on the other side of the world?

'I'll see you outside the hospital. Just give me a chance to have some breakfast.'

Fin delayed leaving and poured some cereal into a bowl. She made herself a cup of tea using a teabag instead of the pot. Her phone pinged.

It was George.

Fin's heart accelerated.

She read the message. *Feeling ghastly. Ebs with neighbour. Promise me you will look after her for me if something happens.*

Fin's thumbs flew over the keys and tapped out a message. *Of course. I'll get a flight and come over. Wait for me and I'll bring you all home. Love you lots. XXXX*

Fin waited for her to reply but the screen remained blank. She wrote a couple more urgent messages, willing George to respond. Nothing. The tea grew cold. Fin glanced at the time. She texted Anthony. *George unwell. Will fly to NY to pick them up. Talk soon.*

Tonight, Fin would talk to Anthony properly. No more secrets. Tomorrow, she would arrange tickets to fly to America and pick George and Damon up. She would bring them and Ebony back home to Brisbane.

Just before heading off, Fin texted Barb to let her know she was still coming.

Fin's phone rang. Barb again.

'Fin, are you far away?'

'I'm heading off now.'

Barb's voice was tight, tearful. 'Your father is not budging. I am so worried. I wonder if you could stay a few nights and help me look after him?'

'Why the rush? Why won't he stay a couple of nights?'

'It's this whole pandemic business. He will not be told what to do and tells the staff to get that ridiculous gear off. They wanted to sedate him, but he went ballistic. Says the world has gone crazy, that it is an attempt to curtail people's freedoms.'

'George just made contact. I can't look after him. I'm flying to New York to bring George and Ebony home.' Fin spared Barb the details.

'I won't be able to cope on my own. Victor listens to you, you have the skills and the training.'

'You married him.'

The minute Fin heard the words escape her mouth, she regretted it. She would apologise, and make it up to Barb when she saw her face to face.

Fin backed out of the driveway and set out on the one-hour journey back to Ipswich Hospital, her muscles aching with fatigue.

Her phone pinged again, and she glanced at it.

It was Anthony.

She used her hands-free to respond. *Talk soon. Heading to hospital.*

Forty-five minutes later, she heard a siren and several police cars. Fifteen minutes from the hospital and there was a roadblock. Fin swore and slowed to a stop. She wound down her window. The police officer pointed to an alternate route.

'Sorry, there's been an accident. You need to take one of the backroads. It might be closed for a few hours.'

Barb would be in a flap with Victor railing at the staff, determined to do things his own way.

Fin tried to call her mother to let her know about the delay, but the phone rang out.

Poor Barb must be trying to appease Victor. Fin's phone rang.

'Am I speaking to Ms Steinbauer?'

'Speaking.'

'Constable Scott Wheeler here. I am sorry to inform you that your parents were involved in a single-vehicle accident…'

Fin pulled off the road and started shaking. She tried to recall the last words she had spoken to Barb. *You married him.*

Fin's mouth tasted bitter with regret.

'The driver has been taken to the Princess Alexandra Hospital with suspected head injuries. Paramedics attempted to resuscitate the female passenger but were unsuccessful.'

39

Adulthood

THE tip of Anthony's tongue paused at the corner of his lip. That was how Fin knew he was about to say something important. Even though they had only been going out for two months, she had already observed so many tiny details about him. Sometimes it felt as if they had been a couple for years.

'I was wondering…' He fiddled with his teacup. 'It seems a waste to be running two households. Perhaps, you might consider… if I'm being too forward, just tell me.'

Fin's heart did a somersault. She leaned across and put a hand on his arm. 'I would love to move in with you.'

His shoulders eased and his eyes softened. 'Are you sure you are happy to leave your place?'

'It suits me perfectly. My sister is living with me for now and it will give her some space while she finds her feet.'

'How about next weekend, Freya can look after the bookshop, and I'll give you a hand?'

'George is away with some friends, so the timing is perfect.'

'I was hoping to meet her. To get to know your family.'

Fin withdrew her hand from his arm. 'There's plenty of time for that. It will be easier not having George underfoot while I move. I would rather keep you all to myself for a while.'

Fin worried that once she introduced Anthony to George, she might find some flaw, that he might come up short. It was safer not to chance it and risk spoiling things. George would tell Victor and Barb. Fin was not ready for that.

She shook away her thoughts, leaned over, and gave Anthony a kiss.

He hired a small van for the move. Fin savoured the moment of watching him walk up to the front door without him seeing her before letting him in. He handed her a white paper bag that smelt delicious.

'I bought us some pastries from that great place in Morningside. I thought we needed breakfast before tackling the move.'

Fin pulled him into a hug, the bag of goodies clutched in his hand. She buried her face in his shirt and inhaled his shaving cream and clean sweat before relieving him of the parcel and taking him to the kitchen.

'Let's enjoy these and make a start.'

She pulled out a couple of mugs and tea bags.

'Where is your teapot?'

Fin blushed. 'I'm afraid I just use bags. I have a range of different types, though.'

Anthony put his hands to his face in horror. 'I am officially in charge of teamaking from now on. I promise you, your life is about to change. You will never go back…' he dangled one of the offending bags in front of her, '…to one of these again.'

They packed in companionable silence, except when Anthony wanted to check if she wanted a particular item or not. She was surprised at how unattached she was to her things. She had just bought stuff when she needed it. George would need the furniture and the functional kitchenware Fin had accumulated.

When Anthony packed up her books, he blushed. 'I really did sell you a lot of books. My apologies. I didn't know how else to keep you coming to the shop. I was too shy to just ask you out.'

Fin laughed. 'It was perfect. It gave me an excuse to keep coming.'

Their hands touched over the half-packed box of books. Fin was frightened of her bubbling happiness and wondered if one person deserved so much of it.

He held her face in his hands, kissed her on the lips and lingered, his tongue touching hers. Fin disappeared into the moment, not wanting it to end.

He let go. 'It's been a long time since I shared my life with someone.'
'Me too.'

His hands dropped and they stayed opposite each other a little longer, the open box waiting between them.

She touched him lightly on his face, his skin still smooth from shaving. 'I'll pack my clothes, and then I think we can head off.'

~

One gorgeous morning, Fin lingered in bed after a late shift. Anthony pulled her close under the doona and kissed her eyelids and lips before whispering goodbye and heading to the bookshop.

'I'll drop past for lunch,' Fin murmured, his tenderness last night still delicious on her skin.

It was after eight when Fin stretched and rolled out of bed. She hummed to herself in the shower and took her time choosing the right dress. The fabric fell soft past her hips and swished against her legs, making her skin come alive. Sunlight sequined across the doona when a breeze billowed the curtain.

She wandered out to the bathroom and shot a text to George. *How's the unit going? Hope all is well.*

Jules moved in the day after Fin moved out. She imagined his big shoes now taking ownership at the front door and wondered what he was like. Men were attracted to George's ethereal and helpless beauty and took possession of it like it was theirs. Fin typed in another text, hoping to get some goss on Jules. *Anthony is the most gorgeous man. Having lunch with him today. Don't tell the folks about him yet.*

Discretion was not George's strong suit.

Fin put her hair up and then let it down again so it touched her shoulders. She caught sight of herself in the hallway mirror, still carrying more weight than she would have liked, but it no longer seemed important. She usually cast her eyes down when passing mirrors and nearly asked Anthony to move this one. Now she was grateful it was there. She barely recognised the radiant woman who stared back at her.

The bookshop was busy. Inside, Anthony was at the back in deep conversation with a tall, silver-haired man who saw Fin and nudged Anthony, then gestured towards her. Anthony smiled, put his hand on the fellow's shoulder and walked over. Just then, Fin saw George milling with a cluster of people near the table of information about upcoming events. George walked out of the bookshop engrossed in one of the brochures. Fin called out. George shoved the brochure into her jeans pocket and looked up.

'Come and meet Anthony,' Fin said.

He shook her hand. 'George? Lovely to meet you.'

Fin was relieved when George left. For a moment she worried Anthony might invite her to join them, and she wanted him all to herself.

It made her smile that George was checking Anthony out, though. It was the sort of thing Fin usually did when she worried about George and her latest beau. Perhaps it was time to introduce Anthony to the family over lunch.

Fin waited until George disappeared around the corner, then squeezed past the patrons huddled around the new releases at the entrance. Anthony was serving a customer, so Fin went over to the noticeboard where he advertised local exhibitions, book events, and festivals. She picked up the brochure George had been studying from the bundle on the table. A heavy metal band, Demons of Dark, were performing tomorrow evening. Was this the sort of music George listened to when she went out?

'Hello, beautiful.'

Anthony glanced over her shoulder, his breath warm on her neck. 'Do you want to go and see them?'

She shook her head, 'Not particularly. I was just checking it out.'

'Come on, let's get ourselves to Lady Marmalade and have lunch. I've booked us a table.'

They sat and ordered their meals, the ubiquitous pot of tea between them. It was difficult to imagine Anthony without a pot of his favourite brew nearby. He held the brochure for Demons of Dark between his thumb and index finger. 'This is my son Damon's band. It's not my sort of thing, but I support him by advertising the band when they play.'

'Have you been to one of their gigs?'

'Once. I think he was embarrassed. He didn't come and say *hi* even though I know he saw me there.'

'Your parents are supposed to be embarrassing.'

Fin thought about Victor and Barb, how she would have done anything for one of them to come along to one of her swimming carnivals.

Their meals arrived and he seemed relieved to change the topic. 'This place never disappoints.'

Fin looked down at her fritters. It was a relief Anthony had his own family issues, after his divorce. It would make meeting Victor and Barb less daunting.

'I thought maybe we could have lunch with my folks on the weekend.'

'I'd love that. I want to thank them for having you.'

Fin stared down at her food. She really needed to warn him about Victor. 'I'll contact them today and make sure my sister comes along as well.'

'Wonderful, I'm looking forward to it.'

Fin's appetite was replaced by a churn of foreboding.

40

One year earlier

FIN leaned on the doorframe of Anthony's study where he seemed to be spending a lot of time lately. 'Would you come with me? I need to make a statement to the police.'

He turned to look at her. 'Of course.'

They learned that Victor discharged himself against medical advice. Barb was meant to drive as he was still under the influence of narcotic medications for his pain. His left lower leg was still in a cast, and his decision-making was impaired.

The orderly who wheeled him outside stated that Barb had driven the truck to the pick-up zone and pleaded with him to help her get Victor into the cabin. Victor refused help and demanded Barb give him the keys. The orderly witnessed Barb hand them over before Victor insisted on pulling himself up, with Barb pushing from behind. She then walked over and got into the passenger side.

Fin trembled. 'It was her final compromise to Victor, who berated and criticised her, blamed her for his shortcomings.'

When they returned home, Fin sat on edge of the sofa with her elbows on her knees and wept. 'I can't believe she's gone. And do you know the last thing I said to her? *You married him.*'

Anthony sat in the single-seater, hands folded between his knees. 'You weren't to know they'd be your final words.' He reached over and squeezed her arm.

'Even worse than that, I've been trying to get in touch with George and she hasn't responded. I'm getting desperate. I'm worried about her. Maybe you could try Damon.'

Anthony stood up, shoved his hands into his pockets and faced away from her. 'You are going to hate me.'

'That's not true.'

'I lied to you. Over months.'

Fin sat up and stared at his back. 'You're scaring me.'

'I've been sending money to George and Damon for a long time. I knew you wouldn't agree, so I did it without telling you.'

His face contorted. 'I never deserved your love, Fin. I've betrayed you.'

'How much money did you send?'

Fin thought about George's pleas on the phone. Her own refusal to keep dipping into her dwindling savings.

Anthony buried his face in his hands, still facing away from her. 'I used up what I had, then borrowed against the bookshop.'

Fin's thoughts scrambled to absorb the information.

'But with everything closed, I'm losing money. I'm going to lose Books at Stones. I've let poor Freya go, even though she'll struggle to get another job. I just can't afford to pay her.'

Fin thought about that day she rang Freya and how stressed Anthony had been over the past weeks. She had thought it was the chemotherapy.

'Books at Stones is your life. We must save it somehow.'

'It's too late.'

Fin stared at the floor their lies creating an uncomfortable space between them. 'I'm sorry, but I have a confession to make too. George swore me to secrecy, but I can't keep her confidence anymore.' Fin scuffed the edge of the rug with her toe. 'Damon is an alcoholic.'

Anthony's voice was barely audible. 'You knew?'

He turned and they stared at each other with fresh realisation.

'That's why I sent so much money over. I paid for rehab and wanted to support George and Ebony. Pip refused to send more money and he refused to communicate with her. I felt so terrible that my son was the cause of so much disruption and was so grateful George loved him enough to stick around. I was his last hope.'

Anthony lowered himself back into the sofa, his head in his hands. 'I'm going to lose everything.'

Fin spoke first. 'We can do this together. We must bring them home. I have some savings left and will arrange a flight.'

'I can't let you go alone. They won't let you fly anyway. Flights are all grounded.'

'Watch me. I'll organise something. I'll tell them we need George here for her Mum's funeral.'

'I should go.'

Fin looked at him. 'You have the last few chemo sessions. You can't go.'

Anthony reached for her hands. 'What have I done to deserve you? I can never repay you.'

'We are a team, remember?'

Anthony pulled her head into the crook of his arm. It felt so good to be close to him again. She pressed her ear against his chest. His heartbeat stilled the ribbons of thought swirling through her head. 'Actually, there is something you can do for me.'

~

The police attendant came out masked and took their temperatures, then wrote down their details, including phone numbers and email addresses. It was half an hour later when Fin and Anthony, both masked, followed the policeman to a room where the morgue attendant waited. Fin trembled, grateful to have Anthony by her side.

'Your mother has extensive bruising on one side of her face. We have taken photographs and we recommend you look at those first.'

There were two pictures lying face down on a small table. Fin turned her face away. The thought of Barb broken and silenced forever was too much to bear.

'I'm sorry, I just need a moment.'

She stepped outside into the hallway, found the toilets, hung her head over the ceramic bowl, and heaved. It was a relief to empty herself. She knelt on the linoleum, panting. A while later she stood and washed her face, scooped water up in one hand. She ducked her head under the tap and drank to dilute the sour taste of vomit in her mouth. Her eyes were red and sat deep in their sockets. Her face was pale, her cheeks hollowed by loss. She was grateful for the mask covering much of her grief. When she returned, Anthony waited outside. 'You don't have to do this. Let me identify her.'

'I need to see her again.'

Fin turned the photo over and gasped. The bruising was extensive on one side, but Barb was recognisable. Fin put the photo down again and whispered, 'I'm ready now.'

Despite the injuries, Barb looked at peace for the very first time. Her lips wore half a Mona Lisa smile, one eye closed and the other so bruised it disappeared into purple flesh. The skin on her exposed hand was much paler than Fin remembered. She reached out to touch her mother. Fin's thoughts stumbled back to those days on the Wynnum foreshore. Those humid evenings where Victor was away and they shared salty, hot chips from butcher's paper before driving back home, sticky with sand clinging rough to their skin.

Tears trickled down Fin's cheeks. Her final words to Barb returned clear and loud. *You married him.* Fin stumbled backwards, the taste of regret acid in her mouth.

41

One year earlier

FIN sat in her old familiar stool in the kitchen and watched Anthony heat up the teapot and reach for the leaves. 'I'm planning to see Victor today. He's still unconscious in ICU.'

Anthony took care measuring the tea leaves and added boiling water. 'I'll come along if you like.'

'It's okay. He won't know. Do you remember the first time you met him at the family lunch?'

'I doubt I'll ever forget that day.'

He placed the strainer over and poured them each a cuppa before adding milk.

'Your face when you saw Damon walk in.'

Anthony handed her a mug. 'I should have been alert to Damon's drinking and intervened then. We had to drive them home, remember?'

'It was a lunch that called for drinking. It was a survival tactic.'

~

Victor looked terrible, his face bruised and purple, his mouth parted as if ready to complain. He looked vulnerable and frightened. For the first time, Fin not only pitied him but recognised the multitude of reasons he pitied himself. She paused, jaw tight, tempted to leave again. He would never know.

Fin looked away from his still form; the only evidence he was still alive were the tracings on the monitors around his bed. Barb would still be here if Fin had arrived at the hospital earlier and driven them home. If only she hadn't delayed and lingered over breakfast. Since that day, Fin's senses had shut down, like she was swimming through murky water

208

fully clothed, heavy and weighted down, the visibility barely enough to see her hand. Her sense of taste disappeared. Everything was mud on the roof of her mouth. Sounds were discordant, loud, and she wanted to cover her ears to the incessant clatter and squeak of trolleys in the hospital. Part of her wanted to scream at the inert, broken body on the bed. *It should be Mum lying here with some glimmer of hope at survival.*

Victor's chances of survival and full recovery seemed more remote by the day. Fin pushed for information, wanting some certainty about the future. One of the doctors came over and typed some notes into the computer.

She interrupted. 'Excuse me, what are his chances of living independently if he wakes up?'

'We will repeat all his blood work and see how he goes when we lighten his sedation. There is nothing of concern on the MRI of his brain.'

The ward round moved on, and Fin realised that she was no closer to getting the answers she needed. She had always found reassurance in protocols, found comfort in the balance and symmetries of fluids and biochemistry, every medical problem a great puzzle to be solved and managed with the right combination of expertly administered treatments. Now, when she needed certainty the most, she realised there was that intangible, unmeasurable part of being human that remained uncaptured by the technologies that kept us alive.

Fin dreaded the thought of Victor surviving in a debilitated state. He would insist on going out to The Estate and she would have to push back.

If only George was here so they could discuss what to do. Fin tried to make contact again. *Please get in touch, it's urgent. George, where are u??? It's about mum and dad, I need to talk to you.*

Fin hesitated, her thumbs hovering over her phone. *Mum died in a car accident. Dad is unconscious in ICU.*

~

The phone call came in the middle of the night. Fin was asleep, wrapped up in a dream, her skin sweaty, and her legs entangled in sheets. It took her a minute to orientate. Her phone informed her it was three in the morning. Anthony was asleep beside her.

Half sitting and half lying down, Fin answered, her voice groggy with fatigue.

'Hello?'

'Is that Fin Steinbauer?'

The accent was American. Fin tried to sit up, her thoughts scrambling to align.

'I've got the baby here with me. I just want to let you know she's fine.'

'Who is this? Who am I speaking to?'

'Cindy, your sister's neighbour. She asked me to take the baby, Ebony.'

Fin was awake now and fumbled for the bedside light, her insides churning, her mind trying to make sense of the conversation. 'I want to talk to George, my sister.'

The pause stretched across continents.

'Oh, hon, I'm sorry, you didn't know? That sickness, the COVID killed her, together with the drinking. Didn't anyone call you?'

Fin's heart hammered. 'No, you must be wrong, there is some sort of mistake. Damon's the drinker, not George.'

'They both put it away.'

Fin was wide awake now. Hands trembling, she shook Anthony awake.

She screamed at him, 'George is dead.'

He sat up, hair askew, eyes wide.

Fin wrenched open the bedside table drawer and scrambled for a pen. Her thoughts jumped like moths trapped inside a lamp. She switched her phone to speaker.

'Look, I'm flying over. Give me all your details.'

~

The next couple of weeks were a blur of tears, desperate phone calls, and endless red tape and barriers.

'It is urgent for me to travel to the United States to pick up my niece, a baby. My sister died of COVID in New York.' Fin spoke into the phone.

'I'm afraid you will have to apply for special circumstances. All international travel was banned from the twenty-fourth of March.'

'These are exceptional circumstances. I need to bring this baby home.'

'Fill out the relevant paperwork, and your case will be considered.'

Fin navigated endless forms and phone calls and attempted to force her way through the layers of bureaucracy brought about by the pandemic. She kept coming up against blank walls. Anthony sat in the living area, paperwork spread out over the coffee table between mugs of cold tea.

Fin threw up her hands. 'Have you had any luck getting in contact with Damon?'

He shook his head. 'He discharged himself from rehab a couple of months ago and there's been nothing since then.'

She hurled a folder across the room. 'This is a nightmare. Surely this is an *exceptional circumstance*. Ebony is staying with George's neighbour, Cindy, in New York. We don't even know her. I keep hitting my head against walls. No one's listening.'

Anthony shrank away from her. 'There is one option I haven't explored yet.'

'Don't keep me in suspense.'

'My ex, Pip. Her husband, Simon, might be able to pull a few strings.'

'How?'

'He has a senior role with immigration and will whisper a word in the right ear.'

'What are we waiting for?'

~

Cindy sent photographs of Ebony every few days. It was the one thing that kept them both going. Fin traced around the outlines of Ebony's mouth, her eyes, her tiny hands reaching for a dangling toy. *I'm coming, baby, I promise.*

Anthony refreshed his emails every half hour or so and checked his phone even more often. 'I just hope Pip doesn't ignore me. We didn't part on the best terms.'

'Does she know about Damon's issues?'

'I haven't told her about the rehab, but he started drinking quite young. She gave him an ultimatum, and he left. I don't know if they keep in touch.'

'How about Ebony?'

'I told her and sent some pictures.'

'If that doesn't yield results, nothing will.'

Fin didn't say anything to Anthony, but she worried Damon might show up on Cindy's doorstep and take Ebony away. He was the father. The possibility that George's little girl could end up living in squalor with an alcohol-addled father made Fin dizzy with fear. Getting the photos every few days from Cindy was a reassurance and she had to stop herself begging for more.

Once again, Fin took indefinite unpaid leave from work, which she could ill afford. Her bag was packed while she spent her time filling in forms for travel exemptions. Anthony applied for a passport for Ebony. They learnt that she was automatically a US citizen by virtue of being born there. The weeks ticked past.

They watched the news feeds coming from New York with horror at the unspeakable numbers of active cases and deaths in the city. The numbers seemed so distant and detached from the reality of grief and loss associated with each one. A sister, mother, brother, father, a friend, reduced to a statistic. It did not seem possible that this was happening today in a rich country with healthcare and hospitals. Fin could have screamed with frustration that their lives depended on a bureaucrat's signature on a piece of paper. It was like being a caged bird, watching everyone through bars, uncertain if the door would ever be unlatched.

When Anthony's phone rang, Fin jumped, her antennae trained towards bad news. He walked away, and Fin forced herself not to follow and eavesdrop. After what seemed like hours, but was in fact ten minutes, Anthony returned grinning.

'You have permission to leave the country.'

She flung her arms around his neck, caused him to take a step backwards. 'I'm not sure how Pip managed it, but I'm forever grateful.'

'It was a word in the right ear.'

After spending just shy of $20,000, she finally checked onto a multileg flight that would get her to New York in three days, arriving on the ninth of June.

Anthony's brow furrowed. 'I only wish I could go with you. I feel so useless.'

'Without your contacts, I wouldn't have been able to leave the country.'

'Please be careful and wear an N95 mask all the time. Wash your hands. I'll never forgive myself if you don't make it back.'

42

One year earlier

IT was two days before Fin was due to fly out to bring Ebony home. Anthony was due to have his final chemotherapy after several delays. They sat on the back deck drinking tea, exhausted after the last frenzied weeks. Anthony's skin was ashen with fatigue. Fin wished she did not have to leave him.

His phone rang.

'Hello. Alec, what's happening?'

Fin frowned. The name sounded familiar, and she tried to place it.

'Someone has made an offer?' Anthony's voice cracked.

Of course, Alec was the agent from Revolution Commercial. Fin had nearly forgotten about Books at Stones.

Anthony ended the call. His face sagged, and he aged ten years. He didn't look at Fin. 'A fellow has offered us the asking price.'

Fin thought of her nearly empty account and the huge cost of travelling to pick up Ebony. The timing was perfect.

'I can't do it. I've changed my mind.'

Fin hardened. 'It's too late. We need the money to support George and Ebony. After the IVF, the airfares, and me taking so much time off work, we're broke.'

Anthony refused to look at her. 'I just didn't think it would happen so fast.'

He stood up, shoulders hunched. 'The buyer wants a short settlement. I'm going to meet Alec at the bookshop. I might ring Freya. She left a few things there. I'd like to pay her a bonus now the place has sold.'

He walked out, a skin of milk forming on his half-drunk tea.

~

Fin sat dutifully beside Victor, who was no longer attached to monitors but only awake for short periods of time. He remained delirious, and his speech was garbled and incomprehensible. She dared not think about what might happen to him. The doctors' earlier optimism was now more guarded, and she had given up asking about the prognosis.

'I'm heading to New York to pick up Ebony.'

She found it hard to talk to Victor when he was awake. It turned out it had been easier when he was unconscious.

He wrenched his sheet off, muttering gibberish when her phone rang.

Relieved to have an excuse to step away, Fin left him exposed, and answered the call. 'Hello.'

'Fin, it's Freya.'

She sounded hesitant.

'Are you alright?'

'I guess you know the shop's been sold.'

'I'm sorry he let you go, Freya, but he had no choice.'

'The new owner has offered me my job back.'

'That's great news.'

'Do you think Anthony will be upset?'

'Of course not. He'll be delighted for you. I know he felt awful letting you go.'

~

Anthony clicked his seatbelt in, and Fin backed out of the driveway, careful to angle the car so the back fender didn't scrape. She pointed the car towards the hospital. 'Your final chemotherapy session. How do you feel?'

'Relieved, a bit anxious. I'm trying not to think about the next scan.'

'I won't be here. I feel so awful about that.'

'Picking up Ebony is more important.'

They were quiet for a moment.

Fin drummed her fingers on the steering wheel at the next red light. 'Freya rang me. She mentioned she has her job back.'

The tip of Anthony's tongue was poised on the side of his lip.

'She was worried you might be upset.'

'No, I'm happy for her.'

There was silence then until they reached the hospital. Fin parked, then turned to Anthony and put her hand on his arm. 'I'm sorry about Books at Stones. I know how much it meant to you.'

He hesitated. 'I know the new owner.'

'Is that good news?'

'I don't know. I just can't think about it right now.'

'Once we have Ebony with us and you get the all-clear, we can borrow some money, get another bookshop.'

Anthony shrugged. 'I just want to worry about one day at a time.'

Fin got out and gave him a hug. She watched him make his way to the entrance and worried how he would cope without her, how she would cope not seeing him for weeks.

~

After three gruelling days in the air and multiple time zones, Fin was ragged. She was so tired she had trouble standing up. The South Bronx address was scrawled on a scrap of paper in her pocket as well as in her phone. The paper seemed more real, scribbled down when Cindy first rang.

When Fin stumbled out of the yellow cab wearing her claustrophobic N95 mask, she felt disorientated, as if she had woken up from a bad dream and was still finding her bearings. There were a surprising number of people in the streets compared to Brisbane, an almost carnival-like atmosphere. Graffiti was painted over boarded shop fronts, black paint bleeding into the grain. *Keep Our Community Safe!!!* And nearby, *RIP George Floyd.* A clutch of police stood in front of the latter, armed with Perspex face shields. Fin swallowed, her confidence evaporating.

She pulled out her phone, nearly collapsing with exhaustion.

'Hello? Is that you, Cindy?'

'Fin. You made it. Hi, hon.'

'Just walk down 149th past Capri Cakes, and I'll be there. Everything's opening again this week. The boards are finally coming off the windows after three months of lockdown, so it's busy again.'

Fin stared around and saw a queue outside a cake shop, half the patrons masked, talking into their phones, talking to each other. The police had subdued a scuffle of Black protestors near the *RIP George Floyd* sign. She pushed on, her backpack sagging off one shoulder, the suitcase hobbling behind her, one wheel broken, the heat rising off the pavement, and rubbish piled up in the streets.

Just when she didn't think she could walk another step, an older woman wearing a faded, floral print sundress with a baby cradled in her arms called out, 'Over here, hon!'

With the last bit of strength she had, Fin dragged her case to the waving woman wearing a cloth mask. She dropped everything and put her arms out for Ebony.

The next scene moved in slow motion. The noise, colour, and heat around Fin faded, and just like that, she was holding George's baby close. Fin pulled her mask down and inhaled Ebony's stale-milk smell, felt her soft baby breath on her cheek, and welcomed the one grubby little hand tugging her hair.

'Ebony, my darling. I'm here, I'm here.'

43

One year earlier

THE building where Cindy lived had nineteen storeys and only two elevators. One was out of order. Fin held Ebony and huddled close to Cindy in the waiting queue. It was unfamiliar standing so close to people again.

'You can see how the virus spread here. Bit hard to social distance when there are so many people. You know, in the Bronx, we have double the infection rate.'

Ebony struggled to get free. Fin lowered herself onto her wobbly suitcase and jiggled Ebony on one knee. Careful to keep her balance, Fin made soothing noises, willing the lift to arrive.

'Here, let me.'

Cindy reached over to Ebony, who stretched her arms out. She settled immediately. Fin bit her lip and stood up, her mask dangling around her neck. 'She really likes you.'

'I'm the only person she knows. George got sick and asked for help. Damon went off to some detox place. I had no luck finding him.'

Finally, the lift arrived, and it was their turn. Fin slipped her mask back on and crowded inside with everyone else. The mask felt like a flimsy protection with so many bodies pressed close. When they shuddered to a stop on the twelfth floor, Fin squeezed past everyone and followed Cindy down the hallway, pulling the broken case behind her.

The corridor was pungent with stale cooking. Fin, dizzy with fatigue, could have laid down on the floor right there and slept for a few hours.

Cindy pointed to doors on either side, still holding Ebony. 'Debbie in number fifty-two died, Chuck and Hudson in fifty-eight, Virginia in

218

sixty-two.' She sounded resigned. 'Every person here has lost someone. It's because we do the risky jobs, driving delivery trucks, working as health aides and public transit workers.'

She fumbled the key into the door, Ebony still propped on one hip. 'The landlord halved the rent, but now everything is opening again, that's stopped.' Cindy nodded to the door across the corridor. 'Georgina lived over there.'

Just when Fin wondered when George started to call herself Georgina, they entered Cindy's apartment. It was tiny. There was a worn couch, a small table with two chairs, and a clutter of baby things. Everything looked as tired and faded as Fin felt. 'I wonder if I could just lie down for a few hours.'

'How about a shower? You sleep in my room, and I'll sleep out here with the baby.'

'I couldn't do that. Let me sleep on the couch.'

'I get up early to get to my cleaning jobs. You'll be on your own until three in the afternoon. I usually take Ebony, but I'll leave her with you.'

Fin stumbled into Cindy's room, too tired to argue. She pulled out a few things from her suitcase and had a shower, washing away several days of grime, grit, and desperation. Finally, she collapsed into the bed, pulled the faded beige blanket over her head, and dissolved into a tumble of strange dreams.

~

Fin felt someone shaking her shoulder and startled awake, disorientated. Cindy was leaning over her. 'I'm heading to work. I've fed Ebony.'

Cindy handed Ebony to a rumpled Fin, who held out her arms while the past day rushed back to meet her. 'What time is it?'

'Tomorrow morning. You slept all afternoon and all night. I've left you bagels and cream cheese. Help yourself. I'll be back around three.'

'Thanks for everything. I really appreciate it.'

And just like that, Fin found herself alone with Ebony, who sat and stared at her with George's big, blue eyes. Fin knelt in front of her and realised how little she knew about looking after babies.

'It's you and me now, kiddo. We're heading home soon.'

Fin remembered something, fumbled in her bag, and pulled out the rabbit Anthony had bought for Scarlett. Ebony reached out a plump hand for it. She grabbed the rabbit and put its ear into her mouth. Fin laughed out loud. She snapped a photo and sent one to Anthony and another one to Cindy.

Cindy sent back a message. *Give her a hug from me. Teeth are giving her a hard time.*

Fin longed for George. What sort of mother would she have been? 'Your daughter is growing new teeth,' Fin whispered, as if George was observing it all from someplace. Fin watched as Ebony let go of the rabbit, leaving it lying helpless on its back. Fin pulled out her phone, trained it on Ebony, and took a short video of her concentrated effort to crawl. It made her clench to think of Anthony, alone now, waiting for results, knowing his bookshop was gone. She decided to distract him with a stream of updates about Ebony.

She is the most beautiful little girl with George's eyes and Damon's long fingers and toes. I think she has bits of me too.

Fin watched Ebony explore. The miracle of Fin being here with George's little girl was overwhelming.

Fin whispered to George as though her spirit hovered between the flimsy walls, watching them. Ebony grabbed the rabbit again and Fin took another reel. Suddenly, her belly grumbled. Her last meal had been something in plastic containers on the final leg of her flight. She scooped Ebony up and headed to the kitchen.

Fin made a mental note to leave Cindy money to cover the costs of staying here for a week, as well as funds to reimburse her for taking care of Ebony. Everything was sparse, the pantry close to empty. There were tins of formula, packet noodles, dry crackers, Oreos, and a half-empty jar of peanut butter. Fin opened the fridge and found a packet of bagels and an unopened tub of cream cheese. She messaged Anthony. *No tea to be found anywhere.*

She would buy some more groceries with Cindy after she finished work today.

After scoffing two bagels and a glass of milk, Fin sat back and watched Ebony try to crawl. That was when Fin saw the three boxes and George's old duffle bag against the wall. Curious, she went over and had a peek inside.

Ebony plonked herself beside Fin with one of the rabbit's ears in her mouth again. 'Now let's see what your mummy has in here.'

Fin burrowed through to find an odd assortment of worldly goods. A jumble of clothes and dress jewellery in the duffle, including absurdly high, skinny-heeled stilettoes coloured bright pink. It made Fin smile to see George had not become more practical after moving here. The pointy, shiny shoes looked incongruous among the leggings, long sweaters, and tees. Fin tugged at a tattered ear. It was Lucky, the toy dog George adored when she was a kid. He was missing not only an eye now, but one ear and his tail. His stuffing leaked where stitching had come loose near his back leg. Seeing him brought a flood of memories back. It still seemed surreal Fin would never hug George again.

The boxes had a few kitchen items, mismatched crockery, and a bundle of photographs including one of the two of them enjoying chips down on the Wynnum foreshore. Fin teared up as she gazed down and saw her arm around George while they smiled up at Mum. In the box, there was an envelope marked, *To Fin*. She ripped it open. Ebony grabbed the envelope and started to chew, the word *Fin* dissolving in drool.

Fin's eyes scanned the letter.

Dearest Fin,

This is my Will. I am writing this down because this virus is killing me, I can't breathe.

Please take my darling Ebony home and raise her as your own. I want her to have a good life, a strong mother and I know that is you. I have not been the best mum to my beautiful girl, and that is something I regret. But you, Fin, you are strong in every way. I love you so much, more than I can ever say. I know you will love my girl and give her opportunities that I have failed to provide. Damon is a dear man, I love him to bits, but he is not capable of looking after our precious daughter.

It is the last thing I will ask of you.

Georgina

XXX

It was the first time Fin had seen George sign herself off with her proper name. There was a pungent smell coming from Ebony, then a loud banging on the door. Fin startled, wondering who it might be and if it was safe to let anyone in. She wrinkled her nose, grabbed Ebony, and tiptoed over.

Bang, bang.

'Hello? Anyone home?'

It was an Australian accent.

Who even knew she was here?

'It's me, Damon.'

Fin went cold. Her instinct was not to let him in. She thought of Anthony and knew he would expect her to be kind, to help and support him. He had, after all, supported George in her hour of need.

'Give me a minute.'

With Ebony on one hip, the smell of the nappy becoming stronger by the minute, Fin fumbled the lock.

They stared at each other. He looked terrible, hair unkempt, face unshaven, a torn shirt that had seen better days. There was fresh ink on his forearm.

'Come in and have a seat. Give me a minute, I just need to change her nappy.'

Fin tried to recall where the change gear was. She didn't want to botch up in front of Damon. She gritted her teeth when he followed her into the room, where she remembered some baby clothes on the dresser. Fin handed Ebony over while she opened drawers, praying one would be full of baby things. Damon held his daughter at arm's length. Fin and Damon looked like the two amateurs they were. Neither of them had a clue how to manage the mundane tasks required to care for a seven-month-old baby.

Then Fin saw them: nappies and wipes on the dresser in front of her nose. Ebony started to cry, her legs peddling furiously. Fin lifted her from Damon's arms and laid her on a towel on the bed, using one hand to keep her there while trying to take her towelling shorts off. The shrieking went up an octave and Damon reached in and held Ebony down while Fin removed the nappy and wiped out all the crevices and creases, hoping she had not missed any. She slid a new nappy underneath Ebony's flailing legs. As he leant in, she caught the scent of Damon's liquored breath.

Nostrils clogged with stale alcohol and poo, Fin marched back out to the living area and wrapped the nappy up in a bag. She read the instructions on the tin of formula, reluctant to appear amateurish in front of Damon but more anxious about making a mistake. Damon stood too close, a shock of greasy hair falling over his face.

Finally, the milk was heated, and Ebony reached for the bottle just as Fin sank into the lounge. Damon sat at the other end and stared at his daughter. 'I've come to take her with me. Cindy's been trying to get in touch.'

'Jesus, Damon. How long before you even got here? You haven't responded, and now you turn up reeking of alcohol. You can't possibly look after a child.'

'Ebony is my daughter.'

'You have no job, no money, and a drinking habit. I thought you were in detox.'

He shrank from her, folded himself into the old sofa, all knees, angles, and elbows. His eyes stared up at her, a lifeless grey, any challenge leaked out of them. His voice was ragged. 'I left detox to pick my daughter up. I'll change.'

Fin took advantage of his faltering stance. 'George asked *me* to take her home. She wants me to raise Ebony.'

'I loved Georgina. She loved me.'

'She loved you enough to know that you were incapable of caring for Ebony.'

Fin turned sideways to face Damon. He kept his gaze down. Ebony was dripping milk onto the floor and let go of the bottle. It landed hard and rolled under the sofa. Fin jumped up and gripped Ebony so hard she started to cry.

A shiver ran through Damon, like wind past a sheet spinning on a Hills Hoist. Fin panicked he might be going through severe withdrawals on Cindy's sofa.

'I am her father. I will fight for her.'

Something exploded inside Fin. This must be what it was to be a mother. To fight for your child, to put yourself on the line and know that you would do anything to keep them safe. 'George left a will and made me Ebony's guardian.'

Damon shrank back into the sofa, his skinny arms shielding his face. Ebony started to thrash and wail. Fin jiggled her up and down.

'How much money do you need to get you through?' Fin couldn't believe she was bribing Damon and offering money for his child. Surely, there were laws about doing that. If Anthony ever found out…

Damon had pulled his legs up to his chest now like a cricket about to jump. 'I wasn't even there when Georgina got sick and died. She didn't tell me she had the virus.'

Fin kept a tight hold on Ebony, who was screaming now, her legs kicking, her face red.

Damon rocked back and forth, his voice splintered. 'They took her body, buried her at Hart Island in a pauper's graveyard. I want to get it back, pay to bring her home to Brisbane.'

The saliva in Fin's mouth dried up, her thoughts in pieces. She had wanted to ask Cindy about the body and assumed it was in a morgue somewhere. Fin lowered herself onto the other side of the couch again and let Ebony wriggle free. Damon's voice was muffled through dirty fingers.

'Give me $10 000. I'll clean myself up, get a place to live, a job, and come home with Georgina's ashes.'

Fin nodded. She would withdraw it from her credit card and worry about the consequences later. 'I'll transfer it over today.'

She hesitated about how she would explain it all to Anthony. This was one instance where she had to follow her gut and do what was right for George and Ebony.

Damon stood, hands deep in his pockets. 'I'll fuckin' do whatever it takes to get my daughter back.'

He walked to the door and left without even turning around, leaving the smell of stale liquor in the room and the taste of ash in Fin's mouth.

44

One year earlier

FIN sat surrounded by more paperwork. She had been in touch with the Australian Consulate-General to confirm Ebony's passport and had an appointment with the American passport agency in New York. It seemed that the grip of bureaucracy had a stranglehold on them and would not let her fly home to Anthony.

She didn't want to give Anthony more to worry about, but she really needed him to intervene.

They won't let me bring Ebony home unless I get a letter from Damon. I've tried to contact him, but he won't respond.

Not that Anthony had any more luck with his son. Months went past without so much as a message from Damon. Fin catapulted between sheer wonder at Ebony and the chilling terror of losing her, and she sent photos to Anthony multiple times a day with messages full of tiny details.

Two huge poos today. Orange. Must be the mashed carrots.

Rabbit is her fave toy.

Terrible night. A new tooth.

This latest was accompanied by a blurry photo of a sawtooth bit of white poking from a gum. He rang. 'I'm in love all over again. I need to grow a new heart to fit you and Ebs in.'

Hearing his voice choked Fin up. 'I can't wait to see you.'

She sent messages to Damon too with photographs of his daughter.

Ebony waving hello

Why not come home too? We'll pay for your flight

As much as Fin would prefer to bring Ebony home alone, she would advocate for Damon if it was the only way to get her out of the country.

225

'I'm sorry we're taking up so much space and that we're still here,' Fin apologised to Cindy.

'I'm enjoying a bit of company. With my three all grown up and their father long gone, life was getting lonely. I'll miss you both when you leave.'

'If we leave.'

'Things will sort out, hon.'

Fin was obsessed with news reports about the pandemic and constantly watched the TV or scrolled through newsfeeds on her phone. On the sixth of July, almost one month since her arrival, New York began phase three of reopening with no indoor dining.

Still no message from Damon. Fin's jaw ached from clenching. She longed to get Ebony back to Brisbane, to a normal life.

On the nineteenth of July, phase four reopening was announced, with malls, museums, and indoor dining still closed. The deaths for New York reached 22,934. Fin clutched Ebony to her and rocked back and forth on the lounge. It seemed this nightmare would never end.

She messaged Anthony. *Any news from Simon?*

A moment later her phone pinged. It was Damon. Trembling, Fin read the message.

I'm sick, COVID has damaged my heart. Won't make it.
Letter sent for Ebony. Take her home.
I want you and dad to raise her.
Sorry for everything
Thanks, Love D.

~

It all happened quickly after that. Ebony's passport was approved, and Fin spent another eye-watering amount to get them both home, again via a multileg flight. She packed her bag and an enormous backpack full of baby things for Ebony, who was now crawling and very active. She kept their passports and a sheaf of documents in a plastic sleeve tucked in an inside pocket, praying it would be enough to get them through customs and back to Brisbane. When the cab pulled up, Fin gave Cindy a hug with one arm while Ebony squirmed in the other. Fin pressed an envelope fat with notes into Cindy's hand. 'Thanks for your kindness. If you ever come to Brisbane, you must promise to stay with us.'

Cindy pressed the envelope to her breasts and did not protest or try to give it back.

The cab pulled away, and Fin turned and held Ebony up to the rear window until Cindy was a tiny black spot that soon disappeared. Fin realised she was travelling without a child seat and pulled the seatbelt over the two of them. She had to start thinking like a mother now and regretted not buying a seat yesterday when she made a last-minute dash for some toys and snacks for the seven-leg flight home.

The streets were busy, with people masked and standing in long queues waiting to be tested for SARS CoV2. The airport, in contrast, was eerily quiet. Fin stood with her battered case, Ebony hoisted onto one hip. If only she had bought a pram. Her arm was already aching. Ebony protested, legs flailing, wanting to be put down. Fin shifted Ebony to the other hip and made her way past uniformed officials to check in and ready herself for the long haul. She held her breath, couldn't quite believe it when her documents were scrutinised, and she was waved through to departures.

After a blur of days and nights, in that twilight zone of empty airport lounges and interminable take-offs and landings, there was a surreal quality to landing in Brisbane. The arrivals area echoed; the usually bustling counters closed. Ebony, asleep, hung like a dead weight off Fin's arms. The wheel on the suitcase had now snapped off. It was a relief to go under police escort into quarantine. Just the thought of a shower and lying horizontal was as close to bliss as Fin could imagine. She stared out at the vast, indifferent blue sky as the escort vehicle passed through familiar streets. She shot Anthony a text. *The girls have landed.*

She drifted off to sleep in the escort vehicle and awoke outside the hotel that would be their home for the next fortnight.

Fin had heard only negative reports about quarantine and the insurmountable challenges of being cooped up with a child. It was easier than she imagined, and helped her transition to her new reality, juggling life with motherhood. Between meals in brown paper bags, weak tea, and ghastly coffee in takeaway paper cups, Fin immersed herself in spending uninterrupted time with Ebony. She even gazed at her splayed limbs when she slept. 'I'm your mummy now. One day we'll bring your first mummy and daddy home and I'll tell you all about her. We'll even go to a special place and lay them to rest near the river.'

Fin had never thought of George as sentimental, but the photographs told a different story. They traced their history from the first picture soon after George's birth in hospital to the days when they shared Fin's unit after the wedding was called off. George had kept all of them, dated the back of each one. Fin planned to scan them all and create books to show Ebony her story, her history.

When they first came out of quarantine, Fin was shocked how thin and tired Anthony looked, but he gave them the biggest smile. It was such a relief to see him, she nearly crushed him in her embrace.

He held Fin close, Ebony squeezed between them. 'My girls are home.'

Fin wept into his shoulder. 'I'm so sorry about Damon. I tried to find out where he was, to see him again. After ringing every hospital in the area, I learnt he had died. They wouldn't have let me visit anyway.'

Anthony pressed her close to him. 'You brought Ebony home and came back safe.'

He had arranged a new car seat, bought formula, and cleaned out the nursery. Exhaustion leaked from his pores, his cheeks hollow, his eyes like a racoon's. He still insisted on making the tea and brought it over, the veins in his neck prominent, his brow wrinkled.

'How have you been? It must have been awful here alone, waiting.' Fin tried not to look worried.

'The blood tests have been normal, and I have another scan in one month. I've been worried sick about you and Ebony and…'

Fin snuggled closer to him, grateful Ebony was fast asleep in the nursery, clutching Bunny. 'We will do something for George and Damon. Once this whole thing settles down, we'll go to Hart Island and find them, bring them home and scatter them with Scarlett.'

Anthony shifted away from her. 'There is something I have to tell you. I've been holding off, not wanting to spoil our time together.' He sighed. 'Victor is awake and demanding to go home to The Estate. He is wheelchair-bound, confused, and angry.'

Fin's mood dropped. 'I'll head to The Estate tomorrow and have a look.'

'He can't live there. Should we all go?'

'You stay. I'll take Ebs and call one of the neighbours. I've had an idea and want time to think about it.'

She rang Arch.

'Fin, it's great to hear your voice. I'm so sorry to hear about your mum.' He sounded so familiar.

'It's been tough. George and her partner Damon died of COVID in New York. I just got back with her daughter, and I'm hoping to sell The Estate. I wondered if you would meet me there and tell me if it's habitable.'

'I'm so sorry to hear that. That really is awful.' There was a moment of silence, and Fin worried Arch was no longer there, until he spoke again. 'And of course, I'll meet you on the property. Always happy to help.'

'See you tomorrow morning.'

The property was in poor repair, with piles of old timber rotting around the sagging, incomplete house. It seemed to know it had been abandoned and had given up. Fin felt like doing the same while she waited for Arch to arrive. She clung to Ebony, noticing how unsafe the whole area was for a child, how easily she could injure herself in this wasteland of derelict buildings.

A shiny new truck crested the hill. Arch must be doing well. He pulled up alongside her and got out, a little older, more sunburnt but still the same. 'Who have we here?'

He reached for Ebony and swirled her high until she squealed, and Fin laughed. 'Well, she has given you the vote of confidence.'

Arch smiled. 'I've got a couple of my own now. Two boys.'

'Congratulations. And thanks so much for coming here to help.'

Fin unlocked the main house and Arch followed with a bundle of mail. 'These arrived for your folks. I've been collecting them.'

'I really appreciate you doing all this.'

'I'm always happy to help.' He looked around, one eyebrow raised. 'It's been really let go.' He put his hand on a rotting windowsill and it gave way. A tendril of cobwebs drifted from the ceiling and Fin cried out.

Arch peered down the hallway at unfinished doorways and kicked aside a broken box of artifacts. 'Whatcha thinking of doing with it?'

Fin shrugged. 'No idea. Victor has lost capacity.'

Arch nudged a hole in the wall with his boot. 'Well, let me know if you sell it. I'm hoping to expand the business. My missus is thinking of running farm stays.'

He knelt and coaxed Ebony over. He dangled one of the macramé pieces over his head and made her giggle, a chubby hand reaching to grab it.

Fin took the mail and walked inside. It smelt musty, full of Victor and Barb and yet empty. She clung to the edge of a sideboard, the realisation that Barb was gone punching her in the gut.

'Hey, are you alright?'

Arch grabbed Ebony, who was eager to explore on all fours.

Fin bit her lip. 'It's so hard. I resent that Victor survived and Mum didn't. It is so unfair.'

'He could be a bit of a bastard. She deserved a medal for putting up with him.'

'I'd always hoped she would get a few years without him and move to a small place in the city.'

'She made choices. Not much you can do about that.'

Fin recalled the meals where Victor dominated the conversation while Barb shrank herself to accommodate his needs. Arch scooped Ebony onto his shoulders and walked to the glass sliding doors, pointing at a magpie perched on the railing with its head tipped to the side.

The place missed Barb's sharp cleanliness. Cobwebs hung from the ceiling like loose threads while dust motes hitchhiked along light shafts before settling on surfaces. Fin's heartbeat paused like traffic at peak hour, her layers of grief a vast, uncharted continent she was not ready to explore.

She distracted herself by sifting through the mail. It was largely bills and junk mail. Then she noticed one envelope with the address handwritten in a beautiful cursive. She turned it around to see who it was from. *Bruce Ward.*

Curious, Fin used her nail to nick the corner and pulled the letter out.

Dear Barbara,

I still regret not running away with you. I was young and foolish. A coward. I should have made a stand, insisted that I marry you knowing you were carrying my child. Forgive me. I still think about you often, more often as I grow old. The last thing I want to do is to cause you distress, to disrupt your family.

My beautiful Barbara, I love you still and always will. I did not want to leave this life without telling you that. I bought Books at Stones recently. An impulsive decision. I would love to talk to you about it one day. Most days, I enjoy a coffee across the road at Stones Throw. Should you ever feel inclined, please drop in, just as a friend, and say hello. You would make me a very happy man.

Love always, Bruce.

She read the words again, more slowly this time to absorb their meaning. Surely, this was some sort of cruel mistake. Barb would have confided in her, whispered that sort of secret in her ear. Fin found it impossible to imagine Barb breaking the rules, being in love, and falling pregnant to someone other than Victor.

Arch's voice pulled her back into the room. 'Hey, Earth to Fin.'

Ebony reached for her. 'Ma, ma.'

Fin shook herself, realised her eyes were wet.

Arch grinned. 'Well, did you hear that?'

Fin buried her face in Ebony's soft blonde hair and squeezed her hard. There was a jumble of feelings jostling for space in her chest.

'Arch, read this, would you?'

There was a long silence after he finished and put it down on the table.

'Jesus. Who is this guy?'

Fin shrugged and pulled Ebony close. She remembered the silhouette of a man at the bookshop, the phone call after the shop was sold, Anthony's friend. Wasn't his name Bruce?

It was too much of a coincidence. She shook her thoughts away. 'I'm not sure.'

'Well, there's only one way to find out. His address is on the back of the envelope. You should get in touch.'

45

Now

THE café sounds disappeared around Fin. Her hand was held in a firm clasp by this tall, distinguished man. Her father. The man she had seen with Anthony at the bookshop. He was familiar, in that way of strangers you have crossed paths with before.

He pulled out a chair for her, looked with love and longing into the pram, then beckoned the waitress for a highchair.

He sat down opposite her and fiddled with a cufflink. Fin wondered when she had last seen anyone wear a cufflink.

He cleared his throat and handed her a menu. 'Let's order. It's so much easier to talk when there is a pot of tea in front of me.'

Just like that, Fin's anxiety evaporated.

'Definitely a pot of tea.' She hesitated. It was now or never. 'You know Anthony, don't you?'

He blushed red, fiddled with his cufflink. 'Let's order some of the mango coconut bread, I recommend it. Some toast fingers for the little one?

Fin nodded and lifted Ebony out of the pram and into the highchair.

The orders placed and formalities done with, Fin waited. 'So?'

He looked relieved when the tea arrived. 'May I?'

He poured milk first and swirled the teapot in a way that made Fin's heart clutch. She looked away and adjusted Ebony's blanket.

'Anthony is an old friend of mine. I knew him before he divorced Pip. I ran a small boutique bookshop, The Vault, and specialised in rare and collectable editions, often doing searches to locate out-of-print or old manuscripts for customers. That was before the internet, of course.

Anthony often came in and we would have a drink together – exchange books for wine. I helped him set up Books at Stones when he finally gave up the wine merchant work and did what he longed to do.'

He sipped his tea and smiled again, this one dancing across his whole face. 'Then I became the one ordering books and wandering in, taking him out for lunch between customers.'

Fin leant forward and watched him. 'What about this?' She pulled out the letter from her bag.

He fiddled with his teacup, and she noticed his fingers were too big to fit through the handle. He blanched. 'It must have been a shock to find my letter. I intended it for Barb, of course, and then heard about the accident and was devastated. I realised my lack of courage meant the woman I loved never learnt the truth about my feelings.'

He looked down into his cup again. 'When I read the letter you wrote to me, I made contact immediately. It was one of my happiest days.'

Fin fed Ebony small bits of toast.

'I adored your mother and just assumed we would marry one day and be together forever. Her family drove to Melbourne for Easter, and I had no idea she was pregnant with my child. By the time she returned a month later, I learnt that she was getting married to Victor, who wanted to stay in Australia and needed permanent residency. He agreed to marry Barb and raise my child as his own.'

'Why didn't they let you marry Mum?'

'They wanted a European man, believing an Australian like me to be uncultured and uncivilised. I tried to get in touch with her to plead my case, but she was forbidden to speak to me. I suspect my correspondence never reached her. I felt so guilty for making her pregnant and then leaving her to marry some man she barely knew.'

Fin wiped Ebony's face clean of avocado. 'Victor was not always nice to Mum.'

She wanted to add that he was not always very nice to her, but hesitated. After all, it was not as if Victor hit them. He just used his intimate knowledge about her vulnerabilities to white-ant her confidence and self-belief.

Bruce reached over and lightly touched her hand. 'That is my greatest shame. I knew and didn't do anything about it. I watched from afar and saw them sometimes. I learnt that they had a second daughter and moved out past Ipswich. Still, I felt paralysed to do anything. Eventually, I married someone else, lost contact for a while, and tried to put it all behind me. My marriage wasn't terrible, but we were not happy and separated after ten years.'

He shook his head sadly and poured another cup of tea. It was cold, so he asked for another pot. His smile faded, his body curved over the table. 'This is a two-pot-of-tea conversation.'

Fin started putting pieces together in her head. How Victor always favoured George. How unkind he could be. When she looked at Bruce, she could see she resembled him: his large frame, his wavy, thick hair, even the shape of his jaw and cheekbones.

She reached into her handbag and pulled out the photograph. 'Tell me about this photograph.'

Bruce stared at it and used his fingers to smooth the corners. A single tear fell onto his hand, and he made no move to wipe it away. 'This was taken the last week before Barb disappeared from my life forever. She was already pregnant with you, although I didn't know. I knew she was heading to Melbourne for three weeks and it seemed an impossible amount of time, so I wanted a picture of us. My uncle took a couple, and this was my favourite. When she stopped speaking to me, I slipped it between the pages of a poetry book to mark Elizabeth Barrett Browning's famous sonnet, *How Do I Love Thee?* I gave it to Barb outside her home and she begged me to leave and to never come again. It is the last time we spoke.'

Fin imagined how different her life might have been if her mother had married Bruce. Then she realised there would be no George and no Ebony.

'I wish I had known you before.'

Bruce hung his head. 'I'm sorry. I was anxious about disrupting your family and thought Barb would be angry if I revealed myself.'

'It's just such a coincidence you know Anthony.'

Bruce nodded. 'I could see how much he liked you, so I vouched for you and suggested he ask you out.'

Fin's skin prickled. 'You didn't.'

'I'm afraid I did, interfering old so-and-so that I am. When I heard about Anthony's cancer, it broke my heart. I was devastated when Freya told me he would have to sell the bookshop. I made enquires and decided to buy the bookshop myself. Something to keep me out of trouble in my old age.'

'I can't believe you bought Books at Stones?'

Bruce nodded. 'Crazy, isn't it? I just couldn't bear for it to disappear.'

'Does Anthony know?'

Bruce nodded. 'He was upset at first, but he is getting used to the idea. I told him I was meeting you today and invited him along, but he thought you might want to get to know me without him hovering.'

'It's all a bit much to take in, to be honest.'

'I worried so much about you after Anthony was diagnosed. I visited him in hospital a few times and he had no idea I was your father. I wanted to talk to him about it, but he had enough going on. I'd left it all so long I had no idea how to reach out without scaring you away.'

Fin's head was whirling now. The impossible coincidences, the improbability yet feasibility of Bruce's story. She took the photograph and slid it back into her bag. Ebony started protesting, her feet kicking the highchair. Fin, grateful for a distraction, reached in, undid the safety belt, then pulled her out. There were splodges of avocado down Ebony's dress, and her headband was askew. When Fin tried to strap Ebony back into the pram, she made her body very stiff and screamed. Other patrons turned around and stared. Bruce stood and stepped forward. 'Why don't we head across the road to my bookshop? You can have a look and see what you think.'

He reached out for Ebony and her screaming stopped. Relieved, Fin pushed the pram out of the cafe. They stood waiting for traffic, Ebony safe in Bruce's arms.

'What if I turn out to be a terrible mother?'

He raised one eyebrow, his eyes twinkling. 'I suspect kids don't arrive with a how-to manual and that it is a learn-on-the-job kind of process. This little girl is doing just fine from what I can see.'

They hurried across to the bookshop. It had been rearranged a little, and Fin stared around and absorbed it all while Bruce put Ebony down.

Freya looked up, saw them, and raised an eyebrow at Bruce. 'We only just opened again. Bruce invited me to come back. I'm making some changes. I hope you don't mind.'

Fin shook her head. 'It's up to Bruce, I guess.' She cast a maternal eye around for Ebony who was pulling books out of the box in the children's corner. 'I suspect Anthony would like what you are doing here.'

'Are you sure? I feel guilty about the bookshop, but when Bruce invited me…'

Fin kept an eye on Ebony. 'No need to feel guilty. Anthony knows and agrees you are perfect for the job.'

Freya picked at her nails. 'I was so sorry to hear about George and your mother.' She hesitated. 'How is Anthony?'

'All going well. We'll be okay.'

Ebony reached towards Fin, who knelt and hoisted her up, grateful to be needed.

Freya hurried away, thankful to serve a customer. Bruce beckoned to Fin and walked to the small office at the back of the store. 'Have a seat and shut the door. You can put Ebony down if you like.'

Ebony crawled into a cardboard box and peered out at them, grinning.

Bruce folded his hands together on the table and cleared his throat. 'I have a proposal.'

Fin stared at him again, taking in the details of his jaw and the curve of his cheekbone. It was uncanny. She looked away again, still not able to comprehend that this man had once loved her mother and was in fact her father.

'I'm too old to be running this place and wonder if you and Anthony would be interested in managing it? It might suit you better than shift work with a young one.'

'I don't know what to say.'

'I let you down in so many ways and for far too long. It is a small way of helping both of you.'

'It's a lot to take in and think about.'

'I'd be happy to provide childcare whenever you need it. I could hang around here and pester you while keeping an eye on this mischievous little girl.'

Fin stared at her hands, thoughts whirring.

'After my decades of silence, I've sprung everything on you at once.

I am being selfish because I long to be a part of your life, however small, but understand if you don't want to see me again.'

Fin watched Ebony crawl towards Bruce, like she was considering his offer. Fin suppressed a smile.

'Let me run it past Anthony and think about it.'

46

Now

'DID you know Bruce was my father?' Fin stared at Anthony over breakfast on the back deck. Ebony lifted her spoon up and flicked porridge everywhere.

Anthony picked up the washer and wiped her face, took the spoon, and fed her a few mouthfuls. 'Of course not. Although now I know, I keep seeing a family likeness. It's uncanny.'

'I wonder why he left it so long to tell me?'

'It would have meant destroying a family, bringing up uncomfortable truths that your mother might not have wanted exposed.'

'Bruce wants you back in the bookshop as a manager. He asked me as well, but I think I'd miss nursing too much.'

Anthony's shoulders slumped. 'Let me think about it. It's not the same.' He gave a wan smile. 'The only thing harder than losing the bookshop was selling my Fiat 124. Not counting Damon and George, of course.'

Fin lingered over her second cup of tea, and used a wet washer to wipe Ebony's face. 'Victor is obsessed with seeing George. I have told him she died but he keeps forgetting. Which reminds me, I must see Victor again. It's been a few days and he hates his new accommodation.'

Anthony put his hand on her arm. 'I should come along with you.'

'No. I need to go alone. He just can't accept he will never walk again, that he can't live on The Estate. It's not habitable. He doesn't realise he has deficits.'

'He didn't realise that before his head injury.'

~

An hour later, Fin sat beside Victor in the sunshine and listened to him rant.

'I insist you tell the bastards that I am going back out to The Estate. I have plans that I never completed. I need to finish the place for George.'

'I told you, George died. There is no way you can manage out there on your own.'

'If you were a half-decent daughter, you would come out with me and support me.'

Fin wanted to say that she was not his daughter, but there was no point. Victor was incapable of processing complex information.

'That Barb was always unreliable. And after everything I did for her.' He leant forward, nearly falling out of the wheelchair, one finger wagging in the air. 'I sacrificed my life. I could have had any woman I wanted.'

'Mum died, remember. After the accident.'

'She did the dirty on me. I'll never forgive her.'

Fin wondered what he remembered and if he had twisted the truth for so long now that he no longer knew what had happened. 'I'll have to head off soon. I've a baby to look after now. I might bring her next time.'

'Tell my beautiful George to come and see her old Dad. She'll get me out of this hole and look after me back home.'

'George died in New York, remember?'

Fin waited for him to doze off and left. It was always a relief when her bi-weekly visits were over and she could go home to Anthony and Ebony.

~

'Do you think Victor will ever get easier to spend time with?' Fin dropped her keys into the bowl on the kitchen bench next to Anthony, who sat on a barstool with the newspaper.

He didn't bother looking up. 'No.'

'I've decided not to bring him to Mum's memorial. He doesn't even remember that Barb died. I might bring Bruce along. He really loved Mum.'

Anthony did look up this time and gave her a grateful smile. 'That is a lovely idea.'

The memorial was a small, private ceremony. Fin was grateful for the restrictions limiting numbers. She kept some of Barb's ashes and gave the rest to Bruce.

'I think she would want to be with you.'

'Are you sure?' He held the urn with reverence, tears in his eyes. 'My beautiful Barb.'

The next day, Fin drove out towards The Estate to her shrine. It was a long time since she had visited. The daisies were dense now, smiling faces scattered between long grasses. Arch preferred to let nature take her course, to allow the plants to find their own place, their own balance. Fin liked to give the smaller, less resilient plants a better chance at survival and an opportunity to shine.

She spent a few hours clearing up. In these days of death tallies and mass graves, being here reminded her that life was brittle as an autumn leaf, a tiny part of an endless cycle of death and renewal. It soothed her to pull up weeds, rearrange the stones she had placed over the years.

She scattered the small handful of ashes she had brought along and imagined Barb here beside Joy, Cliff, and the babies, a mingling of their ashes among the wild blooms, their longings whispering on the wind, the bodies that had carried their ghosts released from the torments of navigating life. And one day, Fin promised, George and Damon would join them.

Fin's feet trod the slope down to the river, a flock of galahs in noisy disagreement overhead. She listened to creek water chattering over rocks, noticed lengthening shadows as the trees huddled closer together near the water, their roots holding the earth tight beneath her sneakers.

Fin found solace in the gurgle of water and watched as a dragonfly landed and made the surface tension quiver. Her eyes flicked back to the hidden space between the shrubs where she had lost her virginity, the memory of Arch inside her still vivid so many years later. She undressed and slid into the inky smooth water and let it flow over her like time. Using her legs to frog kick, she ducked below the surface and listened to the silence underneath until she felt cleansed and ready to drive back home.

On the drive, she had an idea.

Anthony was on the back deck pushing Ebony on a baby swing he'd hung up the back. Fin watched the arc curve through the air before calling out. 'Hi, I'm home.'

She snapped a picture of Ebony, chubby fingers clutching the plastic. Fin sent it to Cindy with a short message. They regularly exchanged news and Fin constantly sent photos of Ebony. *Bloody mamarazzi,* Cindy shot back once with an eyeroll emoji.

'Anthony, I've had an idea.'

He let the arc of the swing slow, undid the safety harness and pulled Ebony, who protested loudly, out.

'It's about the bookshop.'

He tensed and sat down, bouncing Ebony in his lap.

'Victor has a brain injury, won't ever be able to move out there again. His cognitive function is awful. I think we should sell the place, pay off his debts, use some of the money to place him in care and offer to buy half the shop from Bruce.'

'I didn't think the place was liveable.'

'Renovate or detonate. It will be someone's dream. In fact, I know someone who is interested.'

Anthony looked up. 'Have you spoken to Bruce?'

'Not yet. I wanted to check with you first.'

~

Anthony parked, and they got out and walked over to Books at Stones. Ebony clutched Bunny in one hand and reached to be let down. Bruce saw them and came over. 'Let her go. There's a box of books there for her to enjoy.'

Fin's mouth went dry. She was still shocked to think of Bruce as her father.

Anthony spoke first. 'I've given your proposition some thought.' He looked around at the changes since he owned the place. 'Fin has an alternative one to put to you. Maybe over dinner?'

Bruce came and put his hand on Fin's shoulder and looked over at Anthony. 'I'm not much of a cook, but I do a mean roast. How about you come to my place for dinner on Friday and we can discuss it all?'

~

Bruce had a gracious old home with views over the river. The large dining table was set for five. He smelt freshly showered, and his thick, silvery hair was damp. The white shirt he was wearing was open at the neck, and the sleeves were rolled up to the elbow. He was wearing a blue chef's apron. Fin looked away, aware she was staring at her father.

There was a highchair near one of the seats, and Fin strapped Ebony in, grateful for this courtesy.

Bruce nodded at her. 'I went out this morning and bought it. Couldn't have my granddaughter without a place at the table.'

Granddaughter. The word made Fin feel warm inside.

Anthony handed two bottles of wine to Bruce, who studied the labels with approval.

There was another knock at the door. Anthony stood up to answer, glanced at Fin, a worried expression on his face. He'd asked if he could invite Pip and Simon as well. She had lost her son, and was yet to meet her granddaughter. Without Simon, they may never have been able to bring Ebony home. Fin heard their voices. Her belly did flip flops.

A slight, short-haired woman walked in on the arms of a brown-haired fellow of modest build.

The introductions were stiff and unnatural.

Bruce smiled. 'Do have a seat and make yourselves at home.'

He left, and a few minutes later, returned with a large platter of sliced roast lamb and vegetables, which he placed next to a gravy boat before slipping off his blue apron. 'Now help yourselves. No formalities here. I am just thrilled to have you all here. It makes this old place of mine finally feel like a home.'

Fin's heartbeat was sharp and made her chest sting. She occupied herself with cutting up Ebony's food and helped her to eat so she didn't throw bits everywhere.

There was the clatter of cutlery against plates, the conversation strained. Bruce paused and used a knife to tap his glass. 'I just want you all to indulge me a moment. It is such a pleasure to have you all here in my home. I always dreamt of having my own family and I never thought I would have so many people I cared about sitting around my table, enjoying a meal.'

Ebony banged a spoon on the highchair as if to say *hear, hear,* and everyone laughed. The mood eased.

Bruce waited a moment and continued. 'I lost the woman I loved but gained a daughter and a family. I want to share my good fortune with others. In the years I have left, I long to enjoy my newfound family and to leave a positive mark on others' lives.'

Anthony interrupted. 'You've already done that.'

Bruce held up his hand. 'I've been given another chance and I want others to have another chance when they fall on hard times.'

He looked over at Fin, who stared down at her plate of half-finished food. 'I had a chat with my daughter here, who has made a proposition.'

Fin held her breath, the word daughter sounding so right when Bruce said it. Ebony squeezed some potato and it oozed between her fingers.

'My daughter, Fin, advised me that The Estate is in poor repair and needs extensive renovations. A fine young man, Arch, is keen to purchase the place, leaving funds for my old friend Anthony to buy half the bookshop back.'

Anthony looked the best he had for months. Colour in his cheeks, the sunken look around his eyes all but gone. He raised his glass. 'To good friends, to family, to following our dreams.'

Everyone raised their glasses. Pip sat stiffly next to Simon, who had one arm around the back of her chair.

Fin exhaled. Bruce looked over at her, and she gave a nod. He smiled at Pip and Simon who sat together on one side of the vast table. Fin realised her hand was shaking and put it in her lap.

'All of us here have lost someone dear to us,' Fin said. 'I want to thank Simon for going behind the scenes, doing whatever had to be done to get Ebony home to be with her family.' Fin realised she was crying. She reached into the highchair and undid the safety strap, lifted Ebony out. 'It's time you met properly.'

Fin handed Ebony to Pip, who seemed too young to be a grandmother. She stared at Ebony with awe, stroked her soft blonde hair. Ebony grabbed the pearls around her neck, and everyone laughed as Simon turned and prised chubby fingers away. Anthony snapped a picture of the three of them together. Ebony was suddenly aware she was the centre of attention and waved her arms around, saying, 'Ma, Ma.' She somehow managed to get squished potato in Pip's immaculate pixie cut.

Fin took a sip of her wine; let it slide down her tongue. 'Ebony's mum, George, died in New York together with thousands of others. A few weeks later, Damon died. I tried to contact him, rang hospitals, but by the time I found where he had treatment it was too late. One day, when we can travel again, we will go and find them, bring them home.'

Pip buried her face in Ebony's blonde curls and sobbed. 'I should have helped, gone over myself.'

Anthony shook his head. 'He didn't want help and rarely responded to messages.'

Pip hugged Ebony very hard. Simon handed her a napkin, and she wiped her eyes, leaving mascara on the white cloth.

Fin looked at the people sitting around Bruce's table. Her father, Bruce. Anthony, who loved her. Pip, who had lost her son and Ebony's father. Simon, who helped get Ebony back to Brisbane. Sitting among his family was like arriving safely home after a long journey. She realised that the best families were not always the ones who raised you or the ones you were born into. Sometimes, you had to create your own, with people who loved you and accepted you just how you were.

Fin looked over at Pip, whose dark head was bent forward over Ebony, the pearls now safely out of reach in her handbag. 'Would you like to come over and see Ebony regularly? Maybe babysit her. I'm hoping to get back to work.'

Pip's lip quivered.

Anthony blew Fin a kiss.

Pip looked up. 'I would like that very much.'

Bruce looked over at Anthony, who gave a nod. Fin noticed a sheen of perspiration on his forehead and hoped he was alright. Bruce disappeared and came back with a bottle of champagne and five flutes on a tray.

Anthony stood up, his hand trembling. He looked over at Fin, who chose that moment to wiggle her fingers at Ebony. 'Fin.'

She looked up and smiled. He pulled a small box out of his pocket, his voice wobbly. 'I wonder if you would do me the honour of becoming my wife.'

There was a moment of silence, everyone's eyes on Fin. She looked around at the family gathered at her father's table, then stood up and walked over to Anthony, holding up her left hand. He slid the diamond onto her ring finger.

'I take it that is a yes?'

ACKNOWLEDGEMENTS

While writing a book is a solitary pursuit, bringing it to life and releasing it into the world requires a large and dedicated team. I was so fortunate to meet my soulmate in Michael who always encourages and supports my endeavours, no matter how crazy they are. Together we have created three beautiful souls: Lara, Eva, and Jonathan, who inspire me daily with their own creativity.

To Kelly Rigby who read my earliest outline for this book and gave me such positive feedback, thank you. To my fabulous writing group, Brisbane Scribes, I just love our monthly meetings, your frank and fearless feedback, the celebration of every win, no matter how small. You ladies are the oxygen for all my writing. Thank you, Jane Connolly, Jenny Adams, Tatia Power, Bernie Condren, Marnie Bolton, and Rachel Millar. You ladies rock. To my colleague and writing friend, Fiona Robertson, who enthusiastically agreed to meet me for breakfast when I confessed to her that I wanted to write; your advice and feedback have been invaluable.

To The Writers' Studio, Sydney, with whom I did my first creative writing course as well as several novel writing courses – I didn't realise what was missing in my life until I signed up to write and I haven't stopped writing since. To the Queensland Writers Centre and Lori-Jay Ellis who is so supportive of writers of every genre, thank you.

To my wonderful editor, Lauren Elise Daniels, who gives such detailed feedback and always pushes me outside my comfort zone to make my writing better. This book would not exist without your input. And to the Hawkeye family. I pinch myself that I am no longer on the outside peering in but am one of you now. Thank you to everyone at Hawkeye for the work you have done to get my novel published. Kasey Delben for your edits, Nita Delgado, Olivia Griffiths, and Bek Diskett for proofreading, Natalie Chen for designing the cover of my dreams, and Meesha Whittam for coming up to me and telling me you loved my story. Your words still make my heart sing. And thank you, Carolyn Martinez, who makes the dreams of aspiring authors come true. I remember meeting you face-to-face for the first time when you said, *I've had my eye on you.* It encouraged me to keep going.

And thank you to every reader who took a chance on me and read this book. It means the world.

The characters in the book are fictional, but Books at Stones does exist and is owned by Michael and Karen Weibler. If you are in Brisbane, do drop in and say hello.

Jo Skinner

ABOUT THE AUTHOR

Jo Skinner is a Brisbane-based General Practitioner (GP) who writes contemporary women's fiction, and freelance non-fiction articles about women's issues and mental health. She also has a distance running habit. When she is not working or writing you will find her accruing kilometres while plotting her next story.

Jo was once asked if she was a GP who writes or a writer who is a GP. It is an impossible question to answer as she is passionate about both. Her love of writing came first with her first story published when she was in primary school. She has never forgotten the thrill of her story winning a competition and being included in a time capsule. After a prolonged hospitalisation in high school, she chose to study medicine, and writing took a back seat.

It was only after eloping with her soulmate, having a family, and moving more times than she cares to remember, that she could no longer ignore the writing itch and signed up to do the first of many creative writing courses.

Her stories have long and shortlisted in competitions, been published in anthologies, and published by *Medicine Today*, MiNDFOOD, and *The Big Issue*. She has co-edited two anthologies. *The Truth about My Daughter* came second in the Hawkeye Manuscript Development Prize in 2022 and is her first published novel.

She lives with her husband, three children, an elderly Pomeranian Papillon cross, Pippa, and a sprightly rescue cat, Jiji.

Book reviews can make or break a book. If you liked what you read today, please do consider posting a review on Goodreads or your favourite forum.

The Truth About My Daughter is available at www.hawkeyebooks.com.au and all good bookstores and libraries.

If you enjoyed, *The Truth About My Daughter*, Hawkeye believes you'll also enjoy:

New Year's Eve by Sarah Todman
Forgotten by Casey Nott
Me That You See by Anne Freeman
Returning to Adelaide by Anne Freeman
Rosanna by Annie O'Moon-Browning
Between Before and After by Edita Mujkic